Alfred Russel Wallace

On miracles and modern spiritualism

Three essays

Alfred Russel Wallace

On miracles and modern spiritualism
Three essays

ISBN/EAN: 9783741185304

Manufactured in Europe, USA, Canada, Australia, Japa

Cover: Foto ©Andreas Hilbeck / pixelio.de

Manufactured and distributed by brebook publishing software
(www.brebook.com)

Alfred Russel Wallace

On miracles and modern spiritualism

ON MIRACLES

AND

MODERN SPIRITUALISM.

Three Essays.

BY

ALFRED RUSSEL WALLACE,

AUTHOR OF

"THE MALAY ARCHIPELAGO," "CONTRIBUTIONS TO THE THEORY
OF NATURAL SELECTION," ETC., ETC.

———

LONDON:

JAMES BURNS, 15 SOUTHAMPTON ROW.

1875.

CONTENTS

"A presumptuous scepticism that rejects facts without examination of their truth, is, in some respects, more injurious than unquestioning credulity."—HUMBOLDT.

"One good experiment is of more value than the ingenuity of a brain like Newton's. Facts are more useful when they contradict, than when they support, received theories."—Sir HUMPHRY DAVY.

"The perfect observer in any department of science will have his eyes, as it were, opened, that they may be struck at once by any occurrence which, *according to received theories, ought not to happen*, for these are the facts which serve as clues to new discoveries."—Sir JOHN HERSCHELL.

"Before experience itself can be used with advantage, there is one preliminary step to make which depends wholly on ourselves: it is, the absolute dismissal and clearing the mind of all prejudice, and the determination to stand or fall by the result of a direct appeal to facts in the first instance, and of strict logical deduction from them afterwards."—Sir JOHN HERSCHELL.

"With regard to the miracle question, I can only say that the word 'impossible' is not, to my mind, applicable to matters of philosophy. That the possibilities of nature are infinite is an aphorism with which I am wont to worry my friends."—Professor HUXLEY.

PREFACE.

THE Essays which form this volume were written at
different times and for different purposes. The first in
order (though not the earliest in date) was read before
the Dialectical Society, with the intention of inducing
sceptics to reconsider the fundamental question of the
inherent credibility or incredibility of Miracles. The
second was written more than eight years ago for the
pages of a Secularist periodical, and a very limited
number of copies printed, chiefly for private circulation.
The third is the article which recently appeared in the
Fortnightly Review. All have been carefully revised, and
considerable additions have been made of illustrative fact,
argument, and personal experience, together with a few
critical remarks on Dr. Carpenter's latest work.

As the two latter Essays were each intended to give a
general view of the same subject, there is necessarily
some repetition in the matters treated of, and the same
authorities are in many cases quoted; but it is believed
that no actual repetition of details will be found, care
having been taken to introduce new facts and fresh illustrations, so that the one Essay will be found to supplement
and support the other.

I must now say a few words on a somewhat personal
matter.

I am well aware that my scientific friends are somewhat puzzled to account for what they consider to be my
delusion, and believe that it has injuriously affected whatever power I may have once possessed of dealing with
the philosophy of Natural History. One of them—Mr.
Anton Dohrn—has expressed this plainly. I am informed
that, in an article entitled "Englische Kritiker und Anti-
Kritiker des Darwinismus," published in 1861, he has put
forth the opinion that Spiritualism and Natural Selection
are incompatible, and that my divergence from the views
of Mr. Darwin arises from my belief in Spiritualism. He
also supposes that in accepting the spiritual doctrines I
have been to some extent influenced by clerical and religious prejudice. As Mr. Dohrn's views may be those of
other scientific friends, I may perhaps be excused for
entering into some personal details in reply.

From the age of fourteen I lived with an elder brother,
of advanced liberal and philosophical opinions, and I soon
lost (and have never since regained) all capacity of being
affected in my judgments, either by clerical influence or
religious prejudice. Up to the time when I first became
acquainted with the facts of Spiritualism, I was a confirmed philosophical sceptic, rejoicing in the works of
Voltaire, Strauss, and Carl Vogt, and an ardent admirer
(as I am still) of Herbert Spencer. I was so thorough
and confirmed a materialist that I could not at that time
find a place in my mind for the conception of spiritual

existence, or for any other agencies in the universe than
matter and force.　Facts, however, are stubborn things.
My curiosity was at first excited by some slight but inexplicable phenomena occurring in a friend's family, and
my desire for knowledge and love of truth forced me to
continue the inquiry.　The facts became more and more
assured, more and more varied, more and more removed
from anything that modern science taught or modern
philosophy speculated on.　The facts beat me.　They
compelled me to accept them, *as facts*, long before I could
accept the spiritual explanation of them: there was at
that time "no place in my fabric of thought into which
it could be fitted."　By slow degrees a place was made;
but it was made, not by any preconceived or theoretical
opinions, but by the continuous action of fact after fact,
which could not be got rid of in any other way.　So much
for Mr. Anton Dohrn's theory of the causes which led me
to accept Spiritualism.　Let us now consider the statement as to its incompatibility with Natural Selection.

Having, as above indicated, been led, by a strict induc-
tion from facts, to a belief—1stly, In the existence of a
number of preterhuman intelligences of various grades;
and, 2ndly, That some of these intelligences, although
usually invisible and intangible to us, can and do act on
matter, and do influence our minds,—I am surely following a strictly logical and scientific course, in seeing how
far this doctrine will enable us to account for some of
those residual phenomena which Natural Selection alone
will not explain.　In the 10th chapter of my *Contributions*

to the Theory of Natural Selection I have pointed out what
I consider to be some of these residual phenomena; and
I have suggested that they may be due to the action of
some of the various intelligences above referred to. This
view was, however, put forward with hesitation, and I
myself suggested difficulties in the way of its acceptance;
but I maintained, and still maintain, that it is one which
is logically tenable, and is in no way inconsistent with a
thorough acceptance of the grand doctrine of Evolution,
through Natural Selection, although implying (as indeed
many of the chief supporters of that doctrine admit) that
it is not the all-powerful, all-sufficient, and only cause of
the development of organic forms.

GRAYS, ESSEX, *Dec.* 1, 1874.

AN ANSWER

TO THE

ARGUMENTS OF HUME, LECKY, AND OTHERS, AGAINST MIRACLES.

(A PAPER READ BEFORE THE DIALECTICAL SOCIETY IN 1871.)

IT is now generally admitted, that those opinions and beliefs in which men have been educated generation after generation, and which have thus come to form part of their mental nature, are especially liable to be erroneous, because they keep alive and perpetuate the ideas and prejudices of a bygone and less enlightened age. It is therefore in the interest of truth that every doctrine or belief, however well established or sacred they may appear to be, should at certain intervals be challenged to arm themselves with such facts and reasonings as they possess, to meet their opponents in the open field of controversy, and do battle for their right to live. Nor can any exemption be claimed in favour of those beliefs which are the product of modern civilisation, and which have, for several generations, been held unquestioned by the great mass of the educated community; for the prejudice in their favour will be proportionately great, and, as was the case with the doctrines of Aristotle and the dogmas of the school-men, they may live on by mere weight of authority and force of habit, long after they have been shown to be opposed alike to fact and to reason. There have been times when popular beliefs were defended by the terrors of the law, and when the sceptic could only attack them

A

at the peril of his life. Now, we all admit that truth can take care of itself, and that only error needs protection. But there is another mode of defence which equally implies a claim to certain and absolute truth, and which is therefore equally unworthy and unphilosophical—that of ridicule and misrepresentation of our opponents, or a contemptuous refusal to discuss the question at all. This method is used among us even now; for there is one belief, or rather disbelief, whose advocates claim more than papal infallibility, by refusing to examine the evidence brought against it, and by alleging general arguments which have been in use for two centuries to prove that it cannot be erroneous. The belief to which I allude is, that all alleged miracles are false; that what is commonly understood by the term *supernatural* does not exist, or if it does is incapable of proof by any amount of human testimony; that all the phenomena we can have cognisance of depend on ascertainable physical laws, and that no other intelligent beings than man and the inferior animals can or do act upon our material world. These views have been now held almost unquestioned for many generations; they are inculcated as an essential part of a liberal education; they are popular, and are held to be one of the indications of our intellectual advancement; and they have become so much a part of our mental nature that all facts and arguments brought against them are either ignored as unworthy of serious consideration, or listened to with undisguised contempt. Now this frame of mind is certainly not one favourable to the discovery of truth, and strikingly resembles that by which, in former ages, systems of error have been fostered and maintained. The time has, therefore, come when it must be called upon to justify itself.

This is the more necessary, because the doctrine, whether true or false, actually rests upon a most unsafe and rotten foundation; for I propose to show that the best arguments hitherto relied upon to prove it are, one and all, fallacious, and prove nothing of the kind. But a theory or belief may be supported by very bad arguments, and yet be true; while it may be supported by some good arguments, and yet be false. But there never was a true theory which had no good arguments to support it. If, therefore, all the arguments hitherto used against miracles in general can be shown to be bad, it will behove sceptics to discover good ones; and if they cannot do so, the evidence in favour of miracles must be fairly met and judged on its own merits, not ruled out of court as it is now.

It will be perceived, therefore, that my present purpose is to clear the ground for the discussion of the great question of the so-called supernatural. I shall not attempt to bring arguments either for or against the main proposition, but shall confine myself to an examination of the allegations and the reasonings which have been supposed to settle the whole question on general grounds.

One of the most remarkable works of the great Scotch philosopher, David Hume, is *An Inquiry concerning Human Understanding*, and the tenth chapter of this work is *On Miracles*, in which occur the arguments which are so often quoted to show that no evidence can prove a miracle. Hume himself had a very high opinion of this part of his work, for he says at the beginning of the chapter, "I flatter myself that I have discovered an argument which, if just, will with the wise and learned be an everlasting check to all kinds of superstitious delusion, and consequently will be useful as long as the world endures; for so long, I presume, will the accounts of miracles and prodigies be found in all history, sacred and profane."

DEFINITION OF THE TERM "MIRACLE."

After a few general observations on the nature of evidence and the value of human testimony in different cases, he proceeds to define what he means by a miracle. And here at the very beginning of the subject we find that we have to take objection to Hume's definition of a miracle, which exhibits unfounded assumptions and false premises. He gives two definitions in different parts of his essay. The first is, "A miracle is a violation of the laws of nature." The second is, "A miracle is a transgression of a law of nature by a particular volition of the Deity, or by the interposition of some invisible agent." Now both these definitions are bad or imperfect. The first assumes that we know all the laws of nature; that the particular effect could not be produced by some unknown law of nature overcoming the law we do know; it assumes also, that if an invisible intelligent being held an apple suspended in the air, that act would violate the law of gravity. The second is not precise; it should be "some invisible *intelligent* agent," otherwise the action of galvanism or electricity, when these agents were first discovered, and before they were ascertained to form part of the order of nature, would answer accurately to this definition of a miracle. The words "violation" and "transgression" are both improperly used, and really beg the question by the definition. How does Hume know that any particular miracle is a violation of a law of nature? He assumes this without a shadow of proof, and on these words, as we shall see, rests his whole argument.

Before proceeding further, it is necessary for us to consider what is the true definition of a miracle, or what is commonly meant by that word. A miracle, as distinguished from a new and unheard-of natural phenomenon, supposes an intelligent superhuman agent either visible or invisible. It is not necessary that what is done should be beyond the power of man to do. The simplest action, if performed independently of human or visible agency, such as a tea-cup lifted in the air at request as by an invisible hand and without assignable cause, would be universally admitted to be a miracle, as much so as the lifting of a house into the air, the instantaneous healing of a wound, or the instantaneous production of an elaborate drawing. It is true that miracles have been generally held to be, either directly or indirectly, due to the action of the Deity; and some persons will not, perhaps, admit that any event not so caused deserves the name of miracle. But this is to advance an unprovable hypothesis, not to give a definition. It is not possible to prove that any supposed miraculous event is either the direct act of God, or indirectly produced by Him to prove the divine mission of some individual; but it may be possible to prove that it is produced by the action of *some* invisible preterhuman intelligent being. The definition of a miracle, I would propose, is therefore as follows:—" Any act or event necessarily implying the existence and agency of superhuman intelligences," considering the human soul or spirit, if manifested out of the body, as one of these superhuman intelligences. This definition is more complete than that of Hume, and defines more accurately the essence of that which is commonly termed a miracle.

THE EVIDENCE OF THE REALITY OF MIRACLES.

We now have to consider Hume's arguments. The first is as follows :—

" A miracle is a *violation of the laws of nature*; and as a firm and *unalterable experience* has established these laws, the proof against a miracle, from the very nature of the fact, is as entire as any argument from experience can possibly be imagined. Why is it more than probable that all men must die; that lead cannot *of itself remain suspended in the air;* that fire consumes wood, and is extinguished by water; unless it be, that these events are found agreeable to the laws of nature, and there is required a *violation of these laws,* or, in other words, a *miracle,* to prevent them? Nothing is esteemed a miracle, if it ever happened in the *common* course of nature. It is no miracle that a man seemingly in good health should die on a sudden; because such a kind of death, though more unusual than any other, has yet been frequently observed to happen. But it is a miracle that a dead man should come to life; because *that has never been observed in any age or country.* There must, therefore, be an uniform experience against every miraculous event, otherwise the event would not merit that appellation. And as an *uniform* experience amounts to a *proof,* there is here a direct and full proof, from the nature of the fact, against the existence of any miracle; nor can such a proof be destroyed, or the miracle rendered credible, but by an opposite proof, which is superior."

This argument is radically fallacious, because if it were sound, no perfectly new fact could ever be proved, since the first and each succeeding witness would be assumed to have universal experience against him. Such a simple fact as the existence of flying fish could never be proved, if Hume's argument is a good one; for the first man who saw and described one, would have the universal experience against him that fish do not fly, or make any approach to flying, and his evidence being rejected, the same argument would apply to the second, and to every subsequent witness; and thus no man at the present day who has not seen a flying fish alive, and actually flying, ought to believe that such things exist.

Again, painless operations in a state produced by mere passes of the hand, were, twenty-five years ago, maintained to be contrary to the laws of nature, contrary to all human experience, and therefore incredible. On Hume's principles they were miracles, and no amount of testimony could ever prove them to be real. Yet these are now admitted to be genuine facts by most physiologists; and they attempt, not very successfully, to explain them. But miracles do not, as assumed, stand alone—single facts opposed to uniform experience. Reputed miracles abound in all periods of history; every one has a host of others leading up to it; and every one has strictly analogous facts testified to at the present day. The uniform opposing experience, therefore, on which Hume lays so much stress does not exist. What, for instance, can be a more striking miracle than the levitation or raising of the human body into the air without visible cause, yet this fact has been testified to during a long series of centuries.

A few well-known examples are those of St. Francis d'Assisi, who was often seen by many persons to rise in the air, and the fact is testified to by his secretary, who could only reach his feet. Saint Theresa, a nun in a convent in Spain, was often raised into the air in the sight of all the sisterhood. Lord Orrery and Mr. Valentine Greatrak both informed Dr. Henry More and Mr. Glanvil that at Lord Conway's house at Ragley, in Ireland, a gentleman's butler, in their presence and in broad daylight, rose into the air and floated about the room above their heads. This is related by Glanvil in his *Sadducismus Triumphatus*. A similar fact is related by eye-witnesses of Ignatius de Loyola; and Mr. Madden, in his life of Savonarola, after narrating a similar circumstance of that saint, remarks, that similar phenomena are related in numerous instances, and that the evidence upon which some of the narratives rest, is as reliable as any human testimony can be. Butler, in his *Lives of the Saints*, says that many such facts are related by persons of undoubted veracity, who testify that they themselves were eye-witnesses of them. So we all know that at least fifty persons of high character may be found in London, who will testify that they have seen the same thing happen to Mr. Home. I do not here adduce this testimony as proving that the circumstances related really took place; I merely bring it forward now, to show how utterly unfounded is Hume's argument, which rests upon the assumption of universal testimony on the one side, and no testimony on the other.

THE CONTRADICTORY NATURE OF HUME'S STATEMENTS.

I now have to show that in Hume's efforts to prove his point, he contradicts himself in a manner so gross and complete, as is, perhaps, not to be found in the works of any other eminent author. The first passage I will quote is as follows :—

"For, first, there is *not to be found*, in *all history*, any miracle attested by a *sufficient number* of men, of such unquestioned *good sense, education*, and *learning*, as to secure us against all delusion in themselves ; of such undoubted *integrity*, as to place them beyond all suspicion of any design to deceive others; of such credit and reputation in the eyes of mankind, as to have a great deal to lose in case of their being detected in any falsehood ; and at the same time attesting facts performed in such a *public manner*, and in so *celebrated a part of the world*, as to render the detection unavoidable ; all which circumstances are requisite to give us a full assurance in the testimony of men."

A few pages further on, we find this passage :—

"There surely never was a greater number of miracles ascribed to one person than those which were lately said to have been wrought in France upon the tomb of Abbé Paris, the famous Jansenist, with whose sanctity the people were so long deluded. The curing of the sick, giving hearing to the deaf, and sight to the blind, were everywhere talked of as the usual effects of that holy sepulchre. But what is more extraordinary, many of the miracles were *immediately proved upon the spot*, before *judges* of *unquestioned integrity*, attested by *witnesses* of *credit and distinction*, in a *learned age*, and on the most *eminent theatre* that is *now in the world*. Nor is this all. A relation of them was published and dispersed everywhere ; nor were the Jesuits, though a learned body, supported by the civil magistrate, and determined enemies to those opinions, in whose favour the miracles were said to have been wrought, ever able *distinctly to refute or detect them.* Where shall we find such a number of circumstances, agreeing to the corroboration of one fact? And what have we to oppose to such a cloud of witnesses, but the absolute *impossibility*, or *miraculous nature* of the events which they relate? And this, surely, in the eyes of all reasonable people, will alone be regarded as a sufficient refutation."

In the second passage he affirms the existence of every single fact and quality which in the first passage he declared never existed (as shown by the italicised passages), and he entirely changes his ground of argument by appealing to the inherent impossibility of the fact, and not at all to the insufficiency of the evidence. He even makes this contradiction still more remarkable, by a note which he has himself given to this passage, a portion of which is as follows :—

"This book was writ by Mons. Montgeron, councillor or judge of the parliament of Paris, a man of figure and character, who was also a martyr to the cause, and is now said to be somewhere in a dungeon on account of his book. . . .

"Many of the miracles of Abbé Paris were proved immediately by witnesses before the officiality or bishop's court at Paris, under the eye of Cardinal Noailles; whose character for integrity and capacity was never contested, even by his enemies.

"His successor in the archbishopric was an enemy to the Jansenists, and for that reason promoted to the see by the court. Yet, twenty-two rectors or curés of Paris, with infinite earnestness, press him to examine those miracles, which they assert to be known to the whole world, and indisputably certain; but he wisely forbore. . . .

"All who have been in France about that time have heard of the reputation of Mons. Herault, the lieutenant of police, whose vigilance, penetration, activity, and extensive intelligence, have been much talked of. The magistrate who, by the nature of his office, is almost absolute, was invested with full powers, on purpose to suppress or discredit these miracles; and he frequently seized immediately, and examined the witnesses and subjects to them; *but never could reach anything satisfactory against them.*

"In the case of Mademoiselle Thibaut he sent the famous De Sylva to examine her; whose evidence is very curious. The physician declares, that it was impossible that she could have been so ill as was proved by witnesses; because it was impossible she could in so short a time have recovered so perfectly as he found her. He reasoned like a man of sense, from natural causes; but the opposite party told him that the whole was a miracle, and that his evidence was the very best proof of it. . . .

"No less a man than the Duc de Chatillon, a duke and peer of France, of the highest rank and family, gives evidence of a miraculous cure performed upon a servant of his, who had lived several years in his house with a visible and palpable infirmity.

"I shall conclude with observing, that no clergy are more celebrated for strictness of life and manners than the regular clergy of France, particularly the rectors or curés of Paris, who bear testimony to these impostures.

"The learning, genius, and probity of the gentlemen, and the austerity of the nuns of Port-Royal, have been much celebrated all over Europe. Yet they all give evidence for a miracle, wrought on the niece of the famous Pascal, whose sanctity of life, as well as extraordinary capacity, is well known. The famous Racine gives an account of this miracle in his famous history of Port-Royal, and fortifies it with all the proofs, which a multitude of nuns, priests, physicians, and men of the world, all of them of undoubted credit, could bestow upon it. Several men of letters, particularly the Bishop of Tournay, thought this miracle so certain, as to employ it in the refutation of Atheists and Freethinkers. The queen-regent of France, who was *extremely prejudiced against the Port-Royal*, sent *her own physician to examine the miracle*, who returned an *absolute convert*. In short, the supernatural cure was so incontestable, that it saved for a time that famous monastery from the ruin with which it was threatened by the Jesuits. *Had it been a cheat, it had certainly been detected by such sagacious and powerful antagonists, and must have hastened the ruin of the contrivers.*"

It seems almost incredible that this can have been written by the great sceptic David Hume, and written in the same work in which he has already affirmed that in all history no such evidence is to be found. In order to show how very remarkable is the evidence to which he alludes, I think it well to give one of the cases in greater detail, as recorded in the original work of Montgeron, and quoted in Mr William Howitt's *History of the Supernatural*:—

"Mademoiselle Coirin was afflicted, amongst other ailments, with a cancer in the left breast, for twelve years. The breast was destroyed by it, and came away in a mass; the effluvia from the cancer was horrible, and the whole blood of the system was pronounced infected by it. Every physician pronounced the case utterly incurable, yet, by a visit to the tomb, she was perfectly cured; and, what was more astonishing, the breast and nipple were wholly restored, with the skin pure and fresh, and free from any trace of scar. This case was known to the highest people in the realm. When the miracle was denied, Mademoiselle Coirin went to Paris, was examined by the royal physician, and made a formal deposition of her cure before a public notary. Mademoiselle Coirin was daughter of an officer of the royal household, and had two brothers in attendance on the person of the king. The testimonies of the doctors are of the most decisive kind. M. Gaulard, physician to the king, deposed officially, that, 'to restore a nipple absolutely destroyed, and separated from the breast, was an actual *creation*, because a nipple is not merely a continuity of the vessels of the breast, but a particular body, which is of a distinct and peculiar organisation.' M. Souchay, surgeon to the Prince of Conti, not only *pronounced the cancer incurable, but, having examined the breast after the cure*, went of himself to the public notary, and made a formal deposition 'that the cure was perfect; that each breast had its nipple in its natural form and condition, with the colours and attributes proper to those parts.' Such also are the testimonies of Seguier, the surgeon of the hospital at Nanterre; of M. Deshieres, surgeon to the Duchess of Berry; of M. Hequet, one of the most celebrated surgeons in France; and numbers of others, as well as of public officers and parties of the greatest reputation, universally known; all of whose depositions are officially and fully given by Montgeron."

This is only one out of a great number of cases equally marvellous, and equally well attested, and we therefore cannot be surprised at Hume's being obliged to give up the argument of the insufficiency of the evidence for

miracles and of the uniform experience against them, the
wonder being that he ever put forth an argument which
he was himself able to refute so completely.

We have now another argument which Hume brings
forward, but which is, if possible, still weaker than the
last. He says :—

"I may add, as a fourth reason, which diminishes the authority of
prodigies, that there is no testimony for any, even those which have
not been expressly detected, that is not opposed by any infinite number of witnesses; so that not only the miracle destroys the credit of
testimony, but the testimony destroys itself. To make this the better
understood, let us consider that, in matters of religion, whatever is
different is contrary; and that it is impossible the religions of ancient
Rome, of Turkey, and Siam, and of China, should, all of them, be
established on any solid foundation. Every miracle, therefore, pre-
tended to have been wrought in any of these religions (and all of
them abound in miracles), as its direct scope is to establish the particular system to which it is attributed; so has it the same force,
though more indirectly, to overthrow every other system. In destroying a rival system, it likewise destroys the credit of those miracles
on which that system was established; so that all the prodigies of
different religions are to be regarded as contrary facts; and the evidences of these prodigies, whether weak or strong, as opposite to
each other. According to this method of reasoning, when we believe
any miracle of Mahomet or his successors, we have for our warrant
the testimony of a few barbarous Arabians. And, on the other hand,
we are to regard the authority of Titus Livius, Plutarch, Tacitus,
and, in short, of all the authors and witnesses, Grecian, Chinese,
and Roman Catholic, who have related any miracle in their particular religion; I say, we are to regard their testimony in the same
light as if they had mentioned that Mahometan miracle, and had in
express terms contradicted it, with the same certainty as they have
for the miracle they relate."

Now this argument, if argument it can be called, rests
upon the extraordinary assumption that a miracle, if real,
can only come from God, and must therefore support only
a true religion. It assumes also that religions cannot be
true unless given by God. Mr. Hume assumes, therefore,

to know that nothing which we term a miracle can possibly be performed by any of the probably infinite number of intelligent beings who may exist in the universe between ourselves and the Deity. He confounds the evidence for the fact with the theories to account for the fact, and most illogically and unphilosophically argues, that if the theories lead to contradictions, the facts themselves do not exist.

I think, therefore, that I have now shown that—1. Hume gives a false definition of miracles, which begs the question of their possibility. 2. He states the fallacy that miracles are isolated facts, to which the entire course of human testimony is opposed. 3. He deliberately and absolutely contradicts himself as to the amount and quality of the testimony in favour of miracles. 4. He propounds the palpable fallacy as to miracles connected with opposing religions destroying each other.

MODERN OBJECTIONS TO MIRACLES.

We will now proceed to some of the more modern arguments against miracles. One of the most popular modern objections consists of making what is supposed to be an impossible supposition, and drawing an inference from it which looks like a dilemma, but which is really none at all.

This argument has been put in several forms. One is, " If a man tells me he came from York by the telegraph-wire, I do not believe him. If fifty men tell me they came from York by telegraph wires, I do not believe them. If any number of men tell me the same, I do not believe them. Therefore, Mr Home did not float in the air, notwithstanding any amount of testimony you may bring to prove it."

Another is, "If a man tells me that he saw the lion on Northumberland-house descend into Trafalgar-square and

drink water from the fountains, I should not believe him.
If fifty men, or any number of men, informed me of the
same thing, I should still not believe them."

Hence it is inferred that there are certain things so
absurd and so incredible, that no amount of testimony
could possibly make a sane man believe them.

Now, these illustrations look like arguments, and at first
sight it is not easy to see the proper way to answer them;
but the fact is that they are utter fallacies, because their
whole force depends upon an assumed proposition which
has never been proved, and which I venture to assert never
can be proved. The proposition is, that a large number of
independent, honest, sane, and sensible witnesses, *can*
separately and repeatedly testify to a plain matter of fact
which never happened at all.

Now, no evidence has been adduced to show that this
ever has occurred or ever could occur. But the assumption is rendered still more monstrous when we consider the
circumstances attending such cases as those of the cures
at the tomb of the Abbé Paris, and the cases of living
scientific men being converted to a belief in the reality of
the phenomena of modern Spiritualism; for we must assume that, being fully warned that the alleged facts are
held to be impossible and are therefore delusions, and
having the source of the supposed delusion pointed out, and
all the prejudices of the age and the whole tone of educated
thought being against the reality of such facts, yet numbers of educated men, including physicians and men of
science, remain convinced of the reality of such facts
after the most searching personal investigation. Yet the
assumption that such an amount and quality of independent converging evidence *can* be all false, must be proved,
if the argument is to have the slightest value, otherwise it
is merely begging the question. It must be remembered that

we have to consider, not absurd beliefs or false inferences, but plain matters of fact; and it cannot be proved, and never has been proved, that any large amount of cumulative evidence of disinterested and sensible men, was ever obtained for an absolute and entire delusion. To put the matter in a simple form, the asserted fact is either possible, or not possible. If possible, such evidence as we have been considering would prove it; if not possible, such evidence could not exist. The argument is, therefore, an absolute fallacy, since its fundamental assumption cannot be proved. If it is intended merely to enunciate the proposition, that the more strange and unusual a thing is the more and better evidence we require for it, that we all admit; but I maintain that human testimony increases in value in such an enormous ratio with each additional independent and honest witness, that no fact ought to be rejected when attested by such a body of evidence as exists for many of the events termed miraculous or supernatural, and which occur now daily among us. The burden of proof lies on those who maintain that such evidence can possibly be fallacious; let them point out one case in which such cumulative evidence existed, and which yet proved to be false. Let them give not supposition, but proof. And it must be remembered, that no proof is complete which does not explain the exact source of the fallacy in all its details. It will not do, for instance, to say, that there was this cumulative evidence for witchcraft, and that witchcraft is absurd and impossible. That is begging the question. The diabolic theories of the witch mania may be absurd and false; but the facts of witchcraft as proved, not by the tortured witches, but by independent witnesses, so far from being disproved, are supported by a whole body of analogous facts occurring at the present day.

THE UNCERTAINTY OF THE ASSERTED PHENOMENA OF
MODERN SPIRITUALISM.

Another modern argument is used more especially
against the reality of the so-called Spiritual phenomena.
It is said, " These phenomena are so uncertain; you have
no control over them; they follow no law. Prove to us
that they follow definite laws like all other groups of
natural phenomena, and we will believe them." This argument appears to have weight with some persons, and yet
it is really an absurdity.   The essence of the alleged phenomena (whether they be true or not, is of no importance)
is, that they seem to be the result of the action of independent intelligences, and are therefore deemed to be
Spiritual or superhuman.   If they had been found to follow strict law and not independent will, no one would
have ever supposed them to be Spiritual.   The argument,
therefore, is merely the statement of a foregone conclusion,
namely, " As long as your facts go to prove the existence
of distinct intelligences, we will not believe them ; demonstrate that they follow fixed law, and not intelligence, and
then we will believe them." This argument appears to
me to be childish, and yet it is used by some persons who
claim to be philosophical.

THE NECESSITY OF SCIENTIFIC TESTIMONY.

Another objection which I have heard stated in public,
and received with applause, is, that it requires immense
scientific knowledge to decide on the reality of any uncommon or incredible facts, and that till scientific men
investigate and prove them they are not worthy of credit.
Now I venture to say that a greater fallacy than this was
never put forth.   The subject is very important, and the
error is very common, but the fact is the exact opposite of
what is stated ; for I assert, without fear of contradiction,

that whenever the scientific men of any age have denied the facts of investigators on *a priori* grounds, *they have always been wrong.*

It is not necessary to do more than refer to the world-known names of Galileo, Harvey, and Jenner. The great discoveries they made were, as we know, violently opposed by all their scientific contemporaries, to whom they appeared absurd and incredible; but we have equally striking examples much nearer to our own day. When Benjamin Franklin brought the subject of lightning-conductors before the Royal Society, he was laughed at as a dreamer, and his paper was not admitted to the *Philosophical Transactions.* When Young put forth his wonderful proofs of the undulatory theory of light, he was equally hooted at as absurd by the popular scientific writers of the day.* The *Edinburgh Review* called upon the public to put Thomas Gray into a strait jacket for maintaining the practicability of railroads. Sir Humphry Davy laughed at the idea of London ever being lighted with gas. When Stephenson proposed to use locomotives on the Liverpool and Manchester Railway, learned men gave evidence that it was impossible that they could go even twelve miles an hour. Another great scientific authority declared it to be equally impossible for ocean steamers ever to cross the

---

* The following are choice specimens from *Edinburgh Review* articles in 1803 and 1804 :—

"Another Bakerian lecture, containing more fancies, more blunders, more unfounded hypotheses, more gratuitous fictions, all upon the same field, and from the fertile yet fruitless brain of the same eternal Dr. Young."

And again—

"It teaches no truths, reconciles no contradictions, arranges no anomalous facts, suggests no new experiments, and leads to no new inquiries."

One might almost suppose it to be a modern scientific writer hurling scorn at Spiritualism!

Atlantic. The French Academy of Sciences ridiculed the
great astronomer Arago, when he wanted even to discuss
the subject of the electric telegraph. Medical men ridiculed the stethoscope when it was first discovered. Painless operations during the mesmeric coma were pronounced
impossible, and therefore impostures.

But one of the most striking, because one of the most
recent cases of this opposition to, or rather disbelief in facts
opposed to the current belief of the day, among men who
are generally charged with going too far in the other direction, is that of the doctrine of the " Antiquity of Man."
Boué, an experienced French geologist, in 1823, discovered
a human skeleton eighty feet deep in the loess or hardened
mud of the Rhine. It was sent to the great anatomist
Cuvier, who so utterly discredited the fact that he threw
aside this invaluable fossil as worthless, and it was lost.
Sir C. Lyell, from personal investigation on the spot, now
believes that the statements of the original observer were
quite accurate. So early as 1715 flint weapons were found
with the skeleton of an elephant in an excavation in Gray's-
inn-lane, in the presence of Mr. Conyers, who placed them
in the British Museum, where they remained utterly un-
noticed till quite recently. In 1800 Mr. Frere found flint
weapons along with the remains of extinct animals at
Hoxne, in Suffolk. From 1841 to 1846, the celebrated
French geologist, Boucher de Perthes, discovered great
quantities of flint weapons in the drift gravels of the
North of France; but for many years he could convince
none of his fellow scientific men that they were works of
art, or worthy of the slightest attention. At length, however, in 1853, he began to make converts. In 1859-60,
some of our own most eminent geologists visited the spot,
and fully confirmed the truth of his observations and
deductions.

Another branch of the subject was, if possible, still worse treated. In 1825, Mr. McEnery, of Torquay, discovered worked flints along with the remains of extinct animals in the celebrated Kent's Hole Cavern ; but his account of his discoveries was simply laughed at. In 1840, one of our first geologists, Mr. Godwin Austen, brought this matter before the Geological Society, and Mr. Vivian, of Torquay, sent in a paper fully confirming Mr. McEnery's discoveries; but it was thought too improbable to be published. Fourteen years later, the Torquay Natural History Society made further observations, entirely confirming the previous ones, and sent an account of them to the Geological Society of London ; but the paper was rejected, as too improbable for publication. Now, however, for five years past, the cave has been systematically explored under the superintendence of a Committee of the British Association, and all the previous reports for forty years have been confirmed, and have been shown to be even less wonderful than the reality. It may be said that "this was proper scientific caution." Perhaps it was ; but at all events it proves this important fact—that in this, as in every other case, the humble and often unknown observers have been right; the men of science who rejected their observations have been wrong.

Now, are the modern observers of some phenomena, usually termed supernatural and incredible, less worthy of attention than those already quoted ? Let us take, first, the reality of what is called clairvoyance. The men who have observed this phenomenon, who have carefully tested it through long years or through their whole lives, will rank in scientific knowledge and in intellectual ability as quite equal to the observers in any other branch of discovery. We have no less than seven competent medical men—Drs. Elliotson, Gregory, Ashburner, Lee, Herbert Mayo, Esdaile, and Haddock, besides persons of such high ability as Miss Martineau, Mr. H. G. Atkinson, Mr. Charles Bray, and Baron Reichenbach. With the history of previous discoverers before us, is it more likely that these eleven educated persons, knowing all the arguments against the facts, and investigating them carefully, should be all wrong, and those who say *à priori* that the thing is impossible should be all right, or the contrary? If we are to learn anything by history and experience, then we may safely prognosticate that, in this case as in so many others, those who disbelieve other men's observations without enquiry will be found to be in the wrong.

REVIEW OF MR. LECKY'S ASSERTIONS ABOUT MIRACLES.

We now come to the modern philosophic objectors, most eminent among whom is Mr. Lecky, author of the *History of Rationalism* and the *History of Morals*. In the latter work he has devoted some space to this question, and his clear and well-expressed views may be taken to represent the general opinions and feelings of the educated portion of modern society. He says:—

"The attitude of ordinary educated people towards miracles is not that of doubt, of hesitation, of discontent with the existing evidence, but rather of absolute, derisive, and even unexamining incredulity."

He then goes on to explain why this is so:—

"In certain stages of society, and under the action of certain influences, an accretion of miracles is *invariably formed* around every *prominent person* or *institution*. We can analyse the general causes that *have impelled men towards the miraculous;* we can show that these causes have never failed to produce the effect; and we can trace the gradual alteration of mental conditions *invariably accompanying* the decline of the belief.

"When men are *destitute of the critical spirit*, when the notion of *uniform law is yet unborn*, and when their imaginations are still incapable of rising to abstract ideas, histories of miracles are always formed and always believed; and they continue to flourish and to multiply until these conditions are altered. Miracles cease when men cease to believe and expect them. . . ."

Again :—

" We do not say they are impossible, or even that they are not authenticated by as much evidence as many facts we believe. We only say that, *in certain states of society, illusions* of this kind inevitably appear. . . ."

" Sometimes we can discover the precise natural fact which the superstition has misread, but more frequently we can give only a general explanation, enabling us to assign these legends to their place, as the *normal expression* of a *certain stage* of knowledge or intellectual power; and this explanation is their refutation."

Now, in these statements and arguments of Mr. Lecky, we find some fallacies hardly less striking than those of Hume. His assertion that in certain stages of society an accretion of miracles is invariably formed round every prominent person or institution, appears to me to be absolutely contradicted by well-known historical facts.

The Church of Rome has ever been the great theatre of miracles, whether ancient or modern. The most prominent person in the Church of Rome is the Pope; the most prominent institution is the Papacy. We should expect, therefore, if Mr. Lecky's statement be correct, that the Popes would be pre-eminently miracle-workers. But the fact is, that with the exception of one or two very early ones, no miracles whatever are recorded of the great majority of the Popes. On the contrary, it has been generally among the very humblest members of the Romish Church, whether clergy or laity, that the power of working miracles has appeared, and which has led to their being canonized as saints.

Again, to take another instance, the most prominent person connected with the reformed churches is Luther. He himself believed in miracles. The whole world in his day believed in miracles; and miracles, though generally of a demoniac character, continued rife in all Protestant churches for many generations after his death; yet there has been no accretion of miracles round this remarkable man.

Nearer to our own day we have Irving, at the head of a church of miracle-workers; and Joe Smith, the founder of the miracle-working Mormons; yet there is not the slightest sign of any tendency to impute any miracles to either of these men, other than those which the latter individual claimed for himself before his sect was established. These very striking facts seem to me to prove that there must be some basis of truth in nearly every alleged miracle, and that the theory of any growth or accretion round prominent individuals is utterly without evidence to support it. It is one of those convenient general statements which sound very plausible and very philosophical, but for which no proof whatever is offered.

Another of Mr. Lecky's statements is, that there is an alteration of mental conditions invariably accompanying the decline of belief. But this "*invariable accompaniment*" certainly cannot be proved, because the decline of the belief has only occurred once in the history of the world; and, what is still more remarkable, while the mental conditions which accompanied that one decline have continued in force or have even increased in energy and are much more widely diffused, belief has now for twenty years been growing up again. In the highest states of ancient civilisation, both among the Greeks and Romans, the belief existed in full force, and has been testified to by the highest and most intellectual men of every age. The decline which in the last and present centuries has certainly taken place cannot, therefore, be imputed to any general law, since it is but an exceptional instance. *

---

* The decline of the belief may, however, be due (as a friend has suggested to me) to a real decline in the occurrence of the phenomena which

Again, Mr. Lecky says that the belief in the supernatural only exists " when men are destitute of the critical spirit, and when the notion of uniform law is yet unborn." Mr. Lecky in this matter contradicts himself almost as much as Hume did. One of the greatest advocates for the belief in the supernatural was Glanvil; and this is what Mr. Lecky says of Glanvil:—

"The predominating characteristic of Glanvil's mind was an intense scepticism. He has even been termed by a modern critic the first English writer who has thrown scepticism into a definite form; and if we regard this expression as simply implying a profound distrust of human faculties, the judgment can hardly be denied. And certainly it would be difficult to find a work displaying less of credulity and superstition than the treatise on ' The Vanity of Dogmatising,' afterwards published as *Scepsis Scientifica*, in which Glanvil expounded his philosophical views. . . The *Sadducismus Triumphatus* is probably the ablest book ever published in defence of the reality of witchcraft. Dr. Henry Moore, the illustrious Boyle, and the scarcely less eminent Cudworth, warmly supported Glanvil; and no writer comparable to these in ability or influence appeared on the other side; yet the scepticism steadily increased."

---

compelled the belief, due to a well-known natural law. It is certain that witches, and the persons subject to their influence, were what are now termed "mediums;" that is, persons of the peculiar organization required for the manifestation of modern spiritual phenomena. For several centuries all persons endowed in almost any degree with these peculiar powers were persecuted as witches, and burnt or destroyed by thousands all over the so-called *civilised* world. The mediums being destroyed, the production of the phenomena became impossible; added to which the persecution would lead to concealment of all incipient manifestations. Just at this time, too, physical science began to make those rapid strides which have changed the face of the world · and induced a frame of mind which led men to look with horror and loathing at the barbarities and absurdities of the witch-persecutors. A century of repose has allowed the human organism to regain its normal powers; and the phenomena which were formerly imputed to the direct agency of Satan, are now looked upon by Spiritualists as, for the most part, the work of invisible intelligences very little better or worse than ourselves.

Again Mr. Lecky thus speaks of Glanvil :—

" It was between the writings of Bacon and Locke that that latitudinarian school was formed which was irradiated by the genius of Taylor, *Glanvil*, and Hales, and which became the very centre and seedplot of religious liberty."

These are *the men* and these the *mental conditions* which are favourable to *superstition* and *delusion !* *

---

* The Rev. Joseph Glanvil, who witnessed some of the extraordinary disturbances at Mr. Mompesson's, and has given a full account of them, and has also collected the evidence for many remarkable cases of supposed witchcraft, was not the credulous fool many who hear that he wrote in favour of the reality of witches will suppose him to have been, but a man of education, talent, and judgment. Mr. Lecky, in his "History of the Rise and Progress of Rationalism in Europe," says of him :—"A divine who in his own day was very famous, and who I venture to think has been surpassed in genius by few of his successors. The works of Glanvil are far less known than they should be." I here give a few extracts from his "Introduction to the Proof of the Existence of Apparitions, Spirits, and Witches."

"Section IV.—What things the author concedes in this controversy about witches and witchcraft ":—

First : He grants that there are " witty and ingenious men" opposed to him in the matter.

Secondly : He admits that some who deny witches are good Christians.

Thirdly : He says, " I allow that the great body of mankind is very credulous, and in this matter, so that they do believe vain impossible things in relation to it. That converse with the Devil and real transmutation of men and women into other creatures are such. That people are apt to impute the extraordinaries of art or nature to witchcraft, and that their credulity is often abused by subtle and designing knaves through these. That there are ten thousand silly, lying stories of witchcraft and apparitions among the vulgar."

Fourthly: " I grant that melancholy and imagination have very great force and beget strange persuasions; and that many stories of witches and apparitions have been but melancholy fancies."

Fifthly : " I know and yield that there are many strange natural diseases that have odd symptoms, and produce wonderful and astonishing effects beyond the usual course of nature, and that such are sometimes falsely ascribed to witchcraft."

Sixthly : " I own the Popish Inquisitors and other witch-finders have done

The critical spirit and the notion of uniform law are certainly powerful enough in the present day, yet in every country in the civilised world there are now hundreds and thousands of intelligent men who believe, on the testimony

much wrong, that they have destroyed innocent persons for witches, and that watching and torture have extorted extraordinary confessions from some that were not guilty."

Seventhly: He acknowledges that of the facts which he affirms to be real many are very strange, uncouth, and improbable, and that we cannot understand them or reconcile them with the commonly received notions of spirits and the future state.

Having made these concessions to his adversaries he demands others in return.

"Section V.—The postulata which the author demands of his adversaries as his just right are, viz. :—

First: That whether witches are or are not is a question of fact.

Secondly: That matter of fact can only be proved by immediate sense or the testimony of others. To endeavour to demonstrate fact by abstract reasoning or speculation is as if a man should prove that Julius Cæsar founded the Empire of Rome by algebra or metaphysics.

Thirdly: That Scripture is not all allegory, but generally has a plain, literal, and obvious meaning.

Fourthly: That *some* human testimonies are credible and certain, viz. :— They may be so circumstantiated as to leave no reason of doubt; for our senses *sometimes* report truth, and *all mankind* are not liars, cheats, and knaves—at least they are not all liars when they have no interest to be so.

Fifthly: That which is sufficiently and undeniably proved ought not to be denied because we know not how it can be, that is, because there are difficulties in the conceiving of it ; otherwise sense and knowledge is gone as well as faith. For the *modus* of most things is unknown, and the most obvious in nature have inextricable difficulties in the conceiving of them, as I have shown in my *Scepsis Scientifica.*

Sixthly: We know scarcely anything of the nature of Spirits and the conditions of the future state."

And he concludes :—"These are my *postulata* or demands, which I suppose will be thought reasonable, and such as need no more proof."

The evidence adduced by a man who thus philosophically lays down his basis of investigation cannot be despised ; and a perusal of Glanvil's works will well repay anyone who takes an interest in this inquiry.

of their own senses, in phenomena which Mr Lecky and others would term miraculous, and therefore incredible, but which the witnesses maintain to be part of the order of nature. Instead of being, as Mr. Lecky says, an indication of " certain states of society"—" the normal expression of a certain stage of knowledge or intellectual power"—this belief has existed in all states of society, and has accompanied every stage of intellectual power. Socrates, Plutarch, and St. Augustine alike give personal testimony to supernatural facts; this testimony never ceased through the middle ages; the early reformers, Luther and Calvin, throng the ranks of witnesses; all the philosophers, and all the judges of England, down to Sir Matthew Hale, admitted that the evidence for such facts was irrefutable. Many cases have been rigidly investigated by the police authorities of various countries; and, as we have already seen, the miracles at the tomb of the Abbé Paris, which occurred in the most sceptical period of French history, in the age of Voltaire and the encyclopædists, were proved by such an array of evidence, and were so open to investigation, that one of the noblemen of that court—convinced of their reality after the closest scrutiny—suffered the martyrdom of imprisonment in the Bastile for insisting upon making them public. And in our own day we have, at the lowest estimate, many millions of believers in modern Spiritualism in all classes of society; so that the belief which Mr Lecky imputes to a certain stage of intellectual culture, only appears, on the contrary, to have all the attributes of universality.

IS THE BELIEF IN MIRACLES A SURVIVAL OF SAVAGE THOUGHT?

The philosophical argument has been put in another form by Mr. E. B. Tylor, in a lecture at the Royal Institution, and in several passages in his other works. He maintains that all Spiritualistic and other beliefs in the supernatural are examples of the survival of savage thought among civilised people; but he ignores the facts which compel the beliefs. The thoughts of those educated men who know, from the evidence of their own senses, and by repeated and careful investigation, that things called supernatural are true and real facts, are as totally distinct from those of savages as are their thoughts respecting the sun, or thunder, or disease, or any other natural phenomenon. As well might he maintain that the modern belief that the sun is a fiery mass, is a survival of savage thought, because some savages believe so too; or that our belief that certain diseases are contagious, is a similar survival of the savage idea that a man can convey a disease to his enemy. The question is a question of facts, not of theories or thoughts, and I entirely deny the value or relevance of any general arguments, theories, or analogies. when we have to decide on matters of fact.

Thousands of intelligent men now living know, from personal observation, that some of the strange phenomena which have been pronounced absurd and impossible by scientific men, are nevertheless true. It is no answer to these, and no explanation of the facts, to tell them that such beliefs only occur when men are destitute of the critical spirit, and when the notion of uniform law is yet unborn; that in certain states of society illusions of this kind inevitably appear, that they are only the normal expression of certain stages of knowledge and of intellectual power, and that they clearly prove the survival of savage modes of thought in the midst of modern civilisation.

I believe that I have now shown—1. That Hume's arguments against miracles are full of unwarranted assumptions, fallacies, and contradictions, and have no logical force what-

ever.   2. That the modern argument of the telegraph-wire
conveyance and drinking stone-lion are positively no arguments at all, since they rest on false or assumed premises.
3. That the argument that dependence is to be placed upon
the opinions of men of science rather than on the facts observed by other men, is opposed to universal experience
and the whole history of science.   4. That the philosophical argument so well put by Mr. Lecky and Mr. Tylor,
rests on false or unproved assumptions, and is therefore
valueless.

In conclusion, I must again emphatically point out that
the question I have been here discussing is—in no way,
whether miracles are true or false, or whether modern
Spiritualism rests upon a basis of fact or of delusion,—
but solely, whether the arguments that have hitherto been
supposed conclusive against them have any weight or
value.   If I have shown—as I flatter myself I have done—
that the arguments which have been supposed to settle
the general question so completely as to render it quite
unnecessary to go into particular cases, are all utterly
fallacious, then I shall have cleared the ground for the
production of evidence; and no honest man desirous of
arriving at truth will be able to evade an inquiry into
the nature and amount of that evidence, by moving the
previous question—that miracles are unprovable by any
amount of human testimony.   It is time that the "derisive
and unexamining incredulity" which has hitherto existed
should give way to a less dogmatic and more philosophical
spirit, or history will again have to record the melancholy
spectacle of men, who should have known better, assuming
to limit the discovery of new powers and agencies in the
universe, and deciding, *without investigation*, whether other
men's observations are true or false.

THE SCIENTIFIC ASPECT

OF

THE SUPERNATURAL.

THE SCIENTIFIC ASPECT

OF

THE SUPERNATURAL.

I.

INTRODUCTORY.

IN the following pages I have brought together a few examples of the evidence for <u>facts</u> usually deemed miraculous or supernatural, and therefore incredible; and I have prefixed to these some general considerations on the nature of miracle, and on the possibility that much which has been discredited as such is not really miraculous in the sense of implying any alteration of the <u>laws of nature</u>. In that sense I would repudiate miracles as entirely as the most thorough sceptic. It may be asked if I have myself seen any of the wonders narrated in the following pages. I answer that I have witnessed facts of a similar nature to some of them, and have satisfied myself of their genuineness; and therefore feel that I have no right to reject the evidence of still more marvellous facts witnessed by others.*

---

* In Dr. Carpenter's recent work on "Mental Physiology" (p. 627), he refers to me, by name, as one of those who have "committed themselves to the extraordinary proposition, that if we admit the reality of the *lower* phenomena (Class I., defined as "those which are conformable to our previous knowledge," &c.), the testimony which we accept as good for these ought to convince us of the *higher* (Classes II. and III., defined as "those which are in direct contrariety to our existing knowledge," &c). As he must refer to the above passage, and that eight lines further on, my readers will have an opportunity of judging of the accuracy of Dr. C.'s unqualified statement that I refer to different *classes* of facts, when my words are "*facts of a similar nature.*" It will be seen further on that I have

A single new and strange fact is, on its first announcement, often treated as a miracle, and not believed because it is contrary to the hitherto observed order of nature. Half a dozen such facts, however, constitute a little " order of nature" for themselves. They may not be a whit more understood than at first; but they cease to be regarded as miracles. Thus it will be with the many thousands of facts of which I have culled a few examples here. If but one or two of them are proved to be real, the whole argument against the rest, of " impossibility" and " reversal of the laws of nature," falls to the ground. I would ask any man desirous of knowing the truth, to read the following five works carefully through, and then say whether he can believe that the whole of the *facts* stated in them are to be explained by imposture or self-delusion. And let him remember that if but one or two of them are true, there ceases to be any strong presumption against the truth of the rest. These works are—

1. Reichenbach's Researches on Magnetism, Electricity, Heat, Light, &c., in their relations to the vital force. Translated by Dr. Gregory.

2. Dr. Gregory's Letters on Animal Magnetism.

3. R. Dale Owen's Footfalls on the Boundary of Another World.

4. Hare's Experimental Investigation of the Spirit Manifestations.

5. Home's Incidents of my Life.

All these are easily obtained, except the 4th, which may be had from the publisher of this work.

---

witnessed numerous facts quite incredible to Dr. C., because "in direct contrariety to *his* existing knowledge," but that other observers, whom I quote, have witnessed much more remarkable facts of the *same class*, which *I therefore* feel bound to accept on their testimony. This Dr. C. twists into an " extraordinary proposition ! "

I subjoin a list of the persons whose names I have adduced in the following pages, as having been convinced of the truth and reality of most of these phenomena. I presume it will be admitted that they are *honest* men. If, then, these facts, which many of them declare they have repeatedly witnessed, never took place, I must leave my readers to account for the undoubted *fact* of their belief in them, as best they can. I can only do so by supposing these well-known men to have been all fools or madmen, which is to me more difficult than believing they are sane men, capable of observing matters of fact, and of forming a sound judgment as to whether or no they could possibly have been deceived in them. A man of sense will not lightly declare, as many of these do, not only that he has witnessed what others deem absurd and incredible, but that he feels morally certain he was not deceived in what he saw.

LIST.

1. Professor A. DE MORGAN—Mathematician and Logician.
2. Professor CHALLIS—Astronomer.
3. Professor WM. GREGORY, M.D.—Chemist.
4. Professor ROBERT HARE, M.D.—Chemist.
5. Professor HERBERT MAYO, M.D., F.R.S.—Physiologist.
6. Mr. RUTTER—Chemist.
7. Dr. ELLIOTSON—Physiologist.
8. Dr. HADDOCK—Physician.
9. Dr. GULLY—Physician.
10. Judge EDMONDS—Lawyer.
11. Lord LYNDHURST—Lawyer.
12. CHARLES BRAY, Philosophical Writer.
13. Archbishop WHATELY—Clergyman.
14. Rev. W. KERR, M.A.—Clergyman.
15. Hon. Col. E. B. WILBRAHAM—Military Man.

16. Capt. R. F. BURTON—Military Man.
17. NASSAU E. SENIOR—Political Economist.
18. W. M. THACKERAY—Author.
19. T. A. TROLLOPE—Author.
20. R. D. OWEN—Author and Diplomatist.
21. W. HOWITT—Author.
22. S. C. HALL—Author.

II.

MIRACLES AND MODERN SCIENCE.

A MIRACLE is generally defined to be a violation or suspension of a law of nature, and as the laws of nature are the most complete expression of the accumulated experiences of the human race, Hume was of opinion that no amount of human testimony could prove a miracle. Strauss bases the whole argument of his elaborate work on the same ground, that no amount of testimony coming to us through the depth of eighteen centuries can prove that those laws were ever subverted, which the unanimous experience of men now shows to be invariable. Modern science has placed this argument on a wider basis, by showing the interdependence of all these laws, and by rendering it inconceivable that force and motion, any more than matter, can be absolutely originated or destroyed. Prof. Tyndall in his recent paper on *The Constitution of the Universe* in the *Fortnightly Review*, says, " A miracle is strictly defined as an invasion of the law of the conservation of energy.* To create or annihilate matter would be deemed on all hands a miracle; the creation or annihilation of energy would be equally a miracle to those who understand the principle of conservation." Mr. Lecky in his great work on "Rationalism" shows us that during the last two or three centuries, there has been a continually increasing disposition to adopt secular rather than theological views,

---

* This supposed definition of a miracle is a pure assumption. Miracles do not imply any "invasion of the law of the conservation of energy," but merely the existence of intelligent beings invisible to us, yet capable of acting on matter, as explained further on.

in history, politics, and science. The great physical discoveries of the last twenty years have pushed forward this
movement with still greater rapidity, and have led to a firm
conviction in the minds of most men of education that
the universe is governed by wide and immutable laws,
under which all phenomena whatever may be classed, and
to which no fact in nature can ever be opposed. If therefore we define miracle as a contravention of any one of
these laws, it must be admitted that modern science has
no place for it; and we cannot be surprised at the many
and varied attempts by writers of widely different opinions,
to account for or explain away all recorded facts in history
or religion, which they believe could only have happened
on the supposition of miraculous or supernatural agency.
This task has been by no means an easy one. The amount
of direct testimony to miracles in all ages is very great.
The belief in miracles has been, till very recently, almost
universal, and it may safely be asserted that, of those who
are, on general grounds, most firmly convinced of the impossibility of events deemed miraculous, few if any have
thoroughly and honestly investigated the nature and
amount of the evidence that these events really happened.
On this subject, however, I do not now intend to enter.
It appears to me that the very basis of the whole question
has been to some extent misstated and misunderstood, and
that in every well authenticated case of supposed miracle
a solution may be found which will remove many of our
difficulties.

One common fallacy appears to me to run through all
the arguments against facts deemed miraculous, when it is
asserted that they *violate*, or *invade*, or *subvert* the laws of
nature. This is really assuming the very point to be
decided, for if the disputed fact did happen, it could only
be in accordance with the laws of nature, since the only

complete definition of the "laws of nature" is that they are the laws which regulate all phenomena. The very word "supernatural," as applied to a *fact*, is an absurdity; and "miracle," if retained at all, requires a more accurate definition than has yet been given of it. To refuse to admit, what in other cases would be absolutely conclusive evidence of a fact, because it cannot bé explained by those laws of nature with which we are now acquainted, is really to maintain that we have complete knowledge of those laws, and can determine beforehand what is or is not possible. The whole history of the progress of human knowledge shows us, that the disputed prodigy of one age becomes the accepted natural phenomenon of the next, and that many apparent miracles have been due to laws of nature subsequently discovered.

Many phenomena of the simplest kind would appear supernatural to men having limited knowledge. Ice and snow might easily be made to appear so to inhabitants of the tropics. The ascent of a balloon would be supernatural to persons who knew nothing of the cause of its upward motion; and we may well conceive that, if no gas lighter than atmospheric air had ever been discovered, and if in the minds of all (philosophers and chemists included), air had become indissolubly connected with the idea of the lightest form of terrestrial matter, the testimony of those who had seen a balloon ascend might be discredited, on the grounds that a law of nature must be suspended, in order that anything could freely ascend through the atmosphere in direct contravention to the law of gravitation.

A century ago, a telegram from three thousand miles' distance, or a photograph taken in a second, would not have been believed possible, and would not have been credited on any testimony, except by the ignorant and superstitious who believed in miracles. Five centuries ago,

the effects produced by the modern telescope and micro-
scope would have been deemed miraculous, and if related
only by travellers as existing in China or Japan, would
certainly have been disbelieved. The power of dipping
the hand into melted metals unhurt, is a remarkable case
of an effect of natural laws appearing to contravene another
natural law; and it is one‘ which certainly might have
been, and probably has been regarded as a miracle and the
fact believed or disbelieved, not according to the amount
or quality of the testimony to it, but according to the credulity or supposed superior knowledge of the recipient.
About twenty years ago, the fact that surgical operations
could be performed on patients in the mesmeric trance
without their being conscious of pain, was strenuously denied by most scientific and medical men in this country, and
the patients, and sometimes the operators, denounced as
impostors; the asserted phenomenon was believed to be
contrary to the laws of nature. Now, probably every man
of intelligence believes the facts, and it is seen that there
must be some as yet unknown law of which they are a
consequence. ⌊When Castellet informed Réaumur that he
had reared perfect silkworms from the eggs laid by a virgin
moth, the answer was *Ex nihilo nihil fit*, and the fact was
disbelieved. It was contrary to one of the widest and best
established laws of nature; yet it is now universally
admitted to be true, and the supposed law ceases to be
universal.⌉ These few illustrations will enable us to understand how some reputed miracles may have been due to
yet unknown laws of nature. We know so little of what
nerve or life-force really is, how it acts or can act, and in
what degree it is capable of transmission from one human
being to another, that it would be indeed rash to affirm that
under no exceptional conditions could phenomena, such as
the apparently miraculous cure of many diseases, or per-

ception through other channels than the ordinary senses, ever take place.

To illustrate how gradually the natural glides into the miraculous, and how easily our beliefs are determined by preconceived ideas rather than by evidence, take the following pair of cases:—

Some years since an account appeared in the *London Medical Times* of an experiment on four Russians who had been condemned to death. They were made, without knowing it, to sleep in beds whereon persons had died of epidemic cholera, but not one of them caught the disease. Subsequently they were told that they must sleep in the beds of cholera patients, but were put into perfectly clean and wholesome beds, yet three of them now took the disease in its most malignant form, *and died within four hours.*

About two hundred years ago Valentine Greatrak cured people of various diseases by stroking them with his hand. The Rev. Dr. R. Dean, writing an account from personal observation, says:—"I was three weeks together with him at my Lord Conway's, and saw him lay his hands upon (I think) a thousand persons: and really there is something in it more than ordinary, but I am convinced 'tis not miraculous. I have seen deafness cured by his touch, grievous sores of many months date in a few days healed; obstructions and stoppings removed, and cancerous knots in the breast dissolved." The detailed evidence of eyewitness of high character and ability as to these extraordinary cures is overwhelming, but cannot here be given.

Now, of these two cases the first will be generally believed; the second disbelieved. The first is supposed to be a natural effect of "imagination," the second is generally held to be of the nature of a miracle. Yet to impute any definite physical effect to imagination is merely to state

the facts, and to hide our complete ignorance of the causes
or laws which govern them. And to hold that there *can
be* no curative power in the repeated contact of a peculiarly
constituted human being, when the analogy of the admitted
facts of mesmerism proves how powerful and curious are
the effects of human beings on each other, would seem to
be a very great degree of presumption in our present almost
complete ignorance of the relation of the mind to the
body.

But it will be objected that it is only the least important
class of miracles that can possibly be explained in this
manner. In many cases dead matter is said to have been
endowed with force and motion, or to have been suddenly
increased immensely in weight and bulk; things altogether
non-terrestrial are said to have appeared on earth, and the
orderly progress of the great phenomena of nature is
affirmed to have been suddenly interrupted. Now one
characteristic of most of this class of reputed miracles is,
that they seem to imply the action of another power and
intelligence than that of the individual to whose miraculous power they are vulgarly imputed. One of the most
common and best attested of these phenomena is the movement of various solid bodies in the presence of many witnesses, without any discoverable cause. In reading the
accounts of these occurrences by eye-witnesses one little
point of detail often recurs—that an object appears to be
thrown or to fall suddenly, and yet comes down gently
and without noise. This curious point is to be found
mentioned in old trials for witchcraft, as well as in the
most modern phenomena of spiritualism, and is strikingly
suggestive of the objects being *carried* by an invisible agent
To render such things intelligible or possible from the
point of view of modern science, we must, therefore, have
recourse to the supposition that intelligent beings may

exist, capable of acting on matter, though they themselves are uncognisable directly by our senses.

That intelligent beings may exist around and among us, unperceived during our whole lives, and yet capable under certain conditions of making their presence known by acting on matter, will be inconceivable to some, and will be doubted by many more, but we venture to say, that no man acquainted with the latest discoveries and the highest speculations of modern science, will deny its *possibility*. The difficulty which this conception presents, will be of quite a different nature from that which obstructs our belief in the possibility of miracle, when defined as a contravention of those great natural laws which the whole tendency of modern science declares to be absolute and immutable. The existence of sentient beings uncognisable by our senses, would no more contravene these laws, than did the discovery of the true nature of the Protozoa, those structureless gelatinous organisms which exhibit so many of the higher phenomena of animal life without any of that differentiation of parts or specialization of organs which the necessary functions of animal life seem to require. The existence of such preterhuman intelligences if proved, would only add another and more striking illustration than any we have yet received, of how small a portion of the great cosmos our senses give us cognisance. Even such sceptics on the subject of the supernatural as Hume or Strauss, would probably not deny the validity of the conception of such intelligences, or the abstract possibility of their existence. They would perhaps say, " We have no sufficient proof of the fact; the difficulty of conceiving their mode of existence is great; most intelligent men pass their whole lives in total ignorance of any such unseen intelligences: it is amongst the ignorant and superstitious alone that the belief in them prevails. As philosophers we cannot deny the possibility you postulate, but we must have the most clear and satisfactory proof before we can receive it as a fact."

But it may be argued, even if such beings should exist, they could consist only of the most diffused and subtle forms of matter. How then could they act upon ponderable bodies, how produce effects at all comparable to those which constitute so many reputed miracles? These objectors may be reminded, that all the most powerful and universal forces of nature are now referred to minute vibrations of an almost infinitely attenuated form of matter; and that, by the grandest generalisations of modern science, the most varied natural phenomena have been traced back to these recondite forces. Light, heat, electricity, magnetism, and probably vitality and gravitation, are believed to be but "modes of motion" of a space-filling ether; and there is not a single manifestation or force or development of beauty, but is derived from one or other of these. The whole surface of the globe has been modelled and remodelled, mountains have been cut down to plains, and plains have been grooved and furrowed into mountains and valleys, all by the power of ethereal heat vibrations set in motion by the sun. Metallic veins and glittering crystals buried deep down under miles of rock and mountain, have been formed by a distinct set of forces developed by vibrations of the same ether. Every green blade and bright blossom that gladdens the surface of the earth, owes its power of growth and life to those vibrations we call heat and light, while in animals and man the powers of that wondrous telegraph whose battery is the brain and whose wires are nerves, are probably due to the manifestation of a yet totally distinct "mode of motion" in the same all-pervading ether. In some cases we are able to perceive the effects of these recondite forces yet more directly. We see a magnet, without contact, or impact of any ponderable matter capable to our imagination of exerting force, yet overcoming gravity and inertia, raising and moving solid bodies. We behold electricity in the form of lightning riving the solid oak, throwing down lofty towers and steeples, or destroying man and beast, sometimes without a wound. And these manifestations of force are produced by a form of matter so impalpable, that only by its effects does it become known to us. With such phenomena everywhere around us, we must admit that if intelligences of what we may call an ethereal nature do exist, we have no reason to deny them the use of those ethereal forces which are the everflowing fountain from which all force, all motion, all life upon the earth originate. Our limited senses and intellects enable us to receive impressions from, and to trace some of the varied manifestations of ethereal motion under phases so distinct as light, heat, electricity, and gravity; but no thinker will for a moment assert that there can be no other possible modes of action of this primal element. To a race of blind men, how utterly inconceivable would be the faculty of vision, how absolutely unknowable the very existence of light and its myriad manifestations of form and beauty. Without this one sense, our knowledge of nature and of the universe could not be a thousandth part of what it is. By its absence our very intellect would have been dwarfed, we cannot say to what extent; and we must almost believe that our moral nature could never have been fully developed without it, and that we could hardly have attained to the dignity and supremacy of man. Yet it is possible and even probable that there may be modes of sensation as superior to all ours, as is sight to that of touch and hearing. In the next chapter we shall consider the bearings of this view of the subject on the more recent developments of so-called supernaturalism.

III.

MODERN MIRACLES VIEWED AS NATURAL PHENOMENA.

ONE very powerful argument against miracles with men of intelligence (and especially with such as are acquainted with the full scope of the revelations of modern science), is derived from the prevalent assumption that, if real, they are the direct acts of the Deity The nature of these acts is often such, that no cultivated mind can for a moment impute them to an infinite and supreme being. Few if any reputed miracles are at all worthy of a God; and it is the man of science who is best enabled to form a proper conception of the lofty and unapproachable nature of the attributes which must pertain to the supreme mind of the universe. Strange to say, however, he is in most cases illogical enough to consider the difficulties in the way of this assumption as a valid argument against the facts in question having ever occurred, instead of being merely one against the mode of interpreting them. He even carries this objection further, by the equally unfounded assumption that any beings who could possibly produce the asserted phenomena must be mentally of a high order, and therefore, if the phenomena do not accord with his ideas of the dignity of superior intelligences, he simply denies the facts without examination. Yet many of these objectors admit that the mind of man is probably not annihilated at death, and that therefore countless millions of beings are constantly passing into another mode of existence, who, unless a miracle of mental transformation takes place, must be very far inferior to himself. Any argument, therefore, against the reality of phenomena having been produced by preter-human intelligences, on account of the trivial or apparently useless nature of such phenomena, has really no logical bearing whatever upon the question. The assumption that all preter-human intelligences are more intellectual than the average of mankind, is as utterly gratuitous, and as powerless to disprove facts, as that of the opponents of Galileo when they asserted that the planets could not exceed the perfect number, *seven*, and that therefore the satellites of Jupiter could not exist. Let us now return to the consideration of the probable nature and powers of those preter-human intelligences, whose possible existence only it is my object at present to maintain.

I have in the first part of this paper given reasons for supposing that there might be, and probably are, other (and perhaps infinitely varied) forms of matter and modes of ethereal motion, than those which our senses enable us to recognise. We must therefore admit that there may be and probably are, organisations adapted to act upon and to receive impressions from them. In the infinite universe there may be infinite possibilities of sensation, each one as distinct from all the rest as sight is from smell or hearing, and as capable of extending the sphere of the possessor's knowledge and the development of his intellect, as would the sense of sight when first added to the other senses we possess. Beings of an ethereal order, if such exist, would probably possess some sense or senses of the nature above indicated, giving them increased insight into the constitution of the universe, and proportionately increased intelligence to guide and direct for special ends those new modes of ethereal motion, with which they would in that case be able to deal. Their every faculty might be proportionate to the modes of action of the ether. They might have a power of motion as rapid as that of light or the electric current. They might have a power of vision as acute as that of our most powerful telescopes and microscopes. They might have a sense somewhat analogous to the powers of the last triumph of science, the spectroscope, and by it be enabled to perceive instantaneously the intimate constitution of matter under every form, whether in organised beings or in stars and nebulæ. Such existences possessed of such, to us, inconceivable powers, would not be *supernatural*, except in a very limited and incorrect sense of the term. And if those powers were exerted in a manner to be perceived by us, the result would not be a *miracle*, in the sense in which the term is used by Hume or Tyndall. There would be no "violation of a law of nature;" there would be no "invasion of the law of conservation of energy." Neither matter nor force would be created or annihilated, even though it might appear so to us. In an infinite universe the great reservoir of matter and force must be infinite; and the fact that an ethereal being should be able to exert force, drawn perhaps from the boundless ether, perhaps from the vital energies of human beings, and make its effects visible to us as an apparent "creation," would be no more a real miracle, than is the perpetual raising of millions of tons of water from the ocean, or the perpetual exertion of animal force upon the earth, both of which we have only recently traced immediately to the sun, and perhaps remotely to other and varied sources lost in the immensity of the universe. All would be still natural. The great laws of nature would still maintain their inviolable supremacy. We should simply have to confess with a modern man of science, that "our five senses are but clumsy instruments to investigate the imponderables," and might see a new and deeper meaning in the oft-quoted but little heeded words of the great poet, when he reminds us that "there are more things in heaven and earth than are dreamt of in our philosophy."

It would appear then, if my argument has any weight, that there is nothing self-contradictory, nothing absolutely inconceivable, in the idea of intelligences uncognisable directly by our senses, and yet capable of acting more or less powerfully on matter. There is only to some minds a high improbability, arising from the supposed absence of all proof that there are such beings. Let direct proof be forthcoming, and there seems no reason why the most sceptical philosopher should refuse to accept it. It would be simply a matter to be investigated and tested like any other question of science. The evidence would have to be collected and examined. The results of the inquiries of different observers would have to be compared. The previous character of the observers for knowledge, accuracy, and honesty, would have to be weighed, and some, at least, of the facts relied on would have to be re-observed. In this manner only could all sources of error be eliminated, and a doctrine of such overwhelming importance be established as truth. I propose now to inquire whether such proof has been given, and whether the evidence is attainable by any one who may wish to investigate the subject in the only manner by which truth can be reached —by direct observation and experiment.

The first fact capable of proof is this:—That during the last eighteen years, while physical science has been progressing with rapid strides, and the growing spirit of rationalism has led to a very general questioning of all facts of a supposed miraculous or supernatural character, a continually increasing number of persons maintain their belief in the existence of beings of the nature of those we have hitherto postulated as a bare possibility. All these persons declare that they have received direct and oft-repeated proofs of the existence of such beings. Most of them tell us they have been convinced against all their previous notions and prepossessions. Very many have previously been materialists, not believing in the existence of any intelligences disconnected from a visible, tangible form, nor in the continued existence of the mind of man after death. At the present moment there are at least three millions of persons in the United States of America who have received to them satisfactory proofs of the existence of invisible intelligences; and in this country there are many thousands who declare the same thing. A large number of these persons continually receive fresh proofs in the privacy of their own homes, and so much interest is felt in the subject that <u>six</u> periodicals are published in London, several on the Continent, and a very large number in America, which are exclusively devoted to disseminating information relating to the existence of these invisible intelligences and the means of communicating with them. A little enquiry into the literature of the subject, which is already very extensive reveals the startling fact that this revival of so-called supernaturalism is not confined to the ignorant or superstitious, or to the lower classes of society. On the contrary, it is rather among the middle and upper classes that the larger proportion of its adherents are to be found; and among those who have declared themselves convinced of the reality of facts such as have been always classed as miracles, are numbers of literary, scientific, and professional men, who always have borne and still continue to bear high characters, are above the imputation either of falsehood or trickery, and have never manifested indications of insanity. Neither is the belief confined to any one religious sect or party. On the contrary, men of all religions and of no religion are alike to be found in the ranks of the believers; and as already

stated, many entire sceptics as to there being any superhuman intelligences in the universe, have declared that by
the force of direct evidence they have been, however unwill-
ingly, compelled to believe that such intelligences do exist.
Here is certainly a phenomenon altogether unique in
the history of the human mind. In examining the evidence of similar prodigies during past ages, we have to
make much allowance for early education, and the almost
universal pre-existing belief in the possibility and frequent
occurrence of miracles and supernatural appearances. In
the present day it is a notorious fact that among the educated classes, and especially among students of medicine
and science, the scepticism on such subjects is almost universal. But what seems the most extraordinary fact of all,
and one that would appear to be absolutely inconsistent
with any theory of fraud, imposture, or self-delusion, is,
that during the eighteen years which have elapsed since
the revival of a belief in the supernatural in America, not
one single individual has carefully investigated the subject
without accepting the reality of the phenomena, and while
thousands have been converted *to* the belief, not one adhe-
rent has ever been converted back *from* it. While the
peculiarly constituted individuals who are the *media* of
the phenomena may be counted by thousands, not one
has ever exploded the imposture, if imposture it be. And
of the few who receive payment for giving up their time
to those who wish to witness the manifestations, it is
remarkable that no one has yet tried to be first in the
market with a full history of the wonderfully ingenious
apparatus and extraordinary dexterity that must have
been requisite to make dupes of many millions of people
and to establish a new literature and a new religion. They
must be very blind not to see that such a work would be
a most profitable speculation.

D

If there is any one thing which modern philosophy teaches more consistently than another, it is that we can have no *à priori* knowledge of natural phenomena or of natural laws. But to declare that any facts, testified to by several independent witnesses, are impossible, and to act upon this declaration so far as to refuse to examine these facts when opportunity offers, is to lay claim to this very *à priori* knowledge of nature which has been universally given up. One of our most celebrated modern men of science fell into the same error when he made his unfortunate statement that, "before we proceed to consider any question involving physical principles, we should set out with clear ideas of the naturally possible and impossible;" for no man can be sure that, however "clear" his ideas may be in this matter, they will be equally true ones. It was very "clearly impossible" to the minds of the philosophers at Pisa that a great and a small weight could fall from the top of the heavy tower in the same time; and if this principle is of any use, they were right in disbelieving the evidence of their senses, which assured them that they did; and Galileo, who accepted that evidence, was, to use the words of the same eminent authority, "not only ignorant as respects the education of the judgment, but ignorant of his ignorance." Men who repeatedly, and under conditions which render doubt impossible to them, witness plain facts that their scientific teachers declare cannot be real, but yet decline to disprove by the only means possible, that of a full and impartial examination, may be excused for thinking that theirs is a parallel case to that of Galileo and his opponents.

In order that my readers may judge for themselves whether delusion or deception will best account for these facts, or whether we have indeed made a discovery more important and more extraordinary than any that has yet distinguished the nineteenth century, I propose to bring before them a few witnesses, whose evidence it will be well for them to hear before forming a hasty judgment. I shall call chiefly persons connected with science, art, or literature, and whose intelligence and truthfulness in narrating their own observations are above suspicion; and I would particularly insist, that no objections of a general kind can have any weight against direct evidence to special facts, many of which are of such a nature that there is absolutely no choice between believing that they did occur, or imputing to all who declare they witnessed them, wilful and purposeless falsehood.

IV.

OD-FORCE, ANIMAL MAGNETISM, AND CLAIRVOYANCE.

BEFORE proceeding to adduce the evidence of those persons who have witnessed phenomena which, if real, can only be attributed to preter-human intelligences, it will be well to take note of a series of curious observations on human beings, which prove that certain individuals are gifted with unusual powers of perception, sometimes by the ordinary senses leading to the discovery of new forces in nature, sometimes in a manner which no abnormal power of the ordinary senses will account for, but which imply the existence of faculties in the human mind of a nature analogous to those which are generally termed supernatural, and are attributed to the action of unembodied intelligences. It will be seen that we are thus naturally led up to higher phenomena, and are enabled, to some extent, to bridge over the great gulf between the so-called natural and supernatural.

I wish first to call my reader's attention to the researches of Baron Reichenbach, as detailed in Dr. Gregory's translation of his elaborate work. He observed that persons in a peculiar nervous condition experienced well-marked and definite sensations on contact with magnets and crystals, and in total darkness saw luminous emanations from them. He afterwards found that numbers of persons in perfect health and of superior intellect could perceive the same phenomena. As an example, I may mention that among the numerous persons experimented on by Baron Reichenbach were:

DR. ENDLICHER, Professor of Botany and Director of the Botanic Garden of Vienna.

DR. NIED, a physician at Vienna, in extensive practice, very active and healthy.

M. WILHELM, HOCHSTETTER, son of Professor Hochstetter of Esslingen.

M. THEODORE KOTSCHY, a clergyman, botanist, and well-known traveller in Africa and Persia; a powerful, vigorous, perfectly healthy man.

DR. HUSS, Professor of Clinical Medicine, Stockholm, and Physician to the King of Sweden.

DR. RAGSKY, Professor of Chemistry in the Medical and Surgical Josephakademie in Vienna.

M. CONSTANTIN DELHEZ, a French philologist, residing in Vienna.

M. ERNST PAUER, Consistorial Councillor, Vienna.

M. GUSTAV AUSCHNETZ, Artist, Vienna.

BARON VON OBERLAENDER, Forest Superintendent in Moravia.

All these saw the lights and flames on magnets, and described the various details of their comparative size, form, and colour, their relative magnitude on the positive and negative poles, and their appearance under various conditions, such as combinations of several magnets, images formed by lenses, &c.; and their evidence exactly confirmed the descriptions already given by the "sensitive" patients of a lower class, whose testimony had been objected to, when the observations were first published.

In addition to these, Dr. Diesing, Curator in the Imperial Academy of Natural History at Vienna, and the Chevalier Hubert von Rainer, Barrister of Klagenfurt, did not see the luminous phenomena, but were highly sensitive to the various sensations excited by magnets and crystals. About fifty other persons in all conditions of life, of all ages, and of both sexes, saw and felt the same phenomena. In an elaborate review of Reichenbach's work in the " British and Foreign Medico-Chirurgical Review," the evidence of these twelve gentlemen, men of position and science, and three of them medical men, is *completely ignored*, and it is again and again asserted that the phenomena are *subjective*, or purely imaginary. The only particle of argument to support this view is, that a mesmeric patient was *by suggestion* made to see " lights" as well without as with a magnet   It appears to me, that it would be as reasonable to tell Gordon Cumming or Dr. Livingstone that they had never seen a real lion, because, by suggestion, a score of mesmeric patients can be made to believe they see lions in a lecture room. Unless it can be proved that Reichenbach and these twelve gentlemen, have none of them sense enough to apply simple tests (which, however, the details of the experiments show, were again and again applied), I do not see how the general objections made in the above-mentioned article, that Reichenbach is not a physiologist, and that he did not apply sufficient tests, can have the slightest weight against the mass of evidence he adduces. It is certainly not creditable to modern science, that these elaborate investigations should be rejected without a particle of disproof; and we can only impute it to the distasteful character of some of the higher phenomena produced, and which it is still the fashion of professors of the physical sciences to ignore without ex- amination. I have seen it stated also, that Reichenbach's theory has been disproved by the use of an electro-magnet, and that a patient could not tell whether the current was on or off. But where is the detail of this experiment pub- lished, and how often has it been confirmed, and under what conditions ?   And if true in one case, how does it affect the question, when similar tests *were* applied to Reichenbach's patients; and how does it apply to facts like

this, which Reichenbach gives literally by the hundred ?
" Prof. D. Endlicher saw on the poles of an electro-magnet,
flames forty inches high, unsteady, exhibiting a rich play
of colours, and ending in a luminous smoke, which rose to
the ceiling and illuminated it." (Gregory's Trans. p. 342.)
The least the deniers of the facts can do, is to request these
well-known individuals who gave their evidence to Reichenbach, to repeat the experiments again under exactly
similar conditions, as no doubt in the interests of science
they would be willing to do.   If then, *by suggestion*, they
can all be led to describe equally well defined and varied
appearances when only sham magnets are used, the odylic
flames and other phenomena will have been fairly shown
to be very doubtful.   But as long as negative statements
only are made, and the whole body of facts testified to by
men at least equal in scientific attainments to their opponents, are left untouched, no unprejudiced individual can
fail to acknowledge that the researches of Reichenbach have
established the existence of a vast and connected series of
new and important natural phenomena.   Doctors Gregory
and Ashburner in England, state that they have repeated
several of Reichenbach's experiments, under test conditions,
and have found them quite accurate.

Mr Rutter, of Brighton, has made, quite independently,
a number of curious experiments, which he has detailed
in his little work on " Magnetised Currents and the Magnetoscope," and which were witnessed by hundreds of
medical and scientific men.   He showed that the various
metals and other substances, the contact of a male or
female hand, or even of a letter written by a male or
female, each produced distinct effects on the magnetoscope.
And a single drop of water from a glass in which a homœo-
pathic globule had been dissolved, caused a characteristic
motion of the instrument when dropped upon the hand of

the operator, even when he did not know the substance employed. Dr. King corroborates these experiments, and states that he has seen a decillionth of a grain of silex, and a billionth of a grain of quinine cause motion by means of this apparatus. Every caution was taken in conducting the experiments, which were equally successful when a third party was placed between Mr. R. and the magneto-ccope. Magnets and crystals also produced powerful effects, as indicated by Reichenbach. Yet Mr. Rutter's experiments, like Reichenbach's, are ignored by our scientific men, although during several years he offered facility for their investigation.[*]

The case of Jacques Aymar, whose powers were imputed by himself and others to the divining rod, but which were evidently personal, is one of the best attested on record, and one which indisputably proves the possession by him

---

[*] Dr. Carpenter ("Mental Physiology," p. 287) states that Mr. Rutter's experiments were shown to be fallacies by Dr. Madden, who found that unless he knew the substance operated on, no definite indications were given. But this only proves that different operators have different degrees of power. And Dr. Carpenter very unfairly omits to notice three very important classes of test experiments made by Mr. Rutter. In one a crystal is placed on a stand altogether detached from the instrument or the table on which it stands. Yet when this is touched, it sets the pendulum in motion; and the direction of the motion changes as the direction of the axis of the crystal is changed.— (Rutter's "Human Electricity," p. 151). Again, when the pendulum has acquired its full momentum, either rotary or oscillatory, it takes from 7 to 10 *minutes* to come to a state of rest. But if any piece of bone or other dead animal matter is placed in the operator's hand, the pendulum comes to a dead stop in from 5 to 20 *seconds;* a feat which cannot be performed voluntarily or by any amount of "expectant attention" (Op. cit. p. 147 and app. p. lv.) Again, knowledge of the substance operated on is *not necessary* with all operators, to produce definite and correct results (l. c. app. p. lvi.) What are we to think of a writer who comes forward as a master to teach the public, and sets before them such a partial and one-sided account of the evidence as this?

of a new sense in some degree resembling that of many other clairvoyants. Mr. Baring-Gould, in his "Curious Myths of the Middle Ages," gives a full account of the case with a reference to the original authorities. These are, M. Chauvin, a Doctor of Medicine, who was an eye-witness who publishes his narrative; the Sieur Pauthot, Dean of the College of Medicine at Lyons; and the Procès-verbal of the Procureur du Roi. The facts of the case are briefly as follows. On the 5th of July, 1692, a wine-seller and his wife were murdered and the bodies found in their cellar in Lyons, their money having been carried off. A bloody hedging bill was found by the side of the bodies, but no trace of the murderers was discovered. The officers of justice were completely at fault, when they were told of a man named Jacques Aymar, who, four years before had discovered a thief at Grenoble who was quite unsuspected of the crime. The man was sent for and taken to the cellar, where his divining rod became violently agitated, and his pulse rose as though he were in a fever. He then went out of the house, and walked along the streets like a hound following a scent. He crossed the court of the Archbishop's palace and down to the gate of the Rhone, when, it being night, the quest was relinquished. The next day, accompanied by three officers, he followed the track down the bank of the river to a gardener's cottage. He had declared that so far he had followed three murderers, but here two only entered the cottage, where he declared they had seated themselves at a table and had drunk wine from a particular bottle. The owner declared positively no one had been there, but Aymar, on testing each individual in the house, found two children who had been in contact with the murderers, and these reluctantly confessed that on Sunday morning when they were alone, two men

had suddenly entered and had seated themselves and taken
wine from the very bottle which had been pointed out.
He then followed them down the river and discovered the
places where they slept, and the particular chairs or benches
they had used. After a time he reached the military camp
of Sablon, and ultimately reached Beaucaire where the
murderers had parted company, but he traced one of them
into the prison, and among fourteen or fifteen prisoners
pointed out a hunchback (who had only been an hour in
the prison) as the murderer. He protested his innocence,
but on being taken back along the road was recognised in
every house where Aymar had previously traced him.
This so confounded him that he confessed, and was ultimately executed for the murder.

During the process of this wonderful experiment, which
occupied several days, Aymar was subjected to other tests
by the Procurator General. The hedging bill, with which
the murder was committed, with three others exactly like
it, were secretly buried in different places in a garden. The
diviner was then brought in; and his rod indicated where
the blood-stained weapon was buried, but showed no movement over the others. Again they were all exhumed and
reinterred, and the Comptroller of the Province himself
bandaged Aymar's eyes and led him into the garden, with
the same result. The two other murderers were afterwards traced, but they had escaped out of France. Pierre
Garnier, Physician of the Medical College of Montpelier,
has also given an account of various tests to which Aymar
was subjected by himself, the Lieutenant General, and two
other gentlemen to detect imposture; but they failed to
discover a trace of deception, and he traced the course of a
man who had robbed the Lieutenant General some months
before, pointing out the exact side of a bed on which he
had slept with another man.

Here is a case which one would think was demonstrated; the investigation having been carried on under the eyes of magistrates, officers, and physicians, and resulting in the discovery of a murder and the tracking out of his course with more minute accuracy than ever bloodhound tracked a fugitive slave,—yet Mr. Baring-Gould calls the man an " impostor," and speaks of his " *exposé* and downfall." And what are the grounds on which these harsh terms are used ? Merely that at a later period, when brought to Paris to satisfy the curiosity of the great and learned, his power left him, and he seems to have either had totally false impressions or to have told lies to conceal his want of power. But how does this in the least affect the question? The fact that he was so easily found out at Paris, or rather that he there possessed no extraordinary powers, would surely prove rather, that there could not possibly have been any imposture in the former case when he stood every test, and instead of failing, succeeded. He can only be proved an impostor by proving all the witnesses to be also impostors, or by showing that no such crime was ever committed, or ever discovered. This, however, neither Mr. Baring-Gould nor any one else has ever attempted to do; and we must therefore conclude that the murder was really discovered by Jacques Aymar in the manner described, and that he undoubtedly possessed some equivalent to a new sense in many respects resembling the powers of some modern clairvoyants.

The subject of Animal Magnetism is still so much a disputed one among scientific men, and many of its alleged phenomena so closely border on, if they do not actually reach what is classed as supernatural, that I wish to give a few illustrations of the kind of facts by which it is supported. I will first quote the evidence of Dr. William Gregory, late Professor of Chemistry in the University of Edinburgh, who for many years made continued personal investigations into this subject, and has recorded them in his " Letters on Animal Magnetism," published in 1851.   The simpler phenomena of what are usually termed " Hypnotism," and " Electro-Biology," are now universally admitted to be real ; though it must never be forgotten, that they too had to fight their way through the same denials, accusations, and imputations, that are now made against clairvoyance, and phreno-mesmerism.   The same men who advocated, tested, and established the truth of the more simple facts, claim that they have done the same for the higher phenomena ; the same class of scientific and medical men who once denied the former, now deny the latter. Let us see then if the evidence for the one is as good as it was for the other.

Dr. Gregory defines several stages of clairvoyance, sometimes existing in the same, sometimes in different patients. The chief division, however, is into 1. Sympathy or thought-reading, and 2. True clairvoyance. The evidence for the first is so overwhelming, it is to be met with almost everywhere, and is so generally admitted, that I shall not occupy space by giving examples, although it is, I believe, still denied by the more materialistic physiologists. We will, therefore, confine our attention to the various phases of true clairvoyance.

Dr. Haddock, residing at Bolton, had a very remarkable clairvoyante (E.) under his care.   Dr. Gregory says, "After I returned to Edinburgh, I had very frequent communication with Dr. H., and tried many experiments with this remarkable subject, sending specimens of writing, locks of hair, and other objects, the origin of which was perfectly unknown to Dr. H., and in every case, without exception, E. saw and described with accuracy the persons concerned " (p. 403).

Sir Walter C. Trevelyan, Bart., received a letter from a lady in London, in which the loss of a gold watch was mentioned. He sent the letter to Dr. H. to see if E. could trace the watch. She described the lady accurately, and her house and furniture minutely, and described the watch and chain, and described the person who had it, who, she said, was not a habitual thief, and said further that she could tell her handwriting. The lady, to whom these accounts were sent, acknowledged their perfect accuracy, but said, the description of the thief applied to one of her maids whom she did not suspect, so she sent several pieces of handwriting, including that of both her maids. The clairvoyante immediately selected that of the one she had described, and said—"she was thinking of restoring the watch, saying she had found it." Sir W. Trevelyan wrote with this information, but a letter from the lady crossed his, saying, the girl mentioned before by the clairvoyante, *had restored the watch and said she had found it* (p. 405.)

Sir W. Trevelyan communicated to Dr. Gregory another experiment he had made. He requested the Secretary of the Geographical Society to send him the writing of several persons abroad, not known to him, and without their names. Three were sent. E. discovered in each case, where they were; in two of them described their persons accurately; described in all three cases, the cities and countries in which they were, so that they could be easily recognised, and told the time by the clocks, which verified the place by difference of longitude (p. 407.)

Many other cases, equally well tested, are given in great detail by Dr. Gregory; and numerous cases are given of tests of what may be called simple direct clairvoyance. For example, persons going to see the phenomena purchase in any shop they please, a few dozens of printed mottoes, enclosed in nutshells. These are placed in a bag, and the

clairvoyante takes out a nutshell and reads the motto.
The shell is then broken open and examined, and hundreds
of mottoes have been thus read correctly.   One motto thus
read contained ninety-eight words.   Numbers of other
equally severe test cases, are given by Dr. Gregory, devised
and tried by himself and by other well-known persons.

Now will it be believed, that in the very elaborate
article in the "British and Foreign Medico-Chirurgical
Review" already referred to, on Dr. Gregory's and other
works of an allied nature, *not one single experiment of this
kind is mentioned or alluded to ?*   There is a great deal of
general objection to Dr. Gregory's views, because he was a
chemist and not specially devoted to physiology (forgetting
that Dr. Elliotson and Dr. Mayo who testify to similar
facts, were both specially devoted to physiology) and a few
quotations of a general nature only are given; so that no
reader could imagine that the work criticised was the
result of *observation* or *experiment* at all.   The case is a
complete illustration of judicial blindness.   The opponents
dare not impute wilful falsehood to Dr. Gregory, Dr. Mayo,
Dr. Haddock, Sir Walter Trevelyan, Sir T. Willshire, and
other gentlemen who vouch for these facts; and yet the
facts are of such an unmistakable nature, that without
imputing wilful falsehood they cannot be explained away.
They are therefore silently ignored, or more probably the
records of them are never read.   But the silence or contempt of our modern scientific men cannot blind the
world any longer to those grand and mysterious phenomena of mind, the investigation of which can alone conduct us to a kowledge of what we really are.

Dr. Herbert Mayo, F.R.S., late Professor of Anatomy
and Physiology in King's College, and of Comparative
Anatomy in the Royal College of Surgeons, also gives his
personal testimony to facts of a similar nature.   In his

"Letters on the Truths contained in Popular Superstitions" (2nd. Ed. p. 178), he says:—"From Boppard, where I was residing in the years 1845—46, I sent to an American gentleman in Paris a lock of hair, which Col. C—, an invalid then under my care, had cut from his own head and wrapped in writing paper from his own writing desk. Col. C— was unknown even by name to this American gentleman, who had no clue whatever whereby to identify the proprietor of the hair. And all that he did was to place the paper in the hands of a noted Parisian somnambulist. She stated, in the opinion she gave on the case, that Col. C— had partial palsy of the hips and legs, and that for another complaint he was in the habit of using a surgical instrument. The patient laughed heartily at the idea of the distant somnambulist having so completely realised him."

Dr. Mayo also announces his conversion to a belief in the truth of phrenology and phreno-mesmerism, and Dr. Gregory gives copious details of experiments in which special care has been taken to avoid all the supposed sources of fallacy in phreno-mesmerism; yet although Dr. Mayo's work is included in the criticism already referred to, none of the facts he himself testifies to, nor the latest opinions he puts forward, are so much as once mentioned.

Dr. Joseph Haddock, a physician, resident and prac- tising at Bolton, who has been already mentioned, has published a work entitled "Somnolism and Psycheism," in which he endeavours to classify the facts of mesmerism and clairvoyance, and to account for them on physiological and psychical principles. The work is well worth reading, but my purpose here is to bring forward one or two facts from those which he gives in an appendix to his work. Nothing is more common than for those who deny the reality of clairvoyance to ask contemptuously, "If it is

true, why is not use made of it to discover lost property, or
to get news from abroad?" To such I commend the following statement, of which I can only give an abstract.

On Wednesday evening, December the 20th, 1848, Mr.
Wood, grocer of Cheapside, Bolton, had his cash box with
its contents stolen from his counting-house. He applied
to the police and could get no clue, though he suspected
one individual. He then came to Dr. Haddock to see if
the girl, Emma, could discover the thief or the property.
When put in *rapport* with Emma she was asked about the
lost cash box, and after a few moments she began to talk
as if to some one not present, described where the box was,
what were its contents, how the person took it, where he
first hid it; and then described the person, dress, associations of the thief so vividly, that Mr. Wood recognised a
person he had *not the least suspected.* Mr. Wood immediately sought out this person, and gave him the option of
coming at once to Dr. Haddock's or to the police office.
He chose the former, and when he came into the room
Emma started back, told him he was a bad man, and had
not on the same clothes as when he took the box. He at
first denied all knowledge of the robbery, but after a time
acknowledged that he had taken it exactly in the manner
described by Emma, and it was accordingly recovered.

Now as the names, place, and date of this occurrence are
given, and it is narrated by an English physician, it can
hardly be denied without first making some inquiry at the
place where it is said to have happened. The next instance
is of clairvoyance at a much greater distance. A young
man had sailed suddenly from Liverpool for New York. His
parents immediately remitted him some money by the mail
steamer, but they heard, some time afterwards, that he had
never applied for it. The mother came twenty miles to
Bolton to see if, by Emma's means, she could learn any-

thing of him. After a little time Emma found him, described his appearance correctly, and entered into so many details as to induce his mother to rely upon her statements, and to request Dr. Haddock to make enquiries at intervals of about a fortnight. He did so, traced the young man by her means to several places, and the information thus acquired was sent to his parents. Shortly after, Dr. Haddock received information from the father that a letter had arrived from his son, and that "it was a most striking confirmation of Emma's testimony from first to last."

Dr. Edwin Lee, in his work on "Animal Magnetism," gives an account of fourteen séances at Brighton in private houses with Alexis Didier the well known clairvoyant. On every one of these occasions, he played at cards blindfolded, often naming his adversary's cards as well as his own, read numbers of cards written by the visitors and enclosed in envelopes, read any line asked for in any book, eight or ten pages farther on than the page opened, and described the contents of numbers of boxes, card-cases, and other envelopes. Dr. Lee also gives an account of the celebrated Robert Houdin's interview with Alexis when similar tests were applied by that great conjurer, who brought his own cards and dealt them himself, and yet Alexis immediately told him every card in both the hands without turning them up. Houdin took a book from his pocket and opening it asked Alexis to read a line at a particular level eight pages in advance. The clairvoyant stuck a pin in to mark the line and read four words which were found on the corresponding line at the ninth page forward. Houdin proclaimed it "stupefying", and the next day signed this declaration: "I cannot help stating that the facts above related are scrupulously exact, and the more I reflect upon them the more impossible do I find it to class them among the tricks which are the object of my art."

E

A fortnight later he sent a letter to M. de Mirville (by whom he had been introduced to Alexis) giving an account of a second seance where the same results were repeated, and concluding:—"I therefore came away from this seance as astonished as any one can be, and fully convinced that it would be quite *impossible* for any one to produce such surprising effects by mere skill."

Mr. H. G. Atkinson, F.G.S., has shewn me one of the tests of clairvoyance by Adolphe Didier, brother of Alexis, which he saw produced himself at a private house in London. A well known nobleman wrote a word at the bottom of a piece of paper which he folded over repeatedly so that it was covered by five or six layers of paper. It was then given to Adolphe, who was surrounded by a circle of observers while he wrote with a pencil outside what had been written within. The curious point is that he made several trials and crossed them out again but at length wrote the exact word, the others being approximations to it. This is very curious and indicates the existence of a new sense, a kind of rudimentary perception which can only get at the exact truth by degrees, and it corresponds remarkably with the manner in which clairvoyants generally describe objects. They do not say at once: "It is a medal," but "It is metal," "it is round and flat," "it has writing on it," and so on.

Now, when we have the evidence of Dr. Gregory, Dr. Mayo, Dr. Lee, Dr. Haddock, and of hundreds of other equally honest if not equally capable men who have witnessed similar facts, is it a satisfactory solution of the difficulty, that all of these persons in every case were the victims of imposture? Medical men are not very easily imposed on, especially in a matter which they can observe and test repeatedly; and when we find that such a celebrated professor of legerdemain as Houdin not only detected no imposture but declared the phenomena *impossible* to be the effect of skill or trick, we have a complete answer to all who, without investigation, proclaim the whole a che t! In this case it is clear that there is no room for self-dec p-tion. Either every one of the cases of clairvoyance yet recorded (and they certainly number thousands) is the result of imposture, or we have ample proof that cert in individuals possess a new sense of which it is probable we all have the rudiments. If ordinary vision were as rare as clairvoyance, it would be just as difficult to prove its reality as it is now to establish the reality of this wonderful power. The evidence in its favour is absolutely conclusive to any one who will examine it, and who is not deluded by that most unphilosophical dogma that he knows *a priori* what is possible and what is impossible.

In a paper by Dr. T. Edwards Clark, of New York, on the Physiology of Trance, which appeared in the *Quarterly Journal of Psychological Medicine*, it is stated that a cataleptic patient was under the care of M. Despine, late Inspector of the Mineral Waters of Aix, in Savoy, who says of her:—"Not only could our patient hear by means of the palms of her hands, but we have seen her read without the assistance of the eyes, merely with the tips of the fingers, which she passed rapidly over the page that she wished to read. At other times we have seen her copy a letter word for word, reading it with her left elbow while she wrote with her right hand. During these proceedings, *a thick pasteboard completely intercepted* any visual ray that might have reached her eyes. The same phenomenon was manifested at the soles of her feet, on the epigastrium, and other parts of the body."

Dr. Clark adds:—"There are many other cases equally as strange as these, that have been noticed by different persons standing high in the medical profession."

The above test of holding a pasteboard before the eyes, is one which Dr. Carpenter informed me he considered conclusive, as *he* found that supposed clairvoyants always failed to see through it. But it is evident that he had never met with a case of very perfect clairvoyance like that above described.*

We will now pass to the evidence for the facts of what is termed Modern Spiritualism.

---

* Not one of the important *facts* mentioned in this chapter, on the authority of medical men, nor any others of a like nature to be found in the works here quoted, are taken notice of by Dr. Carpenter in his recent volume on "Mental Physiology;" in which he nevertheless boldly attempts to settle the whole question of the reality of such facts! It is, we suppose, owing to his limited space that, in a work of over 700 pp., none of the well-attested facts opposed to his views could be brought to the notice of his readers.

V.

THE EVIDENCE OF THE REALITY OF APPARITIONS.

I NOW propose to give a few instances in which the evidence of the appearance of preter-human or spiritual beings is as good and definite as it is possible for any evidence of any fact to be.   For this purpose I shall use some of the remarkable cases collected and investigated by the Hon. Robert Dale Owen, formerly member of Congress and American Minister at Naples.   Mr. Owen is the author of works of a varied character; * Essays," Moral Physiology," "The Policy of Emancipation," and many others.   He has been, I believe, throughout his life a consistent and philosophical sceptic, and his writings show him to be well educated, logical, and extremely cautious in accepting evidence.

In 1855, during his official residence at Naples, his attention seems to have been first attracted to the subject of the "supernatural," by witnessing the phenomena occurring in the presence of Mr. Home.   He tells us that "sitting in his own well-lighted apartment, in company with three or four friends, all curious observers like himself," a table and lamp weighing ninety-six pounds "rose eight or ten inches from the floor, and remained suspended in the air while one might count six or seven, the hands of all present being laid upon the table."

And on another occasion he states:—"In the dining-room of a French nobleman, the Count d'Ourches, residing near Paris, I saw on the first day of October 1858, in broad daylight, at the close of a *déjeuner à la fourchette*, a dinner-table seating seven persons, with fruit and wine on it, rise and settle down as already described, while all the guests were standing around it, *and not one of them touching it.* All present saw the same thing."

He then commenced collecting evidence of so-called supernatural phenomena, occurring *unsought for*, and has brought together, in his "Footfalls on the Boundary of another World," the best arranged and best authenticated series of facts which have yet been given to the public on this subject.

This work is certainly the most philosophical of its kind that has yet appeared, and perhaps, had it been entitled "A Critical Examination into the Evidence of the Supernatural," which it really is, it would have attracted more attention than it appears to have done.

Nothing is more common than the assertion that all supposed apparitions, when not impostures, are hallucinations; because, it is said, there is no well-authenticated case of an apparition having been seen by two persons at once. It is therefore advisable to give an outline here of one case of this kind, which is given more fully at p. 278 of Mr. Owen's book.

Sir John Sherbroke and General George Wynyard were Captain and Lieutenant in the 33rd Regiment, stationed in the year 1785 at Sydney, in the island of Cape Breton, Nova Scotia. On the 15th of October of that year, about nine in the morning, as they were sitting together at coffee in Wynyard's parlour, Sherbroke, happening to look up, saw the figure of a pale youth standing at a door leading into the passage. He called the attention of his companion to the stranger, who passed slowly through the room into the adjoining bed-chamber. Wynyard, on seeing the figure, turned as pale as death, grasped his friend's arm, and, as soon as it had disappeared, exclaimed, "Great

God! my brother!" Sherbroke thinking there was some trick, had a search immediately made, but could find no one either in the bed-room or about the premises. A brother officer, Lieutenant Gore, coming in at the time, assisted in the search, and at his suggestion Sherbroke made a memorandum of the date, and all waited with anxiety for letters from England, where Wynyard's brother was. The expected letter came to Captain Sherbrooke, asking him to break to his friend the news of his brother John's death, which had occurred on the day and hour when he had been seen by the two officers. In 1823 Lieutenant-Colonel Gore gave this account in writing to Sir John Harvey, Adjutant-General of the Forces in Canada. He also stated that some years afterwards Sir Sherbroke, who had never seen John Wynyard alive, recognised in England a brother of the deceased, who was remarkably like him, by the resemblance to the figure he had seen in Canada. Mr. Owen has obtained additional proof of the correctness of these details from Captain Henry Scott, R.N., who was told by General Paul Anderson, C.B., that Sir John Sherbroke had, shortly before his death, related the story to him in almost exactly the same words as Mr. Owen has given it and which was communicated in manuscript to Captain Scott.

The evidence in this case of the fact of the appearance of the same apparition to two people (one of whom did not know the individual) is very complete; and I cannot rest satisfied with any theory which requires me to reject such evidence, without offering any intelligible explanation of what occurred.

I will now give an abstract of a few more of Mr. Owen's cases, to illustrate their general character and the careful manner in which they have been authenticated and tested. The first is one which he calls "The Fourteenth of November." ("Footfalls," p. 299.)

On the night between the 14th and 15th of November, 1857, the wife of Captain G. Wheatcroft, residing in Cambridge, dreamed that she saw her husband (then in India). She immediately awoke, and looking up, she perceived the same figure standing by her bedside. He appeared in his uniform, the hands pressed across the breast, the hair dishevelled, the face very pale. His large dark eyes were fixed full upon her; their expression was that of great excitement, and there was a peculiar contraction of the mouth, habitual to him when agitated. She saw him, even to each minute particular of his dress, as distinctly as she had ever done in her life. The figure seemed to bend forward as if in pain, and to make an effort to speak, but there was no sound. It remained visible, the wife thinks, as long as a minute, and then disappeared. She did not sleep again that night. Next morning she related all this to her mother, expressing her belief that Captain W. was either killed or wounded. In due course a telegram was received to the effect that Captain W. had been killed before Lucknow on the 15th of November. The widow informed the Captain's solicitor, Mr. Wilkinson, that she had been quite prepared for the fatal news, but she felt sure there was a mistake of a day in the date of his death. Mr. Wilkinson then obtained a certificate from the War Office, which was as follows :—

"9579.
"No.——.

"War Office, 30th January, 1858.

"These are to certify that it appears, by the records in this office, that Captain G. Wheatcroft, of the 6th Dragoon Guards, was killed in action on the 15th of November, 1857.

(Signed)   "B. Hawes."

A remarkable incident now occurred. Mr. Wilkinson was visiting a friend in London, whose wife has all her life had perception of apparitions, while her husband is a "medium." He related to them the vision of the Captain's widow, and described the figure as it appeared to her, when Mrs. N. instantly said, "That must be the very person I saw on the evening we were talking of India." In answer to Mr. Wilkinson's questions, she said they had obtained a communication from him through her husband, and he had said that he had been killed in India that afternoon by a wound in the breast. It was about nine o'clock in the evening; she did not recollect the date. On further inquiry, she remembered that she had been interrupted by a tradesman, and had paid a bill that evening; and on bringing it for Mr. Wilkinson's inspection, the receipt bore date the *Fourteenth* of November. In March, 1858, the family of Captain Wheatcroft received a letter from Captain G—— C——, dated Lucknow, 19th of December, 1857, in which he said he had been close to Captain W. when he fell, and that it was on the *fourteenth in the afternoon*, and not on the 15th, as reported in Sir Colin Campbell's despatches. He was struck by a fragment of a shell in the breast. He was buried at Dilkoosha, and on a wooden cross at the head of his grave are cut the initials G. W., and the date of his death, 14th of November. The War Office corrected their mistake. Mr. Wilkinson obtained another copy of the certificate in April, 1859, and found it in the same words as that already given, only that the 14th of November had been substituted for the 15th.

Mr. Owen obtained the whole of these facts *directly from the parties themselves.* The widow of Captain Wheatcroft examined and corrected his MSS., and showed him a copy of Captain C.'s letter. Mr. Wilkinson did the same; and Mrs. N—— herself related to him the facts which occurred to her. Mrs. N—— had also related the circumstances to Mr. Howitt before Mr. Owen's investigations, as he certifies in his "History of the Supernatural," vol. 2, p. 225.

Mr. Owen also states that he has in his possession both
the War Office certificates, the first showing the erroneous
and the second the corrected date.

Here we have the same apparition appearing to two
ladies unknown to and remote from each other on the same
night; the communication obtained through a third person,
declaring the time and mode of death; and all coinciding
exactly with the events happening many thousand miles
away. We presume the *facts* thus attested will not be
disputed; and to attribute the whole to "coincidence"
must surely be too great a stretch of credulity, even for
the most incredulous.

The next case is one of haunting, and is called

THE OLD KENT MANOR HOUSE (p. 304).

In October, 1857, and for several months afterwards,
Mrs. R., the wife of a field officer of high rank, was residing in Ramhurst Manor House, near Leigh, in Kent. From
her first occupying it, every inmate of the house was more
or less disturbed at night by knocking, and sounds as of
footsteps, but more especially by voices, which could not
be accounted for. Mrs. R.'s brother, a young officer, heard
these voices at night, and tried every means to discover
the source of them in vain. The servants were much
frightened. On the second Saturday in October, Miss S.,
a young lady who had been in the habit of seeing apparitions from her childhood, came to visit Mrs. R., who met
her at the railway station. On arriving at the house Miss
S. saw on the threshold two figures, apparently an elderly
couple, in old-fashioned dress. Not wishing to make her
friend uneasy, she said nothing about them at the time.
During the next ten days she saw the same figures several
times in different parts of the house, always by daylight.
They appeared surrounded by an atmosphere of a neutral
tint. On the third occasion they spoke to her, and said

that they had formerly possessed that house, and that their
name was *Children*. They appeared sad and downcast,
and said that they had idolised their property, and that it
troubled them to know that it had passed away from
their family, and was now in the hands of strangers. On
Mrs. R. asking Miss S. if she had heard or seen anything,
she related this to her. Mrs. R. had herself heard the
noises and voices continually, but had seen nothing, and
after a month had given up all expectation of doing so,
when one day, as she had just finished dressing for dinner,
in a well-lighted room with a fire in it, and was coming
down hastily, having been repeatedly called by her brother,
who was impatiently waiting for her, she beheld the two
figures standing in the doorway, dressed just as Miss S.
had described them, but above the figure of the lady,
written in the dusky atmosphere, in letters of phosphoric
light, the words "Dame Children," and some other words
intimating that she was "earth-bound." At this moment
her brother again called out to her that dinner was waiting,
and, closing her eyes, she rushed through the figures.
Inquiries were made by the ladies as to who had lived in
the house formerly, and it was only after four months
that they found out, through a very old woman, who
remembered an old man, who had told her that he had in
his boyhood assisted to keep the hounds for the Children
family, who then lived at Ramhurst. All these particulars
Mr. Owen received himself from the two ladies, in December, 1858. Miss S. had had many conversations with the
apparitions, and on Mr. Owen's inquiring for any details
they had communicated, she told him that the husband
had said his name was *Richard*, and that he had died in
1753. Mr. Owen now determined, if possible, to ascertain
the accuracy of these facts, and after a long search among
churchyards and antiquarian clergymen, he was directed

to the "Hasted Papers" in the British Museum. From these he ascertained that "*Richard* Children settled himself at Ramhurst," his family having previously resided at a house called "Childrens," in the parish of Tunbridge. It required further research to determine the date. This was found several months later, in an old "History of Kent," by the same "Hasted," published in 1778, where it is stated that "Ramhurst passed by sale to Richard Children, Esq., who resided here, and died possessed of it in 1753, aged eighty-three years." In the "Hasted Papers" it was also stated that his son did not live at Ramhurst, and that the family seat after Richard's time was Ferox Hall, near Tunbridge. Since 1816 the mansion has been occupied as a farm house, having passed away entirely from the Children family.

However much any one of these incidents might have been scouted as a delusion, what are we to say to the combination of them? A whole household hear distinct and definite noises of persons walking and speaking. Two ladies see the same appearances, at different times, and under circumstances the least favourable for delusion. The name is given to one by voice, to the other by writing; the date of death is communicated. An independent enquirer by much research, finds out that all these facts are true; that the christian name of the only "Children" who occupied and died in the house was *Richard*, and that his death took place in the year given by the apparition, 1753.

Mr. Owen's own full account of this case, and the observations on it should be read, but this imperfect abstract will serve to show that none of the ordinary modes of escaping from the difficulties of a "ghost story" are here applicable.

At page 195 of Mr. Owen's volume, we have a most

interesting account of disturbances occurring at the parsonage of Cideville, in the department of Seine Inférieure, France, in the winter of 1850-51.   The circumstances gave rise to a trial, and the whole of the facts were brought out by the examination of a great number of witnesses.   The Marquis de Mirville collected from the legal record all the documents connected with the trial, including the *procès verbal* of the testimony.   It is from these official documents Mr. Owen gives his details of the occurrences.

The disturbances commenced from the time when two boys, aged 12 and 14, came to be educated by M. Tinel, the parish priest of Cideville, and continued *two months and a half* until the children were removed from the parsonage.   They consisted of knockings, as if with a hammer on the wainscot; scratchings, shakings of the house so that all the furniture rattled; a din as if every one in the house were beating the floor with mallets, the beatings forming tunes when. asked, and answering questions by numbers agreed on.   Besides these noises there were strange and unaccountable exhibitions of force.   The tables and desks moved about without visible cause; the fire-irons flew repeatedly into the middle of the room, windows were broken; a hammer was thrown into the middle of the room, and yet fell without noise, as if put down by an invisible hand; persons standing quite alone had their dresses pulled.   On the Mayor of Cideville coming to examine into the matter, a table at which he sat with another person, moved away in spite of their endeavours to hold it back, while the children were standing in the middle of the room; and many other facts of a similar nature were observed repeatedly by numerous persons of respectability and position, every one of whom, going with the intention of finding out a trick, were, after deliberate examination, convinced that the phenomena were not produced by any person present. The Marquis de Mirville was himself one of the witnesses.

The interest of this case consists first, in the evidence having been brought out before a legal tribunal; and secondly, in the remarkable resemblance of the phenomena to those which had occurred a short time previously in America, but had not yet become much known in Europe. There is also the closest resemblance to what occurred at Epworth Parsonage in the family of Wesley's father, and which is almost equally well authenticated.* Now when in three different countries, phenomena occur of an exactly similar nature, and which are all open to the fullest examination at the time, and when no trick or delusion is in either case found out but every individual of many hundreds who go to see them becomes convinced of their reality, the fact of the similarity of the occurrences even

---

* In an article entitled "Spirit Rapping a Century Ago," in an early number of the *Fortnightly Review*, an account is given of the disturbances at Epworth Parsonage, the residence of the Wesley family, and it is attempted to account for them by the supposition that they were entirely produced by Hester Wesley, one of John Wesley's sisters; yet the phenomena, even as related by this writer, are such as no human being could possibly have produced, while the moral difficulties of the case are admitted to be quite as great as the physical ones. Every reader of the article must have perceived how lame and impotent is the explanation suggested; and one is almost forced to conclude that the writer did not believe in it himself, so different is the tone of the first part of the article in which he details the facts, from the latter part in which he attempts to account for them. When taken in connection with other similar occurrences narrated by Mr. Owen, all equally well authenticated, and all thoroughly investigated at the time, it will be impossible to receive as an explanation that they were in every case mere childish tricks, since that will not account for more than a minute fraction of the established facts. If we are to reject all the facts this assumption will not explain, it will be much simpler and quite as satisfactory to deny that there are any facts that need explaining.

in many details, is of great weight as indicating a similar *natural* origin. In such cases we cannot fairly accept the general explanation of "imposture," given by those who have not witnessed the phenomena, when none of those who did witness them, could ever detect imposture.

The examples I have quoted, give a very imperfect idea of the variety and interest of Mr. Owen's work, but they will serve to indicate the nature of the evidence he has in every case adduced, and may lead some of my readers to examine the work itself. If they do so they will see that similar phenomena to those which puzzled our forefathers at Epworth Parsonage, and at Mr. Mompesson's, at Tedworth, have recurred in our own time, and have been subjected to the most searching examination, without any discovery of trick or imposture; and they may, perhaps, be led to conclude, that though often asserted, it is not yet quite proved that "ghosts have been everywhere banished by the introduction of gaslight."

ظ

VI.

MODERN SPIRITUALISM: EVIDENCE OF MEN OF SCIENCE.

WE have now come to the consideration of what is more especially termed " modern spiritualism," or those pheno- mena which occur only in the presence, or through the influence, of peculiarly constituted individuals, hence termed " mediums." The evidence is here so abundant, coming from various parts of the world, and from persons differing widely in education, tastes, and religion, that it is difficult to give any notion of its force and bearing by short extracts. I will first adduce that of three men of the highest eminence in their respective departments—Pro- fessor De Morgan, Professor Hare, and Judge Edmonds.

Augustus De Morgan, many years Professor of Ma- thematics, and latterly Dean of University College, London, was educated at Cambridge, where he took his degree as 4th wrangler. He studied for the bar, and has been a voluminous writer on mathematics, logic, and biography. He was for eighteen years Secretary to the Royal Astronomical Society, and was a strong advocate for a decimal coinage. In 1863, a work appeared entitled " From Matter to Spirit, the result of ten years' experience in Spirit Manifestations," by C. D., with a preface by A. B. It is very generally known that A. B. is Professor De Morgan, and C. D. Mrs. De Morgan. The internal evi- dence of the preface is sufficient to all who know the Professor's style; it has been frequently imputed to him in print without contradiction, and in the *Athenæum* for 1865, in the "Budget of Paradoxes," he notices the work in such a manner as to show that he accepts the imputation of the authorship, and still holds the opinions therein expressed.* From this preface, which is well worth reading for its vigorous and sarcastic style, I proceed to give a few extracts :—

"I am satisfied from the evidence of my own senses, of *some* of the facts narrated (in the body of the work), of some others I have evidence as good as testimony can give. I am perfectly convinced that I have both seen and heard, in a manner that should make unbelief impossible, things *called* spiritual, which cannot be taken by a rational being to be capable of explanation by imposture, coincidence, or mistake. So far I feel the ground firm under me" (p. 1).

. "The Spiritualists, beyond a doubt, are in the track that has led to all advancement in physical science ; their opponents are the representatives of those who have striven against progress." . . .

"I have said that the deluded spirit-rappers are on the right track : they have the spirit and the method of the grand times when those paths were cut through the uncleared forest in which it is now the daily routine to walk. What was that spirit? It was the spirit of universal examination wholly unchecked by fear of being detected in the investigation of nonsense."

"But to those who know the truth of facts, and who do not know what can and what cannot be, it will appear on reflection that the most probable direction of inquiry—the best chance of eliciting a satisfactory result, is that which is suggested by the spirit hypothesis. I mean the hypothesis that some intelligence which is not that of any human beings clothed in flesh and blood, has a direct share in the phenomena.

"Take the hypothesis on its own *à priori* probability,'

---

* The work has been since advertised as by *Professor and Mrs. De Morgan.*

and compare it with that of attraction. Suppose a person wholly new to both subjects, wholly undrilled both in theology and physics. He is to choose between two assertions, one true and one false, and to lose his life if he choose the false one. The first assertion is that there are incorporeal intelligences in the universe, and that they sometimes communicate with men ; the second is that the particles of the stars in the milky way give infinitesimal permanent pulls to the particles of our earth. I suppose that most men among those who have all-existing prepossessions would feel rather puzzled to know which they would have chosen had they been situated as above described." . . .

" My state of mind, which refers the whole either to some unseen intelligence, or something which man has never had any conception of, proves me to be out of the pale of the Royal Society." . . .

" Of the future state we are informed by some theologians, but quite out of their own heads, that all wants will be supplied without effort, and all doubts resolved without thought. This a *state!* not a bit of it; a mere phase of non-existence; annihilation with a consciousness of it. The rapping spirits know better than that; their views, should they really be human impostures, are very, very singular. In spite of the inconsistencies, the eccentricities, and the puerilities which some of them have exhibited, there is a uniform vein of description running through their accounts, which, supposing it to be laid down by a combination of impostors, is more than remarkable—even marvellous. The agreement is one part of the wonder, it being remembered that the ' mediums ' are scattered through the world; but the other and greater part of it is, that the impostors, if impostors they be, have combined to oppose all the current ideas of a future state, in order to gain belief in the genuineness of their pretensions !"

" Ten years ago, Mrs. Hayden, the well-known American medium, came to my house *alone*. The sitting began immediately after her arrival. Eight or nine persons were present, of all ages and of all degrees of belief and unbelief in the whole thing being imposture. The raps began in the usual way. They were to my ear clear, clean, faint sounds such as would be said to *ring* had they lasted. I likened them at the time to the noise which the ends of knitting-needles would make if dropped from a small distance upon a marble slab, and instantly checked by a damper of some kind. . . . Mrs. Hayden was seated at some distance from the table, and her feet were watched. . . . On being asked to put a question to the first spirit, I begged that I might be allowed to put my question mentally—that is, without speaking it, or writing it, or pointing it out to myself on an alphabet—and that Mrs. Hayden might hold both arms extended while the answer was in progress. Both demands were instantly granted by a couple of raps. I put the question, and desired the answer might be in one word, which I assigned, all mentally. I then took the printed alphabet, put a book upright before it, and bending my eyes upon it, proceeded to point to the letters in the usual way. The word *chess* was given by a rap at each letter. I had now reasonable certainty of the following alternative : either some *thought-reading* of a character wholly inexplicable, or such superhuman acuteness on the part of Mrs. Hayden that she could detect the letter I wanted by my bearing, though she (seated six feet from the book which hid my alphabet) could see neither my hand nor my eye, nor at what rate I was going through the letters. I was fated to be driven out of the second alternative before the evening was done.

" At a later period of the evening, when another spirit was under examination, I asked him whether he remembered a certain review which was published soon after his death, and whether he could give me the initials of an epithet (which happened to be in five words) therein applied to himself. Consent having been given, I began my way through the alphabet as above; the only difference of circumstances being that a bright table lamp was now between me and the medium. I expected to be brought up, at say, the letter F; and when my pencil passed that letter without any signal, I was surprised, and by the time I came to K, or thereabouts, I paused, intending to announce a failure. But some one called out, 'You have passed it; I heard a rap long ago.' I began again, and distinct raps came first at C. then at D. I was now satisfied that the spirit had failed; but stopping to consider a little more, it flashed into my mind that C. D. were his own initials, and that he had chosen to commence the *clause which contained the epithet.* I then said nothing but 'I see what you are at; pray go on,' and I then got T (for *The*), then the E. I wanted—of which not a word had been said—and then the remaining four initials. I was now satisfied that contents of my mind had been read which could not have been detected by my method of pointing to the alphabet, even supposing that could have been seen. . . . The things which I have set down were the beginning of a long series of experiences, many as remarkable as what I have given."—" From Matter to Spirit," Preface, pp. xli. xlii.

From the body of the same work I give one short extract:—" The most remarkable instance of *table moving* with a purpose, which ever came under my notice, occurred at the house of a friend, whose family like my own were staying at the seaside. My friend's family consisted of six persons, and a gentleman, now the husband of one of the daughters, joined them, and I was accompanied by a young

member of my own family.   No paid person was present.
A gentleman who had been expressing himself in a very
sceptical manner, not only with reference to spirit manifestations, but on the subject of spiritual existence generally, sat on a sofa two or three feet from the dining-room
table, round which we were placed.   After sitting some
time we were directed by the rapping to join hands, and
stand up round the table *without touching* it.   All did so
for a quarter of an hour; wondering whether anything
would happen, or whether we were hoaxed by the unseen
power.   Just as one or two of the party talked of sitting
down, the old table, which was large enough for eight or
ten persons, moved *entirely by itself* as we surrounded and
followed it with our hands joined, went towards the gentleman out of the circle, and literally pushed him up to
the back of the sofa till he called out ' Hold, enough.' "—
(From Matter to Spirit, p. 26.)

J. W. EDMONDS, commonly called Judge EDMONDS, is a
man of considerable eminence.   He has been elected a
member of both branches of the State Legislature of New
York, and was for some time President of the Senate.   He
has been Inspector of Prisons, and made great improve-
ments in the penitentiary system.   After passing through
various lower offices, he was made a Judge of the Supreme
Court of New York.   This is the highest judicial office in
the State ; he held it for six years, and then resigned,
solely on account of the outcry raised against him on its
being known that he had become convinced on the subject
of Spiritualism.   Since then he has resumed his practice at
the bar, and was elected to the important office of Recorder
of New York, which, however, he declined to accept.

The Judge was first induced by some friends to visit a
medium, and being astonished at what he saw, determined
to investigate the matter, and discover and expose what

he then believed to be a great imposture. The following are some of his experiences given in his work on "Spirit Manifestations":—

"On the 23rd April, 1851, I was one of a party of nine who sat round a centre table, on which a lamp was burning, and another lamp was burning on the mantelpiece. And then, in plain sight of us all, that table was lifted at least a foot from the floor, and shaken backwards and forwards as easily as I could shake a goblet in my hand. Some of the party tried to stop it by the exercise of their strength, but in vain; *so we all drew back from the table,* and by the light of those two burning lamps we saw the heavy mahogany table suspended in the air."

At the next *séance* a variety of extraordinary phenomena occurred to him. "As I stood in a corner where no one could reach my pocket, I felt a hand thrust into it, and found afterwards that six knots had been tied in my handkerchief. A bass viol was put into my hand, and rested on my foot, and then played upon. My person was repeatedly touched, and a chair pulled from under me. I felt on one of my arms what seemed to be the grip of an iron hand. I felt distinctly the thumb and fingers, the palm of the hand, and the ball of the thumb, and it held me fast by a power which I struggled to escape from. in vain. With my other hand I felt all round where the pressure was, and satisfied myself that it was no earthly hand that was thus holding me fast, nor indeed could it be, for I was as powerless in that grip as a fly would be in the grasp of my hand. It continued with me till I thoroughly felt how powerless I was, and had tried every means to get rid of it." Again, as instances of the intelligence and knowledge of the unseen power, he says that during his journey to Central America, his friends in New York were almost daily informed of his condition. On

returning, he compared his own journal with their notes, and found that they had accurately known the day he landed, days on which he was unwell or well; and on one occasion it was said he had a headache, and at the very hour he was confined to his bed by a sick headache 2000 miles away." As another example, he says, "My daughter had gone with her little son to visit some relatives 400 miles from New York. During her absence, about four o'clock in the morning, I was told through this spiritual intercourse that the little fellow was very sick. I went after him, and found that at the very hour I received that intelligence he was very sick; his mother and aunt were sitting up with him, and were alarmed for the result."
. . . "This will give a general idea of what I was witnessing two or three times a week for more than a year. I was not a believer seeking confirmation of my own notions. I was struggling against conviction. I have not stopped to detail the precautions which I took to guard against deception, self or otherwise. Suffice it to say that in that respect I omitted nothing which my ingenuity could devise. There was no cavil too captious for me to resort to, no scrutiny too rigid or impertinent for me to institute, no inquiry too intrusive for me to make."

In a letter published in the *New York Herald*, August 6th, 1853, after giving an abstract of his investigations, he says—"I went into the investigation originally thinking it a deception, and intending to make public my exposure of it. Having, from my researches, come to a different conclusion, I feel that the obligation to make known the result is just as strong. Therefore it is, mainly, that I give the result to the world. I say mainly, because there is another consideration which influences me, and that is, the desire to extend to others a knowledge, which I am conscious cannot but make them happier and better."

I would now ask whether it is possible that Judge Edmonds can have been deceived as to these facts, and not be insane. Yet he practiced at the bar, and was in the highest repute as a lawyer till his death, about a year ago.

ROBERT HARE, M.D., Emeritus Professor of Chemistry in the University of Pennsylvania, was one of the most eminent scientific men of America. He distinguished himself by a number of important discoveries (among which may be mentioned the Oxy-Hydrogen blowpipe), and was the author of more than 150 papers on scientific subjects, besides others on political and moral questions. In 1853 his attention was first directed to table-turning and allied phenomena, and finding that the explanation of Faraday, which he had at first received as sufficient, would not account for the facts, he set himself to work to devise apparatus which should, as he expected, conclusively prove that no force was exerted but that of the persons at the table. The result was not as he expected, for however he varied his experiments he was in every case only able to obtain results which proved that there *was* a power at work not that of any human being present. But, in addition to the *power* there was an *intelligence*, and he was thus compelled to believe that existences not human did communicate with him.

It is often asserted by the disbelievers in these phenomena, that no scientific man has fully investigated them. This is not true. No one who has not himself inquired into the facts has a right even to give an opinion on the subject till he knows what has been done by others in the investigation; and to know this it will be necessary for him to read carefully, among other works, "Hare's Experimental Investigation of the Spirit Manifestations," which has passed through five editions. It is a volume of 460 closely-printed 8vo. pages, and contains, besides the details of his experiments, numerous discussions on philosophical, moral, and theological questions, which manifest great acuteness and logical power.   The experiments he made were all through private mediums, and his apparatus was so contrived that the medium could not possibly, under the test condition, either produce the motions, or direct the communications that ensued.   For example, the table by its movements caused an index to revolve over an alphabet on a disc; yet, when the medium could not see the disc, the index moved to such letters as to spell out intelligent and accurate communications.   And when the medium's hands were placed upon a truly plane metal plate, supported on accurately turned metal balls, so that not the slightest impulse could be communicated by her to the table, yet the table still moved easily and intelligently.   In another case a medium's hands were suspended in water, so as to have no connection with the board on which the water vessel was placed, and yet, at request, a force of 18lbs. was exerted on the boards, as indicated by a spring balance (see pages 40 to 50).   A considerable space is devoted to communications received through the means of the above-named apparatus, describing the future life of human beings; and as far as my own judgment goes, these descriptions, taken as a whole, give us a far more exalted, and at the same time, more rational and connected view of spirit life, than do the doctrines of any other religion or philosophy; while they are certainly more conducive to morality, and inculcate most strongly the importance of cultivating to the uttermost every mental faculty with which we are endowed.   Even if it be possible to prove that the supposed superhuman source of these communications is a delusion, I would still maintain, that standing on their own merits they give us the best, the highest, the most rational, and the most acceptable ideas of a future state, and must prove the best incentive to intellectual and moral advancement; and I would call upon every thinker to examine the work on this account alone, before deciding against it.

I shall next adduce, very briefly, the testimony of a number of well-known and intelligent Englishmen, to facts of a similar nature witnessed by themselves.

VII.

EVIDENCE OF LITERARY AND PROFESSIONAL MEN TO THE FACTS OF MODERN SPIRITUALISM.

T. ADOLPHUS TROLLOPE was educated at Oxford, and is the well-known author of numerous works of high excellence in the departments of travels, fiction, biography, and history. In 1855 he wrote a letter to Mr. Rymer, of Ealing, which was published in the *Morning Advertiser*, and is reproduced in " Incidents of my Life," 2nd ed., p. 252, in which he shows the inaccuracy and unfairness of Sir David Brewster's account of phenomena occurring in the presence of both, at Mr. Rymer's house, and concludes with these words: " I should not, my dear sir, do all that duty, I think, requires of me, in this case, were I to conclude without stating very solemnly, that after very many opportunities of witnessing and investigating the phenomena caused by, or happening to Mr. Home, I am wholly convinced, that be what may their origin, and cause, and nature, they are not produced by any fraud, machinery, juggling, illusion, or trickery, on his part." Again in a letter to the *Athenæum*, eight years later (dated Florence, March 21, 1863) he says, " I have been present at very many ' sittings ' of Mr. Home in England, many in my own house in Florence, some in the house of a friend in Florence. . . . My testimony then is this: I have seen and felt physical facts, wholly and utterly inexplicable, as I believe, by any known and generally received physical laws. I unhesitatingly reject the theory which considers such facts to be produced by means familiar to the best professors of legerdemain."

An opinion so positive as this, from a man of such
eminence, who during eight years has had repeated opportunities of witnessing, examining, and reflecting on the
phenomena, must surely be held as of far more value than
the opposite opinion, so frequently put forward by those
who have either not witnessed them at all, or only on one
or two occasions.

JAMES M. GULLY, M.D., author of "Neuropathy and
Nervousness," "Simple Treatment of Disease," "The Water
Cure in Chronic Diseases." Of the last work the *Athenæum*
said: "Dr. Gully's book is evidently written by a well-
educated medical man. This work is by far the most
scientific that we have seen on Hydropathy." Dr. Gully
was one of the persons present at the celebrated *séance*
described in the *Cornhill Magazine* in 1860, under the
title "Stranger than Fiction," and he wrote a letter to the
Morning Star newspaper, confirming the entire truthfulness of that article. He says: "I can state with the
greatest positiveness that the record made in the article
'Stranger than Fiction' is in every particular correct; that
the phenomena therein related actually took place in the
evening meeting; and moreover, that no trick, machinery,
sleight-of-hand, or other artistic contrivance, produced what
we heard and beheld. I am quite as convinced of this last
as I am of the facts themselves." He then goes on to
show the absurdity of all suggested explanations of such
phenomena as Mr. Home's floating across the room, which
he both saw and felt; and the playing of the accordion in
several persons' hands, often three yards distance from Mr.
Home. But the most important fact is, that Dr. Gully is
now one of Mr. Home's most esteemed friends. He receives Mr. Home frequently in his house, and has had
ample opportunities of testing the phenomena in private,
and of certainly detecting the gigantic and complicated

system of deception, if it be such. To most minds this will be stronger proof of the reality of the phenomena, than any facts observed at a single *séance*, or than any unsupported assertion that the thing is impossible.

WILLIAM HOWITT, the well-known author of " Rural Life in England," of several historical works exhibiting great research, of many excellent works of fiction, and recently of a " History of Discovery in Australia," has had extensive opportunities of investigating the phenomena, and can hardly be supposed to be incapable of judging of such palpable facts as these:—" Mrs. Howitt had a sprig of geranium handed to her by an invisible hand, which we have planted, and it is growing; so that it is no delusion, no fairy money turned into dross or leaves. I saw a spirit hand as distinctly as I ever saw my own. I touched one several times, once when it was handing me a flower." . . . " A few evenings afterwards a lady desiring that the ' Last Rose of Summer' might be played by a spirit on the accordion, the wish was complied with, but in so wretched a style that the company begged that it might be discontinued. This was done, but soon after, evidently by another spirit, the accordion was carried and suspended over the lady's head, and there, without any visible support or action on the instrument, the air was played through most admirably, in the view and hearing of all."—Letter from William Howitt to Mr. Barkas, of Newcastle, reprinted in Home's " Incidents of my Life," 2nd ed., p. 189.

Here the fact of the spectators not receiving bad music for good, because they believed it to proceed from a super-human source, is decidedly in favour of their coolness and judgment; and the fact was one which the senses of ordinary mortals are quite capable of verifying.

The HON. COLONEL WILBRAHAM sent the following letter to Mr. Home. I extract it from the *Spiritual Magazine:*—

"46 Brook Street, April 14th, 1863.

"My dear Mr. Home,—I have much pleasure in stating that I have attended several *séances*, in your presence, at the houses of two of my intimate friends and at my own, when I have witnessed phenomena similar to those described in your book, which I feel certain could not have been produced by any trick or collusion whatever. The rooms in which they occurred were always perfectly lighted; and it was impossible for me to disbelieve the evidence of my own senses.—Believe me, yours very truly,

"E. B. WILBRAHAM."

S. C. HALL, F.S.A., Barrister-at-Law, Editor of the *Art Journal*, and well known in literary, artistic, and philanthropic circles, has written the following letter to the Editor of the *Spiritual Magazine* (1863, p. 336):—

"Sir,—I follow the example of Colonel Wilbraham, and desire to record my belief in the statements put forth by Mr. D. D. Home ('Incidents of my Life'). I have myself seen nearly all the marvels he relates; some in his presence, some with other mediums, and some when there was no medium-aid (when Mrs. Hall and I sat alone). Not long ago I must have confessed to disbelief in all miracles; I have seen so many that my faith as a Christian is now not merely outward profession, but entire and solemn conviction. For this incalculable good I am indebted to 'Spiritualism;' and it is my bounden duty to induce knowledge of its power to teach and to make happy. That duty may, for the present, be limited to a declaration of confidence in Mr. Home.—Yours, &c.,

"S. C. HALL."

NASSAU WILLIAM SENIOR, late Master in Chancery, and twice Professor of Political Economy in the University of Oxford, was one who, it will astonish many persons to hear, had become convinced of the truth and reality of what they in their superior knowledge suppose to be a gross delusion. In his "Historical and Philosophical Essays," vol. ii. pp. 256-266, he gives a careful summary of the amount and kind of evidence in favour of Phrenology, Homœopathy, and Mesmerism, and concludes thus:—"No one can doubt that phenomena like these deserve to be

observed, recorded, and arranged; and whether we call by
the name of Mesmerism, or by any other name, the science
which proposes to do this, is a mere question of nomen-
clature.   Among those who profess this science there
may be careless observers, prejudiced recorders, and rash
systematisers; their errors and defects may impede the
progress of knowledge, but they will not stop it.   And we
have no doubt that, before the end of this century, the
wonders which now perplex almost equally those who
accept and those who reject modern Mesmerism will be
distributed into defined classes, and found subject to ascertained laws—in other words, will become the subjects of
a science."

These views will prepare us for the following statement,
made in the *Spiritual Magazine*, 1864, p. 336, and which
can be, no doubt, authoritatively denied if incorrect:—
" We have only to add, as a further tribute to the attainments and honours of Mr. Senior, that he was by long
inquiry and experience a firm believer in Spiritual power
and manifestations.   Mr. Home was his frequent guest,
and Mr. Senior made no secret of his belief among his
friends.   He it was who recommended the publication of
Mr. Home's recent work by Messrs. Longmans, and he
authorised the publication, under initials, of one of the
striking incidents there given, which happened to a near
and dear member of his family."

The REV. WILLIAM KERR, M.A., Incumbent of Tipton,   ✳
in his recent work on "Future Punishment, Immortality,
and Modern Spiritualism," thus gives his testimony to the
facts:—"The writer of these pages has, for a length of
time, bestowed great attention upon the subject, and is in
a position to affirm with all confidence, from his own experience, and repeated trials, that the alleged phenomena
of Spiritualism are, for by far the most part, the products

neither of imposture nor delusion. They are true, and that to the fullest extent. The marvels which he himself has witnessed, in the private retirement of his own home, with only a few select friends, and *without having even so much as ever seen a public medium*, are in many respects fully equal to any of the startling narratives that have appeared in print."

THACKERAY, though a cool-headed man of the world, and a close student of human nature, could not resist the evidence of his senses in this matter. Mr. Weld, in his "Last Winter in Rome," p. 180, states, that at a dinner shortly after the appearance in the *Cornhill Magazine* of the article entitled "Stranger than Fiction," Mr. Thackeray was reproached with having permitted such a paper to appear. After quietly hearing all that could be said on the subject, Thackeray replied: "It is all very well for you, who have probably never seen any spiritual manifestations, to talk as you do; but had you seen what I have witnessed, you would hold a different opinion." He then proceeded to inform Mr. Weld, and the company, that when in New York, at a dinner party, he saw the large and heavy dinner table, covered with decanters, glasses, and a complete dessert, rise fully two feet from the ground, the *modus operandi* being, as he alleged, spiritual force. No possible jugglery, he declared, was or could have been employed, on the occasion; and he felt so convinced that the motive force was supernatural, that he then and there gave in his adhesion to the truth of Spiritualism, and consequently accepted the article on Mr. Home's *séance*.

The late CHANCELLOR, LORD LYNDHURST, was another eminent convert to Spiritualism. In the *Spiritual Magazine*, 1863, p. 519, it is said: "He was a careful and scrutinizing observer of all facts which came under his notice, and had no predilections or prejudices against any, and

during the repeated interviews which he has had with Mr.
Home, he was entirely satisfied of the nearness of the
spiritual world, and of the power of spirits to communicate
with those still in the flesh. As to the truth of the mere
physical phenomena, he had no difficulty in acknowledging
them to the fullest extent, neither did he, like many, make
any secret of his conviction, as his friends can testify."

ARCHBISHOP WHATELY was a Spiritualist.   Mr. Fitz- ✱
patrick in his " Memoirs of Whately " tells us, that the
Archbishop had been long a believer in Mesmerism, and
latterly in clairvoyance and Spiritualism.   " He went from
one extreme to another, until he avowed an implicit belief
in clairvoyance, induced a lady who possessed it to become
an inmate of his house, and some of the last acts of his life
were excited attempts at table-turning, and enthusiastic
elicitations of spirit-rapping." This converted into plain
language means, that the Archbishop examined into the
facts before deciding against their possibility; and having
satisfied himself by personal experiment of their reality,
saw their immense importance, and pursued the investigation with ardour.

Dr. ELLIOTSON, who for many years was one of the most
determined opponents of Spiritualism, was at length convinced by the irresistible logic of facts. Mr. Coleman thus
writes in the *Spiritual Magazine*, 1864, p. 216 :—" ' I am,'
Dr. Elliotson said to me, and it is with his sanction that I
make the announcement, ' now quite satisfied of the reality
of the phenomena. I am not yet prepared to admit that
they are produced by the agency of spirits. I do not deny
this, as I am unable to satisfactorily account for what I
have seen on any other hypothesis. The explanations
which have been made to account for the phenomena do
not satisfy me, but I desire to reserve my opinion on that
point at present. I am free, however, to say that I regret

the opportunity was not afforded me at an earlier period. What I have seen lately has made a deep impression on my mind, and the recognition of the reality of these manifestations, from whatever cause, is tending to revolutionise my thoughts and feelings on almost every subject.' "

Captain BURTON, of Mecca and Salt Lake City, is not a man to be taken in by a "gross deception," yet note what he says about the Davenport Brothers, who are supposed to have been so often exposed. In a letter to Dr. Ferguson, and published by him, Captain Burton states that he has seen these manifestations under the most favourable circumstances, in private houses, when the spectators were all sceptics, the doors bolted, and the ropes, tape, and musical instruments provided by themselves. He goes on to say—" Mr. W. Fay's coat was removed while he was securely fastened hand and foot, *and a lucifer match was struck at the same instant, showing us the two gentlemen fast bound, and the coat in the air on its way to the other side of the room.* Under precisely similar circumstances, another gentleman's coat was placed upon him." And he concludes thus—" I have spent a great part of my life in Oriental lands, and have seen there many magicians. Lately I have been permitted to see and be present at the performances of Messrs. Anderson and Tolmaque. The latter showed, as they profess, clever conjuring, *but they do not even attempt what the Messrs. Davenport and Fay succeed in doing.* Finally, I have read and listened to every explanation of the Davenport ' tricks' hitherto placed before the English public, and, believe me, if anything would make me take that tremendous leap ' from matter to spirit,' *it is the utter and complete unreason of the reasons by which the manifestations are explained.*"

Professor CHALLIS, the Plumierian Professor of Astronomy at Cambridge, is almost the only person who, as far

I know, has stated his belief in some of these phenomena solely from the weight of testimony in favour of them. In a letter to the *Clerical Journal* of June, (?) 1862, he says: —" But although I have no grounds, from personal observation, for giving credit to the asserted spontaneous movements of tables, I have been unable to resist the large amount of testimony to such facts, which has come from many independent sources, and from a vast number of witnesses. England, France, Germany, the United States of America, with most of the other nations of Christendom, contributed simultaneously their quota of evidence. . . . *In short, the testimony has been so abundant and consentaneous, that either the facts must be admitted to be such as are reported, or the possibility of certifying facts by human testimony must be given up"*

VIII.

. THE THEORY OF SPIRITUALISM.

MANY of my readers will, no doubt, feel oppressed by the strange and apparently supernatural phenomena here brought before their notice. They will demand that, if indeed they are to be accepted as facts, it must be shown that they form a part of the system of the universe, or at least range themselves under some plausible hypothesis.

There is such an hypothesis—old in its fundamental principle, new in many of its details—which links together all these phenomena as a department of nature hitherto entirely ignored by science and but vaguely speculated on by philosophy; and it does so without in any way conflicting with the most advanced science or the highest philosophy. According to this hypothesis, that which, for want of a better name, we shall term "spirit," is the essential part of all sensitive beings, whose bodies form but the machinery and instruments by means of which they perceive and act upon other beings and on matter. It is "spirit" that alone feels, and perceives, and thinks—that acquires knowledge, and reasons and aspires—though it can only do so by means of, and in exact proportion to, the organisation it is bound up with. It is the "spirit" of man that is man. Spirit is mind; the brain and nerves are but the magnetic battery and telegraph, by means of which spirit communicates with the outer world.

Though the spirit is in general inseparable from the living body to which it gives animal and intellectual life (for the vegetative functions of the organism could go on without spirit), there not unfrequently occur individuals

so constituted that the spirit can perceive independently
of the corporeal organs of sense, or can perhaps wholly or
partially quit the body for a time and return to it again.
At death it quits the body for ever. The spirit like the
body has its laws, and definite limits to its powers. It
communicates with spirit easier than with matter, and in
most cases can only perceive and act on matter through
the medium of embodied spirit. The spirit which has
lived and developed its powers clothed with a human
body, will, when it leaves that body, still retain its
former modes of thought, its former tastes, feelings,
and affections. [The new state of existence is a natural continuation of the old one. There is no sudden acquisition
of new mental proclivities, no revolution of the moral
nature. Just what the embodied spirit had made itself, or
had become—*that* is the disembodied spirit when it begins
its life under new conditions.] It is the same in character
as before, but it has acquired new physical and mental
powers, new modes of manifesting the moral sentiments,
wider capacity for acquiring physical and spiritual knowledge. The great law of "continuity," so ably shown by
Mr. Grove in his recent address to the British Association
at Nottingham, to pervade the whole realm of nature, is
thus, according to the Spiritual theory, fully applicable to
our passage into, and progress through a more advanced
state of existence,—a view which should recommend itself
to men of science as being in itself probable, and in striking contrast with the doctrines of theologians, which place
a wide gulf between the mental and moral nature of man,
in his present, and in his future state of existence.

Now this hypothesis, taken as a mere speculation, is as
coherent and intelligible as any speculation on such a subject can be. But it claims to be more than a speculation,
since it serves to explain and interpret that vast accumula-

tion of facts of which a few examples only have been here given, and to furnish a more intelligible, consistent, and harmonious theory of the future state of man, than either religion or philosophy has yet put forth.

And first; as to the interpretation of facts. In the simplest phenomena of Animal Magnetism, when the muscles, the senses, and the ideas of the patient, are subject to the will of the operator, spirit acts upon spirit, through the intermediation of a peculiar relation between the magnetic or life power of the two organisms; and thus the magnetiser is enabled by his *will* to affect both the mind and the body of the patient and to induce in him for a time an ideal world. In the higher phenomenon of "simple clairvoyance," the spirit appears to be to some extent released from the trammels of body, and is enabled to perceive by some other processes than those of the ordinary senses. In the still higher clairvoyant state termed "mental travelling" the spirit would appear to quit the body (still connected with it however by an ethereal link) and traverse the earth to any distance, communicating with persons in remote countries if it has any clue by which to distinguish them, and (perhaps through the mediation of their organisation) perceiving and describing events occurring around them.

Under certain conditions disembodied spirit is able to form for itself a visible body out of the emanation from living bodies in a proper magnetic relation to itself; and, under certain still more favourable conditions, this body can be made tangible. Thus all the phenomena of "mediumship" take place. Gravity is overcome by a form of life-magnetism, induced between the spirit and the medium; visible hands or visible bodies are produced, which sometimes write, or draw, or even speak. Thus departed friends come to communicate with those still living, or at the moment of death the spirit appears visibly, and sometimes, tangibly to the loved ones in a distant land. All these phenomena would take place far more frequently were the conditions that alone render communication possible more general, or more cultivated.

It appears, then, that all the strange facts, denied by so many because they suppose them "supernatural," may be due to the agency of beings of a like mental nature to ourselves—who *are*, in fact, ourselves—but one step advanced on the long journey through eternity. The trivial and fantastic nature of the acts of some of these disembodied spirits, is not to be wondered at, when we consider the myriads of trivial and fantastic human beings who are daily becoming spirits, and who retain, for a time at least, their human natures in their new condition. But the *generally* trivial nature of the acts and communications of spirits (admitting them to be such) may be totally denied. If we saw two or three persons making strange gestures in perfect silence, we might probably think they were idiots; but if we found that two of them were deaf and dumb, and the three were conversing in the language of signs, we should become aware than the gesticulations of their bodies were no more intrinsically absurd than the movements of our lips and features during speech. So, if we realise to ourselves the fact, that spirits can in most cases only communicate with us in certain very limited modes, we shall see that the true "triviality" consists in objecting to any *mode* of mental converse as being trivial or undignified. Then again, as to the matter of the communications, said to be generally "unworthy of a spirit;" the real question is, are they generally such as would have been unworthy of the same spirit when in the body? We should remember, too, that in most cases the spirit has first to satisfy the inquirer of its existence, and in many cases to do so in the face of a strong prejudice against the very possibility of spirit communication, or even of the very existence of spirit. And the undoubted fact that hundreds and thousands of persons have been so convinced by the phenomena they have witnessed in the presence of mediums, shows, that trivial though they may be, these phenomena are well adapted to satisfy many minds, and thus lead them to receive and inquire into the higher phenomena, which they could otherwise never have been induced to examine.

This hypothesis of the existence of spirit, both in man and out of man, and their possible and actual inter-communication, must be judged exactly in the same way as we judge any other hypothesis—by the nature and variety of the facts it includes and accounts for, and by the absence of any other mode of explaining so wide a range of facts. The truth and reality of the facts, however, is one thing—the goodness of the hypothesis is another, and to find a flaw in the hypothesis is not to disprove the facts. I maintain that the facts have now been proved, in the only way in which facts are capable of being proved—viz., by the concurrent testimony of honest, impartial, and careful observers. Most of the facts are capable of being tested by any earnest inquirer. They have withstood the ordeal of ridicule and of rigid scrutiny for twenty-six years, during which their adherents have year by year steadily increased, including men of every rank and station, of every class of mind, and of every degree of talent; while not a single individual who has yet devoted himself to a detailed examination of these facts, has denied their reality. These are characteristics of a new truth, not of a delusion or imposture. The facts therefore are proved.

Before proceeding to consider the nature of the doctrine which Spiritualism unfolds, I would wish to say a few words on a recent work by a well known philosophic author, in which the facts of Spiritualism are for the most part admitted, but are accounted for by a different hypothesis from that which I have here briefly explained. Mr. Charles Bray, author of the "Philosophy of Necessity," "Education of the Feelings," &c., has just published a small volume whose title is—"On Force, its mental and moral correlates; and on that which is supposed to underlie all phenomena; with speculations on Spiritualism, and other abnormal conditions of mind." The latter half of the work is entirely devoted to a consideration of the facts of modern Spiritualism, and to an attempt to account for them on philosophical principles. Mr. Bray tells us that he has himself witnessed but few of the phenomena, yet enough to satisfy him that they may be true. He seems to rely more on the overwhelming testimony to the facts by men of admitted intelligence, and to the facts themselves being often of such a nature that they cannot be explained away. He has doubtless been led to this less sceptical frame of mind than is usual in philosophic writers, by his acquaintance with cases of clairvoyance, of one of which he states his experience as follows: "*I have heard* a young girl in the mesmeric state, minutely describe all that was seen, by a person with whom she was *en rapport*, and in some cases more than was seen or could be seen, such as the initials in a watch which had not been opened, and also describe persons and scenes at a distance, which I afterwards discovered were correctly described, *beyond a possibility of doubt.*" The italics in this sentence are his own.

Judging from the works mentioned in his book, Mr. Bray seems to have but a limited acquaintance with the literature of Spiritualism, which is the more to be regretted as he has so little personal experience of the phenomena, and is therefore hardly in a position to form a satisfactory hypothesis. He considers, however, that he has formed one which "will account for such facts as are genuine," although he admits that he has not made that searching examination which would alone entitle him to decide which facts were genuine, and which were due to fraud or self-delusion. The theory which he propounds is not at all easy to exhibit in a few words. He says that the force which produces the phenomena of Spiritualism "is an emanation from all brains, the medium increasing its density so as to allow others present to come into communion with it, and the intelligence new to every person present, is that of some brain in the distance, acting through this source upon the mind of the medium, or others of the circle" (p. 107). Again, he speaks of " a mental or thought atmosphere the result of cerebration, but devoid of consciousness till it becomes reflected in our own organisations " (p. 98). It seems to me that this theory labours under the great objection of being unintelligible. How are we to understand an "emanation from all brains," a "thought atmosphere," producing force and motion, visible and tangible forms, intelligent communications by sounds or motions, and all the other varied phenomena imperfectly sketched in these pages ? How does this "unconscious thought atmosphere " form a visible, tangible, force-exerting hand, which can carry flowers, write, or play complete tunes on an instrument ? Does it even account for the simpler, yet still marvellous phenomena of clairvoyance ? Let us take one of the best authenticated cases observed by Dr. Gregory. Mottoes enclosed in nutshells are purchased at a shop, and the clairvoyant reads them accurately. Now we may safely assume that in this case no human mind knows the particular nutshell in which each motto is enclosed. How then does the theory of an "emanation from all brains," or that the clairvoyant is through this emanation acted on by " some mind in the distance," explain the reading of these mottoes? If this "emanation" has the power of reading them itself, and communicates them to the clairvoyant, how can we deny it personality, and in what does it differ from that which we term spirit? If the theory of "spirit" is, as Professor De Morgan says, "ponderously difficult," is not this theory of "brain emanation" still more so? I submit, therefore, that Mr. Bray's hypothesis is not tenable, and that nothing but the supposition of personal minds, existing without, as well as with a human body, and capable, under certain conditions only, of acting on us and on matter, is able to account for the whole range of the phenomena. And this supposition has, I maintain, the advantage of being both intelligible and philosophically probable.

It is, however, very satisfactory to find a philosopher of Mr. Bray's standing recognising the subject at all, as one which possesses so much truth in it as to require an elaborate theory to account for the phenomena. This alone is a proof of the convincing nature of the evidence for those facts which our men of science neglect to investigate as à priori absurd and impossible. The appearance of Mr. Bray's book may perhaps indicate that a change is taking place in public opinion on the subject of clairvoyance and Spiritualism; and it will certainly do good service in drawing the attention of thinkers to a class of phenomena which, above all others, seem calculated to lead to the partial solution of the most difficult of all problems—the origin of consciousness, and the nature of mind.

IX.

THE MORAL TEACHINGS OF SPIRITUALISM.

WE have now to consider whether this vast array of phenomena which claims to put us into communication with beings who have passed into another phase of existence, teaches us anything which may make us wiser and better men. I myself believe that it does, and shall endeavour, as briefly as possible, to set forth what the doctrines of modern Spiritualism really are.

The hypothesis of Spiritualism not only accounts for all the facts (and is the only one that does so), but it is further remarkable as being associated with a theory of a future state of existence, which is the only one yet given to the world that can at all commend itself to the modern philosophical mind. There is a general agreement and tone of harmony in the mass of facts and communications termed "spiritual," which has led to the growth of a new literature, and to the establishment of a new religion. The main doctrines of this religion are: That after death man's spirit survives in an ethereal body, gifted with new powers, but mentally and morally the same individual as when clothed in flesh. That he commences from that moment a course of apparently endless progression, which is rapid, just in proportion as his mental and moral faculties have been exercised and cultivated while on earth. That his comparative happiness or misery will depend entirely on himself; just in proportion as his higher human faculties have taken part in all his pleasures here, will he find himself contented and happy in a state of existence in which they will have the fullest exercise. While he who has depended, more on the body than on the mind for his pleasures, will, when that body is no more, feel a grievous want, and must slowly and painfully develop his intellectual and moral nature till its exercise shall become easy and pleasurable. Neither punishments nor rewards are meted out by an external power, but each one's condition is the natural and inevitable sequence of his condition here. He starts again from the level of moral and intellectual development to which he has raised himself while on earth.

Now here again we have a striking supplement to the doctrines of modern science. The organic world has been carried on to a high state of development, and has been ever kept in harmony with the forces of external nature, by the grand law of "survival of the fittest" acting upon ever varying organisations. In the spiritual world, the law of the "progression of the fittest" takes its place, and carries on in unbroken continuity that development of the human mind which has been commenced here.

The communion of spirit with spirit is said to be by thought-reading and sympathy, and to be perfect between those whose beings are in harmony with each other. Those who differ widely have little or no power of intercommunion, and thus are constituted "spheres," which are divisions, not merely of space, but of social and moral sympathetic organisation. Spirits of the higher "spheres" can, and do sometimes communicate with those below; but these latter cannot communicate at will with those above. But there is for all an eternal progress, a progress solely dependent on the power of will in the development of spirit nature. There are no evil spirits but the spirits of bad men, and even the worst are surely if slowly progressing. Life in the higher spheres has beauties and pleasures of which we have no conception. Ideas of beauty and power become realised by the will, and the infinite cosmos becomes a field where the highest developments of intellect may range in the acquisition of boundless knowledge.

It may be thought, perhaps, that I am here giving merely my own ideal of a future state, but it is not so. Every statement I have made is derived from those despised sources, the rapping table, the writing hand, or the entranced speaker. And to show that I have not done justice either to the ideas themselves, or to the manner in which they are often conveyed to us, I subjoin a few extracts from the spoken addresses of one of the most gifted "trance-mediums," Mrs. Emma Hardinge.

In her address on "Hades," she sums up in this passage her account of our progress through the spheres :—" Of the nature of those spheres and their inhabitants we have spoken from the knowledge of the spirits, dwellers still in Hades. Would you receive some immediate definition of your own condition, and learn how *you* shall dwell, and what your garments shall be, what your mansion, scenery, likeness, occupations ? Turn your eyes within, and ask what you have learned, and what you have done in this, the school-house for the spheres of spirit land. There— there is an aristocracy, and even royal rank and varying degree, but the aristocracy is one of merit, and the royalty of soul. It is only the truly wise who govern, and as the wisest soul is he that is best, as the truest wisdom is the highest love, so the royalty of soul is truth and love. And within the spirit world all knowledge of this earth, all forms of science, all revelations of art, all mysteries of space, must be understood. The exalted soul that is then fully ready for his departure to a higher state than Hades, must know all that earth can teach, and have practised all that Heaven requires. The spirit never quits the spheres of earth until he is fully possessed of all the life and knowledge of this planet and its spheres. And though the progress may be here commenced, and not one jot of what you learn, or think, or strive for here, is lost, yet all achievements must be ultimated there, and no soul can wing its flight to that which you call, in view of its perfection, Heaven, till you have passed through Earth and Hades, and stand ready in your fully completed pilgrimage to enter on the new and unspeakable glories of the celestial realms beyond."

Could the philosopher or the man of science picture to himself a more perfect ideal of a future state than this ? Does it not commend itself to him as what he could wish, if he could by his wish form the future for himself ? Yet this is the teaching of that which he scouts as an imposture or a delusion—as the trickery of knaves or the ravings of madmen—modern Spiritualism. I quote another passage from the same address, and I would ask my readers to compare the modesty of the first paragraph with the claims of infallibility usually put forward by the teachers of new creeds or new philosophies :—"It is true that man is finite and imperfect; hence his utterances are too frequently the dictation of his own narrow perceptions, and his views are limited by his own finite capacity. But as you judge him, so also ye 'shall judge the angels.' Spirits only present you with the testimony of those who have advanced *one step* beyond humanity, and ask for no credence from man without the sanction of man's judgment and reason. Spirits, then, say that their world is as the soul or spiritual and sublimated essence of this human world of yours—that, in locality, the spirit world extends around this planet, as all spirit spheres encircle in zones and belts all other planets, earths, and bodies in space, until the sphere of each impinges upon the other, and they form in connection one vast and harmonious system of natural and spiritual worlds throughout the universe."

The effects of vice and ungoverned passions are thus de-
picted :—"Those spirits have engraved themselves with a
fatal passion for vice, but, alas! they dwell in a world
where there is no means for its gratification. There is the
gambler, who has burnt into his soul the fire of the love of
gain ; he hovers around earth's gamblers, and, as an unseen
tempter, seeks to repeat the now lost joys of the fatal game.
The sensualist, the man of violence, the cruel and angry
spirit; all who have steeped themselves in crime, or pained
their souls with those dark stain spots which they vainly
think are of the body only—all these are there, no longer
able to enact their lives of earthly vice, but retaining on
their souls the deadly mark, and the fatal though ungrati-
fied desire for habitual sin; and so these imprisoned spirits,
chained by their own fell passions in the slavery of hopeless criminal desires, hover round those who attract them
as magnets draw the needle, by vicious inclinations similar
to their own. But you say, the soul, by tempting others,
must thus sink deeper into crime. Ay, but remember that
another point of the spiritual doctrine is the universal
teaching of eternal progress." And then she goes on to
depict in glowing language how these spirits too, in time,
lose their fierce passions, and learn how to begin the upward path of knowledge and virtue. But I must leave the
subject, as I wish to give one extract from the address
of the same gifted lady, on the question, " What is
Spirit ?" as an example of the high eloquence and moral
beauty with which all her discourses are inspired :—
"Small, and to some of us even insignificant, as seems
the witness of the spirit-circle, its phenomenal gleams are
lights which reveal, in their aggregate, these solemn truths,
to us. There we behold foregleams of the powers of soul,
which so vastly do transcend the laws of matter. That
soul's continued existence and triumph over death ; our

own embodied spirit's power of communication with the
invisible world around us, and its various occult forces.
Clairvoyance, clairaudience, prophecy, trance, vision, psy-
chometry, and magnetic healing; how grand and wonderful
appears the soul, invested even in its earthly prison house,
with all these gleams of powers so full of glorious promise
of what we shall be, when the prison gates of matter open
wide and set the spirit free! Oh! fair young girls, whose
forms of supremest loveliness are nature's crowning gems,
forget not, when the great Creator's bounteous hand adorned
your blooming spring with the radiance of summer flowers,
that He shrined within that casket of tinted beauty, a soul
whose glory shall survive the decay of all earthly things,
and live in weal or woe, as your generation stamps it with
beauty or stains it with sinful ugliness, when springs shall
no more return, nor summers melt in the vast and change-
less evermore. Lift up your eyes from the beautiful dust
of to-day, which to-morrow shall be foul in death's corrup-
tion, to the ever-living soul which *you*, not *destiny*, must
adorn with immortal beauty. Remember you are spirits,
and that the hours of your earthly life are only granted you
to shape and form those spirits for eternity. Young men,
who love to expand the muscles of mind, and wrestle in
mental gladiatorial combats for the triumphant crowns of
science, what are all these to the eternal conquests to be
won in fields of illimitable science in the realms of immortality? Press on through earth as a means, but only to
attain to the nobler, higher colleges of the never-dying life,
and use mortal aims as instruments to gild your souls with
the splendour that never fades, but which yourselves must
win here or hereafter, ere you are fit to pass as graduates
in the halls of eternal science. To understand that we are
spirits, and that we live for immortality, to know and
insure its issues; is not this, to Spiritualists, the noblest

H

though last bright page which God has revealed to us ?   Is
not to read and comprehend this page the true mission of
modern Spiritualism ?   All else is but the phenomenal
basis of the science which gives us the assurance that
spirit lives.   This is one great aim and purpose of modern
Spiritualism, to know what the spirit is, and what it must
do—how best to live, so that it may most surely array itself
in the pure white robes of an immortality which is purged
of all mortal sin and earthly grossness."

The teachings of Mrs. Hardinge agree in substance with
those of all the more developed mediums, and I would ask
whether it is probable that these teachings have been
evolved from the conflicting dogmas of a set of impostors ?
Neither does it seem a more probable solution, that they
have been produced "unconsciously" from the minds of
self-deluded men and weak women, since it is palpable to
every reader that these doctrines are essentially different
in every detail, from those taught and believed by any
school of modern philosophers or any sect of modern
Christians.

This is well shown by their opposing statements as to
the condition of mankind after death.   In the accounts of
a future state given by, or through the best mediums, and
in the visions of deceased persons by clairvoyants, spirits
are uniformly represented in the form of *human* beings,
and their occupations as analogous to those of earth.   But
in most religious descriptions, or pictures of heaven, they
are represented as *winged* beings, as resting on, or surrounded by clouds, and their occupations to be playing on
golden harps, or perpetual singing, prayer and adoration
before the throne of God.   How is it, if these visions and
communications are but the remodelling of pre-existing, or
preconceived ideas by a diseased imagination, that the
popular notions are never reproduced?   How is it that

whether the medium be man, woman, or child, whether
ignorant or educated, whether English, German, or American, there should be one and the same consistent repre-
sentation of these preterhuman beings, at variance with
popular notions of them, but such as strikingly to accord
with the modern scientific doctrine of "continuity"?   I
submit that this little fact is of itself a strong corroborative
argument, that there is some objective truth in these communications.

All popular religions, all received notions of a future
state of existence, alike ignore one important side of human
nature, and one which has a large share in the happiness of
our present existence.   Laughter, and the ideas that produce it, are never contemplated as continuing to exist in
the spirit world.   Every form of jovial merriment, of
sparkling wit, and of that humour which is often akin to
pathos, and many of the higher feelings of our nature, are
alike banished from the Christian's Heaven. Yet if these
and all the allied feelings vanish from our natures, when
we "shuffle off this mortal coil," how shall we know ourselves, how retain our identity?   A poet, writing on the
death of Artemus Ward in the *Spectator*, well asks:—

> "Is he gone to the land of no laughter,
>   This man who made mirth for us all?
> Proves death but a silence hereafter,
>   From the sounds that delight and appal?
> Once closed, have the lips no more duty,
>   No more pleasure the exquisite ears,
> Has the heart done o'erflowing with beauty,
>   As the eyes have with tears?"

Now it is noteworthy that the communications which the
spiritualist believes to be verily the words of our departed
friends, give us full assurance that their individual characters
remain unchanged; that mirth, and wit, and laughter, and
every other human emotion and source of human pleasure,

are still retained by them; and that even those small incidents of the domestic circle, which had become a source
of innocent mirth when they were with us in the body, are
still capable of exciting pleasurable feelings. And this has
been held by some to be an objection to the reality of these
communications instead of being, as it really is, a striking
confirmation of them. Continuity, has been pre-eminently
the law of our mental development, and it rests with those
who would abruptly sever this continuity to prove their
case. They have never even attempted to show that it
accords with the facts or with the analogies of nature.

Equally at variance with each other are the popular and
the spiritualistic doctrines as regards the Deity. Our
modern religious teachers maintain that they know a great
deal about God. They define minutely and critically his
various attributes; they enter into his motives, his feelings,
and his opinions; they explain exactly what he has done,
and why he has done it; and they declare that after death
we shall be with him, and shall see and know him. In
the teaching of the "spirits" there is not a word of all this.
They tell us that they commune with higher intelligences
than themselves, but of God they really *know* no more than
we do. They say that above these higher intelligences are
others higher and higher in apparently endless gradation,
but as far as they know, no absolute knowledge of the Deity
himself is claimed by any of them. Is it possible, if these
"spiritual" communications are but the workings of the
minds of weak, superstitious, or deluded human beings, that
they should so completely contradict one of the strongest
and most cherished beliefs of the superstitious and the religious, and should agree with that highest philosophy (of
which most mediums have certainly never heard), which
maintains, that we can know nothing of the almighty, the
eternal, the infinite, the *absolute* Being, who must necessarily

be not only unknown and unknowable, but even *unthink-able* by finite intelligences.

It is often asked, "What has Spiritualism done—what new facts, or what useful information have the supposed spirits ever given to man?" The true answer to this demand probably is, that it is no part of their mission to give knowledge to man which his faculties enable him to acquire for himself, and the very effort to acquire which is part of his education and preparation for the spiritual life. Direct information on matters of fact is however occasionally given, as the records of Spiritualism abundantly show; for example the recent discovery of an inexhaustible supply of pure water in the great city of Chicago (the want of which rendered it notoriously unhealthy) obtained from an artesian well sunk under the guidance of a medium, after it had been pronounced impracticable by men of science. These and all similar facts are however invariably disbelieved *without inquiry.* I prefer therefore to rest the claims of Spiritualism on its moral uses. I would point to the thousands it has convinced of the reality of another world, to the many it has led to devote their lives to works of philanthropy, to the eloquence and the poetry it has given us, and to the grand doctrine of an ever progressive future state which it teaches. Those who will examine its litera- ture will acknowledge these facts. Those who will not examine for themselves either the literature or the pheno- mena of Spiritualism, should at least refrain from passing judgment on a matter of which they are confessedly and wilfully ignorant.

The subject, of which I have here endeavoured to sketch the outlines in a few pages which may perhaps be read when larger volumes would lie unopened, is far too wide and too important for this mode of treatment to do any justice to it. I have been obliged entirely to leave out all mention of the historical proofs of similar phenomena occurring in unbroken succession from the earliest ages to the present day. I could not allude to the spread of Spiritualism on the continent with its numbers of eminent converts. I could not refer to the numbers of scientific and medical men, who have been convinced of its truth, but have not made public their belief. But I claim to have shown cause for investigation; to have proved that it is not a subject that can any longer be contemptuously sneered at as unworthy of a moment's enquiry. I feel myself so confident of the truth and objective reality of many of the *facts* here narrated, that I would stake the whole question on the opinion of any man of science desirous of arriving at the truth, if he would only devote two or three hours a week for a few months to an examination of the phenomena, *before pronouncing an opinion;* for, I again repeat, not a single individual that I have heard of, has done this without becoming convinced of the reality of these phenomena. I maintain, therefore, finally—that whether we consider the vast number and the high character of its converts, the immense accumulation and the authenticity of its facts, or the noble doctrine of a future state which it has elaborated—the so-called supernatural, as developed in the phenomena of animal magnetism, clairvoyance, and modern Spiritualism, is an experimental science, the study of which must add greatly to our knowledge of man's true nature and highest interests.

X.

NOTES OF PERSONAL EVIDENCE.

IN the first edition of this Essay I did not introduce any of my own observations, because I had not then witnessed any such facts in a private house, and without the intervention of paid mediums, as would be likely to satisfy my readers. Having now had the opportunity of investigating the subject under more favourable conditions, I will give some account of my early personal experience, which many of my friends are so polite and illogical as to say will have more weight with them than all the other witnesses I have alluded to. I will begin with what first led me to enquiries outside the pale of what is generally recognised as science.

My earliest experiences on any of the matters treated of in this little work was in 1844, at which time I was teaching in a school in one of the Midland Counties. Mr. Spencer Hall was then lecturing on Mesmerism, and visited our town, and I and many of my pupils attended. We were all greatly interested. Some of the elder boys tried to mesmerize the younger ones, and succeeded; and I myself found several who, under my influence, exhibited many of the most curious phenomena we had witnessed at the lecture. I was intensely interested in the subject, and pursued it with ardour, carrying out a number of experiments to guard against deception and to test the nature of the influence. Many of the details of these experiments are now stamped as vividly on my memory as if they were events of yesterday; and I will briefly give the substance of a few of the more remarkable.

1. *Phenomena during the Mesmeric Trance.*—I produced
the trance state in two or three boys, of twelve to sixteen
years of age, with great ease, and could always be sure
that it was genuine, first, by the turning of the eyeball in
the orbit, so that the pupil was not visible when the eye-
lid was raised ; secondly, by the characteristic change of
countenance; and, thirdly, by the readiness with which I
could produce catalepsy and loss of sensation in any part
of the body. The most remarkable observations during
this state were on phreno-mesmerism and sympathetic sensation. By placing my finger on the part of the head
corresponding to any given phrenological organ, the corresponding faculty was manifested with wonderful and
amusing perfection. For a long time I thought that the
effects produced on the patient were caused by my wishing
the particular manifestation ; but I found by accident that
when, by ignorance of the position of the organs, I placed
my finger on a wrong part, the manifestation which followed was not that which I expected, but that which was
due to the position touched. I was particularly interested
in phenomena of this kind, and by experiments made alone
and silently, completely satisfied myself that the effects
were not due to suggestion or to the influence of my own
mind. I had to buy a little phrenological bust for my
own use, and none of the boys had the least knowledge of
or taste for, phrenology ; yet, from the very first, almost
all the organs touched, in however varied order and in
perfect silence, were followed by manifestations too striking to be mistaken, and presenting more wonderful repre-
sentations of varied phases of human feeling than the
greatest actors are able to exhibit.

The sympathy of sensation between my patient and myself was to me then the most mysterious phenomenon I had
ever witnessed. I found that when I had hold of his hand

he felt, tasted, or smelt exactly the same as I did. I had already produced all the phenomena of suggestion, and could make him tipsy with a glass of water by calling it brandy, and cause him strip off all his clothes by telling him he was on fire; but this was quite another thing. I formed a chain of several persons, at one end of which was the patient; at the other myself. And when in perfect silence I was pinched or pricked, he would immediately put his hand to the corresponding part of his own body, and complain of being pinched or pricked too. If I put a lump of sugar or salt in my mouth, he immediately went through the action of sucking, and soon showed by gestures and words of the most expressive nature what it was *I* was tasting. I have never to this day been satisfied with any of the explanations given of this fact by our physiologists—for they resolve themselves into this, that the boy neither felt nor tasted anything, but acquired a knowledge of what I was feeling and tasting by a preternatural acuteness of *hearing*. That he had any such preternatural acuteness was, however, contrary to all my experience, and the experiment was tried so as expressly to prevent his gaining any knowledge of what I felt or touched by means of the ordinary senses.

2. *Phenomena during the Waking State.*—After I had induced the state of coma several times, some of the boys became very susceptible during their ordinary waking condition. I could induce catalepsy of any of the limbs with great ease; and some curious little facts showed that it was real, not imaginary, rigidity that was produced. Once a boy was in my room in a state of complete rigidity when the dinner-bell rang. I hastily made passes to relax the body and limbs, and we went down together. When his plate was before him, however, he found that he could not bend one of his arms, and not liking to say anything,

sat some time trying to catch my eye. I then had to go
to him, and by two or three passes rendered him able to
eat his dinner. This is a curious and important fact,
because the boy went down *thinking* he was all right.
The rigidity was therefore in no way caused by his
"expectation," since it existed in opposition to it. In
this boy and another one I could readily produce the temporary loss of any of the senses, as hearing or smelling;
and could even so completely take away the memory that
the patient could not tell his own name, greatly to his
disgust and confusion, and this by nothing more than a
simple pass across the face, and saying in an ordinary tone
of voice, "Now, you can't tell me your name." And after
he had remained utterly puzzled for some minutes, if I
made a reverse pass, and said, "Now, you know your name
again," his whole countenance would change—a look of
relief coming over it as the familiar words recurred suddenly to his memory.

Such facts as these were at that period generally imputed
to acting and trick on the part of the patients. Now, most
of our physiologists admit them to be genuine mental phenomena, and attempt to explain them by "abstraction"
and "suggestion"—denying any specific action of the operator on the patient. This appears to me to be really no
explanation at all; and I am confirmed in this view when
I find that those who put it forward deny the reality of all
facts that do not square with it. All such phenomena as
phreno-mesmerism, and sympathetic sensation, and true
clairvoyance, which have been elaborately examined and
tested by a score of good observers, are nevertheless denied
a place in the repertory of established scientific facts by
those who profess to study all the phenomena of the organism or of the mind of man. These personal experiences
having enabled me to detect the more subtle indications

of the mesmeric coma, I have taken every opportunity of witnessing the phenomena in public and private, and am quite satisfied that, in the more remarkable manifestations, there is, or can be, very rarely any deception practised.

As Dr. Carpenter and other men of science still maintain the view that all the higher phenomena of Spiritualism which are not imposture are due to subjective impressions, analogous to those produced in his patients by the mesmeriser, I will here point out certain characteristic differences between the two classes of facts which I first adduced in reply to Mr. E. B. Tylor, in a letter in *Nature* (1872, p. 364).

1. The mesmerised patient never has *doubts* of the reality of what he sees or hears. He is like a dreamer, to whom the most incongruous circumstances suggest no idea of incongruity, and he never inquires if what he thinks he perceives harmonises with his actual surroundings. He has, moreover, lost his memory of what and where he was a few moments before; and can give no account, for instance, of how he managed to get from a lecture room in London to which he came as a spectator half an hour ago, on to an Atlantic steamer in a hurricane, or into the presence of a tiger in a tropical jungle. The assistants at the *séances* of Mr. Home or Mrs. Guppy are not in this state, as even our opponents will admit, and as the almost invariable *suspicion of fraud* with which the phenomena are at first regarded, clearly demonstrates. They do not lose all memory of immediately preceding events; they criticise; they examine; they take notes; they suggest tests— none of which things the mesmerised patient ever does.

2. The mesmeriser has the power of acting on certain sensitive individuals (not on assemblies of people, as Mr. Tylor had assumed), and all experience shows that those who are thus sensitive to any one operator are but a small

proportion of any body of people, and even these almost always require previous manipulation, with an almost passive submission to the operator. The number who can be acted on without such previous manipulation is very small, probably less than one per cent. But there is no such limitation to the number of persons who simultaneously witness most of the mediumistic phenomena. The visitors to Mr. Home or Mrs. Guppy all see whatever occurs of a physical nature, as the records of hundreds of sittings, and even the evidence of sceptics, demonstrates.

The two classes of phenomena, therefore, differ fundamentally; yet there is a connection between them, but in an opposite direction to that suggested. It is the mediums, not the assistants, who are "sensitives." They are almost always subject to the mesmeric influence, and they often exhibit all the characteristic phenomena of coma, trance, rigidity, and abnormal sense-power. Conversely the most sensitive mesmeric patients are almost always mediums.

The differences now pointed out are so radical and so important that it does not say much for the logical clearness of those who persist in classing the two phenomena as identical.' But the manner in which men of great eminence fail to see the bearing of facts when that bearing is against their pet theories, will be further illustrated by a few examples in the appendix to this volume.

3. *Experiences and Tests of Modern Spiritual Phenomena.*
—During twelve years of tropical wanderings, occupied in the study of natural history, I heard occasionally of the strange phenomena said to be occurring in America and Europe under the general names of " table-turning " and " spirit-rapping;" and being aware, from my own knowledge of Mesmerism, that there were mysteries connected with the human mind which modern science ignored because it could not explain, I determined to seize the first

opportunity on my return home to examine into these matters. It is true, perhaps, that I ought to state that for twenty-five years I had been an utter sceptic as to the existence of any preter-human or super-human intelligences, and that I never for a moment contemplated the possibility that the marvels related by Spiritualists could be literally true. If I have now changed my opinion, it is simply by the force of evidence. It is from no dread of annihilation that I have gone into this subject; it is from no inordinate longing for eternal existence that I have come to believe in facts which render this highly probable, if they do not actually prove it. At least three times within the last twenty-five years I have had to face death as imminent or probable within a few hours, and what I felt on those occasions was at most a gentle melancholy at the thought of quitting this wonderful and beautiful earth to enter on a sleep which might know no waking. In a state of ordinary health I did not feel even this. I knew that the great problem of conscious existence was one beyond man's grasp, and this fact alone gave some hope that existence might be independent of the organised body. I came to the inquiry, therefore, utterly unbiassed by hopes or fears, because I knew that my belief could not affect the reality, and with an ingrained prejudice against even such a word as " spirit," which I have hardly yet overcome.

It was in the summer of 1865 that I first witnessed any of the phenomena of what is called Spiritualism, in the house of a friend,—a sceptic, a man of science, and a lawyer, with none but members of his own family present. Sitting at a good-sized round table, with our hands placed upon it, after a short time slight movements would commence— not often "turnings" or " tiltings," but a gentle intermittent movement, like steps, which after a time would bring the table quite across the room. Slight but distinct tapping sounds were also heard. The following notes made at the time were intended to describe exactly what took place :— " July 22nd, 1865.—Sat with my friend, his wife, and two daughters, at a large loo table, by daylight. In about half an hour some faint motions were perceived, and some faint taps heard. They gradually increased; the taps became very distinct, and the table moved considerably, obliging us all to shift our chairs. Then a curious vibratory motion of the table commenced, almost like the shivering of a living animal. I could feel it up to my elbows. These phenomena were variously repeated for two hours. On trying afterwards, we found the table could not be voluntarily moved in the same manner without a great exertion of force, and we could discover no possible way of producing the taps while our hands were upon the table."

On other occasions we tried the experiment of each person in succession leaving the table, and found that the phenomena continued the same as before, both taps and the table movement. Once I requested one after another to leave the table; the phenomena continued, but as the number of sitters diminished, with decreasing vigour, and just after the last person had drawn back leaving me alone at the table, there were two dull taps or blows, as with a fist on the pillar or foot of the table, the vibration of which I could feel as well as hear. No one present but myself could have made these and I certainly did not make them. These experiments clearly indicated, that all were concerned in producing the sounds and movements, and that if there was any wilful deception the whole party were engaged in deceiving me. Another time we sat half an hour at the large table but had no manifestations whatever. We then removed to the small table where taps immediately commenced and the table moved. After some time we returned to the large table, and after a few minutes the taps and movements took place as at the small one.

The movement of the table was almost always in curves as if turning on one of the claws, so as to give a progressive motion. This was frequently reversed, and sometimes regularly alternate, so that the table would travel across the room in a zigzag manner. This gives an idea of what took place with more or less regularity during more than a dozen sittings. Now there can be no doubt that the whole of the *movements* of the table could have been produced by any of the persons present if not counteracted by the others, but our experiments showed that this could not *always* be the case, and we have therefore no right to conclude that it was *ever* the case. The taps, on the other hand, we could not make at all. They were of about the quality that would be produced by a long finger nail tapping underneath the leaf of the table. As all hands were on the table and my eyes at least always open, I know they were not produced by the hands of any one present. They might possibly have been produced by the feet if properly armed with some small hard point to strike with, but if so, the experiments already related show that *all* must have practised the deception. And the fact that we often sat half an hour in one position without a single sound, and that the phenomena never progressed farther than I have related, weigh I think very strongly against the supposition, that a family of four highly intelligent and well educated persons should occupy themselves for so many weary hours in carrying out what would be so poor and unmeaning a deception. The following remark occurs at the end of my notes made at the time:—"These experiments have satisfied me that there is an unknown power developed from the bodies of a number of persons placed in connection by sitting round a table with all their hands upon it."

Some time before these observations I had met a gentle-man who had told me of most wonderful phenomena occurring in his own family—among them the palpable motion of solid bodies when ·no person was touching them or near them; and he had recommended me to go to a public medium in London (Mrs. Marshall), where I might see things equally wonderful. Accordingly, in September 1865, I began a series of visits to Mrs. Marshall, generally accompanied by a friend—a good chemist and mechanic, and of a thoroughly sceptical mind. What we witnessed may be divided into two classes of phenomena—physical and mental. Both were very numerous and varied; but I shall only select from each a few which are of a clear and definite nature.

1st. A small table, on which the hands of four persons were placed (including my own and Mrs. Marshall's), rose up vertically about a foot from the floor, and remained suspended for about twenty seconds, while my friend, who was sitting looking on, could see the lower part of the table with the feet freely suspended above the floor.

2nd. While sitting at a large table, with Miss T. on my left and Mr. R. on my right, a guitar which had been played in Miss T.'s hand slid down on to the floor, passed over my feet, and came to Mr. R., against whose legs it raised itself up till it appeared above the table. I and Mr. R. were watching it carefully the whole time, and it behaved as if alive itself, or rather as if a small invisible child were by great exertions moving it and raising it up. These two phenomena were witnessed in bright gaslight.

3rd. A chair, on which a relation of Mr. R.'s sat, was lifted up with her on it. Afterwards, when she returned to the table from the piano, where she had been playing, her chair moved away just as she was going to sit down, on drawing it up, it moved away again. After this had happened three times, it became apparently fixed to the floor, so that she could not raise it. Mr. R. then took hold of it, and found that it was only by a great exertion he could lift it off the floor. This sitting took place in broad daylight, on a bright day, and in a room on the first floor with two windows.

However strange and unreal these few phenomena may seem to readers who have seen nothing of the kind, I positively affirm that they are facts which really happened just as I have narrated them, and that there was no room for any possible trick or deception. In each case, before we began, we turned up the tables and chairs, and saw that they were ordinary pieces of furniture, and that there was no connection between them and the floor, and we placed them where we pleased before we sat down. Several of the phenomena occurred entirely under our own hands, and quite disconnected from the " medium." They were as much realities as the motion of nails towards a magnet, and, it may be added, not in themselves more improbable or more incomprehensible.

The mental phenomena which most frequently occur are the spelling out of the names of relations of persons present, their ages, or any other particulars about them. They are especially uncertain in their manifestation, though when they do succeed they are very conclusive to the persons who witness them. The general opinion of sceptics as to these phenomena is, that they depend simply on the acuteness and talent of the medium in hitting on the letters which form the name, by the manner in which persons dwell upon or hurry over them—the ordinary mode of receiving these communications being for the person interested to go over a printed alphabet, letter by letter—loud taps indicating the letters which form the required names. I shall select a few of our experiences,

I

which will show how far this explanation is likely to
be a true one.

When I first received a communication myself I was
particularly careful to avoid giving any indication, by going
with steady regularity over the letters; yet there was spelt
out correctly, first, the place where my brother died, Para;
then his Christian name, Herbert; and lastly, at my request, the name of the mutual friend who last saw him,
Henry Walter Bates. On this occasion our party of six
visited Mrs. Marshall for the first time, and my name, as
well as those of the rest of the party, except one, were unknown to her. That one was my married sister, whose
name was no clue to mine.

On the same occasion a young lady, a connection of Mr.
R.'s, was told that a communication was to be made to her.
She took the alphabet, and instead of pointing to the letters
one by one, she moved the pencil smoothly over the lines
with the greatest steadiness. I watched her, and wrote
down the letters which the taps indicated. The name produced was an extraordinary one, the letters being Thomas
Doe Thacker. I thought there must be an error in the
latter part; but the names were Thomas Doe Thacker, the
lady's father, every letter being correct. A number of
other names, places, and dates were spelt out on this
occasion with equal accuracy; but I give only these two,
because in these I am *sure* that no clue was given by
which the names could have been guessed by the most
preternaturally acute intellect.

On another occasion, I accompanied my sister and a
lady who had never been there before to Mrs. Marshall's,
and we had a very curious illustration of the absurdity of
imputing the spelling of names to the receiver's hesitation
and the medium's acuteness. She wished the name of a
particular deceased relation to be spelled out to her, and

pointed to the letters of the alphabet in the usual way, while I wrote down those indicated. The first three letters were y r n. "Oh!" said she, "that's nonsense; we had better begin again." Just then an e came, and thinking I saw what it was, I said—"Please go on, I understand it." The whole was then spelt out thus—yrnehkcocffej. The lady even then did not see it, till I separated it thus— yrneh kcocffej, or Henry Jeffcock, the name of the relation she had wanted accurately spelt backwards.

Another phenomenon, necessitating the exertion both of force and intellect, is the following :—The table having been previously examined, a sheet of note paper was marked privately by me, and placed with a lead pencil under the centre foot of the table, all present having their hands upon the table. After a few minutes taps are heard, and on taking up the paper I find written on it in a free hand—William. On another occasion, a friend from the country—a total stranger to the medium, and whose name was never mentioned—accompanied me ; and, after receiving what purported to be a communication from his son, a paper was put under the table, and in a few minutes there was found written on it Charley T. Dodd, the correct name. In these cases it is certain there was no machinery under the table; and it simply remains to ask, if it were possible for Mrs. Marshall to slip off her boots, seize the pencil and paper with her toes, and write on it a name she had to guess at, and again put on her boots without removing her hands from the table, or giving any indication whatever of her exertions?

I now for some months left off going to Mrs. Marshall's, and endeavoured to produce the phenomena at home. My friend Mr. R. soon found he had the power to produce slight movements of the table, but they were never of such a nature as to satisfy an observer that they were not pro-

duced consciously or unconsciously by our own muscles.
The style and character of the communications obtained
through these movements were, however, such as to satisfy
me that our own minds had no part in producing them.

We tried among all our friends to find one who had power
to produce distinct taps, a class of phenomena that appeared
to us much more satisfactory, because we could not produce them ourselves, either consciously or unconsciously,
under the same conditions. It was in November, 1866,
that my sister discovered that a lady living with her had
the power of inducing loud and distinct taps and other
curious phenomena; and I now began a series of observations in my own house, the most important of which I
shall briefly narrate.

When we sat at a large loo table without a cloth, with
all our hands upon it, the taps would generally commence
in a few minutes. They sound as if made on the under
side of the leaf of the table, in various parts of it. They
change in tone and loudness, from a sound like that produced by tapping with a needle or a long finger nail, to
others like blows with a fist or slaps with the fingers of a
hand. Sounds are produced also like scraping with a
finger nail, or like the rubbing of a damp finger pressed
very hard on the table. The rapidity with which these
sounds are produced and are changed is very remarkable.
They will imitate, more or less exactly, sounds which we
make with our fingers above the table; they will keep
good time to a tune whistled by one of the party; they
will sometimes, at request, play a very fair tune themselves, or will follow accurately a hand tapping a tune upon
the table. When these sounds are heard repeatedly in
one's own well-lighted room, upon one's own table, and
with every hand in the room visible, the ordinary explanations given of them seem utterly untenable. Of course

the first impression on hearing a few taps only is, that some one is making them with their feet.   To set this doubt at rest, we have on several occasions all knelt down round the table, and yet the taps have continued, and have not only been heard as if on the leaf of the table, but have been felt vibrating through it.   Another view is, that the sounds are produced by the slipping of tendons or the cracking of joints in some parts of the medium's body; and this explanation is, I believe, the one most commonly accepted by scientific men.   But surely, if this be so, some one case can be brought forward in which a person's bones or tendons can make sounds like tapping, rapping, thumping, slapping, scratching, and rubbing, and can repeat some of these so rapidly as to follow every tap of an observer's fingers, or to keep time to music; and further, that all these sounds shall appear to every one present not to come from the individual's body, but from the table at which he is sitting, and which shall often vibrate when the sounds are heard.   Until such a case is produced I must be excused for marvelling at the credulity of those who accept so absurd and inadequate an explanation.

A still more remarkable phenomenon, and one which I have observed with the greatest care and the most profound interest, is the exhibition of considerable force under conditions which preclude the muscular action of any of the party. We stand round a small work-table, whose leaf is about twenty inches across, placing our hands all close together near the centre.   After a short time the table rocks about from side to side, and then, appearing to steady itself, rises vertically from six inches to a foot, and remains suspended often fifteen or twenty seconds. During this time any one or two of the party can strike it or press on it, as it resists a very considerable force.   Of course, the first impression is that some one's foot is lifting up the table.   To answer this objection I prepared the table before our second trial without telling any one, by stretching some thin tissue paper between the feet an inch or two from the bottom of the pillar, in such a manner that any attempt to insert the foot must crush and tear the paper.   The table rose up as before, resisted pressure downwards, as if it was resting on the back of some animal, sunk to the floor, and in a short time rose again, and then dropped suddenly down.   I now with some anxiety turned up the table, and, to the surprise of all present, showed them the delicate tissue stretched across altogether uninjured!   Finding that this test was troublesome as the paper or threads had to be renewed every time, and were liable to be broken accidentally before the experiment began, I constructed a cylinder of hoops and laths, covered with canvas.   The table was placed within this as in a well, and, as it was about eighteen inches high, it effectually kept feet and ladies' dresses from the table.   This apparatus in no way checked its upward motion, and as the hands of the medium are always close under the eyes of all present, and simply resting on the top of the table, it would appear that there is some new and unknown power here at work. These experiments have been many times repeated by me, and I am satisfied of the correctness of my statement of the facts.

On two or three occasions only, when the conditions appear to have been unusually favourable, I have witnessed a still more marvellous phenomenon.   While sitting at the large table in our usual manner, I placed the small table about four feet from it, on the side next the medium and my sister.   After some time, while we were talking, we heard a slight sound from the table, and looking towards it found that it moved slightly at short intervals, and after a little time it moved suddenly up to the table by the side of the medium, as if it had gradually got within the sphere of a strong attractive force. Afterwards, at our request, it was thrown down on the floor without any person touching it, and it then moved about in a strange life-like manner, as if seeking some means of getting up again, turning its claws first on one side and then on the other. On another occasion a very large leather arm-chair which stood at least four or five feet from the medium, suddenly wheeled up to her after a few slight preliminary movements. It is, of course, easy to say that what I relate is impossible. I maintain that it is accurately true : and that no man, whatever be his attainments, has such an exhaustive knowledge of the powers of nature as to justify him in using the word impossible with regard to facts which I and many others have repeatedly witnessed.

On Wednesday evening, February 27, 1867, some very remarkable phenomena occurred. The parties present were, my sister, and Miss Nichol (now Mrs. Guppy), her father, Mr. H. T. Humphreys, and two young friends of mine, Mr. and Miss M. My wife and her sister also sat in the room at some distance from the table looking on. There was no fire, and we lowered the gas so as to give a subdued light, which enabled everything to be seen. The moment we were all in our places taps were heard indicating that the conditions were favourable. We now sent for a single wineglass which was placed on the floor between Miss Nichol and her father, and we requested it might be struck. After a short time it was gently tapped producing a clear ringing sound. This soon changed to a sound as if two glasses were gently struck together ; and now we were all astonished by hearing in succession almost every possible sound that could be produced by two glasses one inside the other, even to the clang of one dropped into another. They were in every respect identical with such sounds as we could produce with two glasses and with two only, manipulated in a variety of ways, and yet I was quite sure that only one wineglass was in the room, and every person's hands were distinctly visible on the table.

We now took up the glass again and put it on the table, where it was held by both Miss N. and Mr. Humphreys, so as to prevent any vibration it might produce. After a short interval of silence an exquisitely delicate sound as of tapping a glass was heard, which increased to clear silvery notes like the tinkling of a glass bell. These continued in varying degrees for some minutes, and then became fainter and gradually died away. We afterwards placed a rude bamboo harp from the Malay Archipelago under the table, and, after several alterations of position, the strings were twanged as clearly and loudly as any of us could do it with our fingers. Having had such success with the glass we asked if the harp could also be imitated, and having received permission to try, placed it also on the table. After a little time faint vibrating taps were heard, and these soon changed into very faint twangs which formed a distinct imitation of the harp strings, although by no means so successfully as in the case of the wineglass.

We were informed by taps in the ordinary way that it was through the peculiar influence of Mr. Nichol that this extraordinary production of imitative musical sounds without any material object was effected. I may add that the imitation of the sound produced by *two* glasses was so perfect that some of the party turned up the table immediately after we left it, under the impression that the unseen power had brought in a second glass, but none could be found.

It has been objected that we too often use the expression that the phenomena we witness " could not possibly have been produced by any of the persons present." I maintain that in this instance they could not, and I shall continue in that conviction until they are produced under similar conditions and the *modus operandi* explained.

I have since witnessed a great variety of phenomena, some of which are alluded to in other parts of this volume : but I attach most importance to those which I have carefully and repeatedly tested, and which give me a solid basis of fact by which to judge of what others relate or of what I have myself seen under less favourable conditions.

A DEFENCE OF MODERN SPIRITUALISM.*

(REPRINTED WITH NOTES AND ADDITIONS FROM THE "FORTNIGHTLY
REVIEW.")

IT is with great diffidence, but under an imperative sense
of duty, that the present writer accepts the opportunity
afforded him of submitting to the readers of the *Fortnightly Review* some general account of a wide-spread
movement, which, though for the most part treated with
ridicule or contempt, he believes to embody truths of the
most vital importance to human progress. The subject to
be treated is of such vast extent; the evidence concerning
it is so varied and so extraordinary; the prejudices that
surround it are so inveterate, that it is not possible to do
it justice without entering into considerable detail. The
reader who ventures on the perusal of the succeeding
pages may, therefore, have his patience tried; but if he is
able to throw aside his preconceived ideas of what is possible and what is impossible, and in the acceptance or
rejection of what is submitted to him will carefully weigh

---

* The following are the more important works which have been
used in the preparation of this article:—Judge Edmond's "Spiritual
Tracts," New York, 1858—1860. Robert Dale Owen's "Footfalls on the
Boundary of Another World," Trübner and Co., 1861. E. Hardinge's
"Modern American Spiritualism," New York, 1870. Robert Dale
Owen's "Debateable Land between this World and the Next," Trübner,
and Co., 1871. "Report on Spiritualism of the Committee of the Lon-
don Dialectical Society," Longmans and Co., 1871. "Year Book of
Spiritualism," Boston and London, 1871. Hudson Tuttle's "Arcana of
Spiritualism," Boston 1871. *The Spiritual Magazine*, 1861—1874. *The
Spiritualist Newspaper*, 1872—1874. *The Medium and Daybreak*, 1869—
1874.

and be solely guided by the nature of the concurrent testimony, the writer ventures to believe that he will not find his time and patience ill-bestowed.

Few men, in this busy age, have leisure to read massive volumes devoted to special subjects. They gain much of their general knowledge, outside the limits of their profession or of any peculiar study, by means of periodical literature; and, as a rule, they are supplied with copious and accurate, though general information. Some of our best thinkers and workers make known the results of their researches to the readers of magazines and reviews; and it is seldom that a writer whose information is meagre or obtained at second-hand, is permitted to come before the public in their pages as an authoritative teacher. But as regards the subject we are now about to consider, this rule has not hitherto been followed. Those who have devoted many years to an examination of its phenomena have been, in most cases, refused a hearing; while men who have bestowed on it no adequate attention, and are almost wholly ignorant of the researches of others, have alone supplied the information to which a large proportion of the public have had access. In support of this statement it is necessary to refer, with brief comments, to some of the more prominent articles in which the phenomena and pretensions of Spiritualism have been recently discussed.

At the beginning of the present year the readers of the *Fortnightly Review* were treated to "Experiences of Spiritualism," by a noble lord of no mean ability, and of thoroughly advanced views. He assures his readers that he "conscientiously endeavoured to qualify himself for speaking on this subject" by attending five séances, the details of several of which he narrates; and he comes to the conclusion that mediums are by no means ingenious deceivers, but "jugglers of the most vulgar order;" that the "spiritualistic mind falls a victim to the most patent frauds," and greedily " accepts jugglery as manifestations of spirits;" and, lastly, that the mediums are as credulous as their dupes, and fall straightway into any trap that is laid for them. Now, on the evidence before him, and on the assumption that no more or better evidence would have been forthcoming had he devoted fifty instead of five evenings to the inquiry, the conclusions of Lord Amberley are perfectly logical; but, so far from what he witnessed being a "specimen of the kind of manifestations by which spiritualists are convinced," a very little acquaintance with the literature of the subject would have shown him that no spiritualist of any mark was ever convinced by any quantity of such evidence. In an article published since Lord Amberley's—in *London Society* for February—the author, a barrister and well-known literary man, says :—

"It was difficult for me to give in to the idea that solid objects could be conveyed, invisibly, through closed doors, or that heavy furniture could be moved without the interposition of hands. Philosophers will say these things are absolutely impossible; nevertheless, it is absolutely certain that they do occur. I have met in the houses of private friends, as witnesses of these phenomena, persons whose testimony would go for a good deal in a court of justice. They have included peers, members of parliament, diplomatists of the highest rank, judges, barristers, physicians, clergymen, members of learned societies, chemists, engineers, journalists, and thinkers of all sorts and degrees. They have suggested and carried into effect tests of the most rigid and satisfactory character. The media (all non-professional) have been searched before and after séances. The precaution has even been taken of providing them unexpectedly with other apparel. They have been tied; they have been sealed ; they have been secured in every cunning and dexterous manner that ingenuity could devise, but no deception has been discovered and no imposture brought to light. Neither was there any motive for imposture. No fee or reward of any kind depended upon the success or non-success of the manifestations."

Now here we have a nice question of probabilities. We

must either believe that Lord Amberley is almost infinitely
more acute than Mr. Dunphy and his host of eminent
friends,—so that after five séances (most of them failures)
he has got to the bottom of a mystery in which they, notwithstanding their utmost endeavours, still hopelesly
flounder—or, that the noble lord's acuteness does not surpass the combined acuteness of all these persons; in which
case their much larger experience, and their having witnessed many things Lord Amberley has not witnessed,
must be held to have the greater weight, and to show at
all events, that all mediums are not "jugglers of the most
vulgar order."

In October, 1873, the New Quarterly Magazine, in its
opening number, had an article entitled, " A Spiritualistic
Séance;" but which proved to be an account of certain
ingenious contrivances by which some of the phenomena
usual at séances were imitated, and both spiritualists and
sceptics deceived and confounded. This appears at first
sight to be an exposure of Spiritualism, but it is really
very favourable to its pretensions; for it goes on the
assumption that the marvellous phenomena witnessed do
really occur, but are produced by various mechanical contrivances. In this case the rooms above, below, and at the
side of that in which the séance was held had to be prepared with specially constructed machinery, with assistants
to work it. The apparatus, as described, would cost at
least £100, and would then only serve to produce a few
fixed phenomena, such as happen frequently in private
houses and at the lodgings of mediums who have not
exclusive possession of any of the adjoining rooms, or the
means of obtaining expensive machinery and hired assistants. The article bears internal evidence of being altogether a fictitious narrative; but it helps to demonstrate, if
any demonstration is required, that the phenomena which

occur under such protean forms and varied conditions, and in private houses quite as often as at the apartments of the mediums, are in no way produced by machinery.

Perhaps the most prominent recent attack on Spiritualism was that in the *Quarterly Review* for October, 1871, which is known to have been written by an eminent physiologist, and did much to blind the public to the real nature of the movement. This article, after giving a light sketch of the reported phenomena, entered into some details as to planchette writing and table-lifting,—facts on which no spiritualist depends as evidence to a third party, and then proceeded to define its stand-point as follows:—

" Our position, then, is that the so-called spiritual communications come from *within*, not from without, the individuals who suppose themselves to be the recipients of them ; that they belong to the class termed 'subjective' by physiologists and psychologists, and that the movements by which they are expressed, whether the tilting of tables or the writing of planchettes, are really produced by their own muscular action exerted independently of their own wills and quite unconsciously to themselves."

Several pages are then devoted to accounts of séances which, like Lord Amberley's, were mostly failures; and to the experiences of a Bath clergyman who believed that the communications came from devils ; and, generally, such weak and inconclusive phenomena only are adduced as can be easily explained by the well-worn formulæ of "unconscious cerebration," "expectant attention," and "unconscious muscular action." A few of the more startling physical phenomena are mentioned merely to be discredited and the judgment of the witnesses impugned ; but no attempt is made to place before the reader any information as to the amount or the weight of the testimony to such phenomena, or to the long series of diverse phenomena which lead up to and confirm them. Some of the experiments of Professor Hare and Mr. Crookes are quoted, and criticised in the spirit of assuming that these experienced physicists were ignorant of the simplest principles of mechanics, and failed to use the most ordinary precautions. Of the numerous and varied cases on record of heavy bodies being moved without direct or indirect contact by any human being, no notice is taken, except so far as quoting Mr. C. F. Varley's statement, that he had seen, in broad daylight, a small table moved ten feet, with no one near it but himself, and not touched by him, " as an example of the manner in which minds of this limited order are apt to become the dupes of their own imaginings."

This article, like the others here referred to, shows in the writer an utter forgetfulness of the maxim, that an argument is not answered till it is answered at its best. Amid the vast mass of recorded facts now accumulated by spiritualists there is, of course, much that is weak and inconclusive, much that is of no value as evidence, except to those who have independent reasons for faith in them. From this undigested mass it is the easiest thing in the world to pick out arguments that can be refuted, and facts that can be explained away; but what is that to the purpose? It is not these that have convinced any one; but those weightier, oft-repeated, and oft-tested facts which the writers referred to invariably ignore.

Professor Tyndall has also given the world (in his " Fragments of Science," published in 1871) some account of his attempt to investigate these phenomena. Again we have a minute record of a séance which was a failure; and in which the Professor, like Lord Amberley, easily imposed on some too credulous spiritualists by improvising a few manifestations of his own. The article in question is dated as far back as 1864. We may therefore conclude that the Professor has not seen much of the subject; nor can he have made himself acquainted with what others

have seen and carefully verified, or he would hardly have
thought his communication worthy of the place it occupies
among original researches and positive additions to human
knowledge.   Both its facts and its reasonings have been
well replied to by Mr. Patrick Fraser Alexander, in his
little work entitled, "Spiritualism; a Narrative and a Discussion," which we recommend to those who care to see how
a very acute yet unprejudiced mind looks at the phenomena; and how inconclusive, even from a scientific stand-
point, are the experiences adduced by Professor Tyndall.

The discussion in the *Pall Mall Gazette* in 1868, and a
considerable private correspondence, indicates, that scientific men almost invariably assume that in this inquiry
they should be permitted at the very outset to impose
conditions; and if, under such conditions, nothing happens,
they consider it a proof of imposture or delusion.   But
they well know that, in all other branches of research,
nature, not they, determines the essential conditions, without a compliance with which no experiment will succeed.
These conditions have to be learnt by a patient questioning
of nature, and they are different for each branch of science.
How much more may they be expected to differ in an
inquiry which deals with subtle forces of the nature of
which the physicist is wholly and absolutely ignorant!
To ask to be allowed to deal with these unknown phenomena as he has hitherto dealt with known phenomena, is
practically to prejudge the question, since it assumes that
both are governed by the same laws.

From the sketch which has now been given of the recent
treatment of the subject by popular and scientific writers,
we can summarise pretty accurately their mental attitude
in regard to it.   They have seen very little of the phenomena themselves, and they cannot believe that others have
seen much more.   They have encountered people who are

easily deceived by a little unexpected trickery, and they
conclude that the convictions of spiritualists generally are
founded on phenomena produced, either consciously or
unconsciously, in a similar way. They are so firmly convinced on *à priori* grounds, that the more remarkable
phenomena said to happen do not really happen, that they
will back their conviction against the direct testimony of
any body of men, preferring to believe that they are all
the victims of some mysterious delusion whenever imposture is out of the question. To influence persons in this
frame of mind, it is evident that *more* personal testimony
to isolated facts is utterly useless. They have, to use the
admirable expression of Dr. Carpenter, "no place in the
existing fabric of their thought into which such facts can
be fitted." It is necessary, therefore, to modify the "fabric
of thought" itself; and it appears to the present writer
that this can best be done by a general historic sketch of
the subject; and by showing, by separate lines of inquiry,
how wide and varied is the evidence, and how remarkably
these lines converge towards one uniform conclusion. The
endeavour will be made to indicate, by typical examples
of each class of evidence and without unnecessary detail,
the cumulative force of the argument.

HISTORICAL SKETCH.

Modern Spiritualism dates from March, 1848; it being
then that, for the first time, intelligent communications
were held with the unknown cause of the mysterious
knockings and other sounds similar to those which had
disturbed the Mompesson and Wesley families in the
seventeenth and eighteenth centuries. This discovery was
made by Miss Kate Fox, a girl of nine years old,* and the

---

* Miss K. Fox (now Mrs. Jencken) states that she was only five years
old at this time. Her parents, however, appear to have given the age as
nine to several inquirers at this time.

first recognised example of an extensive class now known
as mediums. It is worthy of remark that this very first
" modern spiritual manifestation" was subjected to the test
of unlimited examination by all the inhabitants of the
village of Hydesville, New York. Though all were utter
sceptics, no one could discover any cause for the noises,
which continued, though with less violence, when all the
children had left the house. Nothing is more common
than the remark, that it is absurd and illogical to impute
noises, of which we cannot discover the cause, to the
agency of spirits. So it undoubtedly is when the noises are
merely noises; but is it so illogical when these noises turn
out to be signals, and signals which spell out a fact, which
fact, though wholly unknown to all present, turns out to
be true ? Yet, on this very first occasion, twenty-six years
ago, the signals declared that a murdered man was buried
in the cellar of the house; it indicated the exact spot in
the cellar under which the body lay; and upon digging
there, at a depth of six or seven feet, considerable portions
of a human skeleton were found. Yet more, the name of
the murdered man was given, and it was ascertained that
such a person had visited that very house and had disappeared five years before, and had never been heard of
since. The signals further declared that he, the murdered
man, was the signaller; and as all the witnesses had
satisfied themselves that the signals were not made by
any living person, or by any assignable cause, the logical
conclusion from the facts was, that it *was* the spirit* of
the murdered man; although such a conclusion might be

---

* It may be as well here to explain that the word "spirit," which is
often considered to be so objectionable by scientific men, is used throughout
this article (or, at all events, in the earlier portions of it) merely to avoid
circumlocution, in the sense of the " intelligent cause of the phenomena,"
and not as implying "the spirits of the dead," unless so expressly stated.

to some in the highest degree improbable, and to others in
the highest degree absurd.

The Misses Fox now became involuntary mediums, and
the family (which had removed to the city of Rochester)
were accused of imposture, and offered to submit the
children to examination by a committee of townsmen
appointed in public meeting. Three committees were successively appointed; the last, composed of violent sceptics
who had accused the previous committees of stupidity or
connivance. But all three, after unlimited investigation,
were forced to declare that the cause of the phenomena
was undiscoverable. The sounds occurred on the wall and
floor while the mediums, after being thoroughly searched
by ladies, "stood on pillows, barefooted, and with their
clothes tied round their ankles." The last and most sceptical committee reported that "They had heard sounds,
and failed utterly to discover their origin. They had
proved that neither machinery nor imposture had been
used; and their questions, *many of them being mental*, were
answered correctly." When we consider that the mediums
were two children under twelve years of age, and the
examiners utterly sceptical American citizens, thoroughly
resolved to detect imposture, and urged on by excited
public meetings, it may perhaps be considered that even
at this early stage the question of imposture or delusion
was pretty well settled in the negative.

In a short time persons who sat with the Misses Fox
found themselves to have similar powers in a greater or
less degree; and in two or three years the movement had
spread over a large part of the United States, developing
into a variety of strange forms, encountering the most
violent scepticism and the most rancorous hostility; yet
always progressing, and making converts even among the
most enlightened and best educated classes. In 1851,

some of the most intelligent men in New York—judges, senators, doctors, lawyers, merchants, clergymen, and authors—formed themselves into a society for investigation. Judge Edmonds was one of these; and a sketch of the kind and amount of evidence that was required to convince him will be given further on. In 1854 a second spiritual society was formed in New York. It had the names of four judges and two physicians among its vice-presidents, showing that the movement had by this time become respectable, and that men in high social positions were not afraid of identifying themselves with it. A little later Professor Mapes, an eminent agricultural chemist, was led to undertake the investigation of Spiritualism. He formed a circle of twelve friends, most of them men of talent and sceptics, who bound themselves to sit together weekly, with a medium, twenty times. For the first eighteen evenings the phenomena were so trivial and unsatisfactory, that most of the party felt disgusted at the loss of time; but the last two sittings produced phenomena of so startling a character, that the investigation was continued by the same circle *for four years, and all became spiritualists.*

By this time the movement had spread into every part of the Union, and, notwithstanding that its adherents were abused as impostors or dupes, that they were in several cases expelled from colleges and churches, were confined as lunatics, and that the whole thing was "explained" over and over again, it has continued to spread up to the present hour. The secret of this appears to have been, that the explanations given never applied to the phenomena continually occurring, and of which there were numerous witnesses. A medium was raised in the air in a crowded room in full daylight. ("Modern American Spiritualism," p. 279.) A scientific sceptic prepared a small portable apparatus, by which he could produce an instantaneous

illumination; and, taking it to a dark séance at which
numerous musical instruments were played, suddenly
lighted up the room while a large drum was being violently
beaten, in the certain expectation of revealing the impostor
to the whole company. But what they all saw was the
drumstick itself beating the drum, with no human being
near it. It struck a few more blows, then rose into the
air and descended gently on to the shoulder of a lady.
(Same work, p. 337.) At Toronto, Canada, in a well-lighted
room, an accompaniment to a song was played on a closed
and locked piano. (Same work, p. 463.) Communications
were given in raised letters on the arm of an ignorant
servant girl, who often could not read them. They sometimes appeared while she was at her household work, and
after being read by her master or mistress, would disappear.
(Same work, p. 196.)   Letters closed in any number of
envelopes, sealed up or even pasted together over the
whole of the written surface, were read and answered by
certain mediums in whom this special power was developed. It mattered not what language the letters were
written in; and it is upon record that letters in German,
Greek, Hebrew, Arabic, Chinese, French, Welsh, and Mexi-
can, have been correctly answered in the corresponding
languages by a medium who knew none of them. (Judge
Edmonds' "Letters on Spiritualism," pp. 59—103, Appendix.) Other mediums drew portraits of deceased persons
whom they had never known or heard of. Others healed
diseases. But those who helped most to spread the belief
were, perhaps, the trance speakers, who, in eloquent and
powerful language, developed the principles and the uses
of Spiritualism; answered objections; spread abroad a
knowledge of the phenomena, and thus induced sceptics to
inquire into the facts; and inquiry was almost invariably
followed by conversion. Having repeatedly listened to

three of these speakers who have visited this country, I can bear witness that they fully equal, and not unfrequently surpass, our best orators and preachers; whether in finished eloquence, in close and logical argument, or in the readiness with which appropriate and convincing replies are made to all objectors. They are also remarkable for the perfect courtesy and sauvity of their manner, and for the extreme patience and gentleness with which they meet the most violent opposition and the most unjust accusations.

Men of the highest rank and greatest ability became convinced by these varied phenomena. No amount of education, of legal, medical, or scientific training, were proof against the overwhelming force of the facts, whenever these facts were systematically and perseveringly inquired into. The number of Spiritualists in the Union is, according to those who have the best means of judging, from eight to eleven millions.* This is the estimate of Judge Edmonds, who has had extensive correspondence on the subject with every part of the United States. The Hon. R. D. Owen, who has also had great opportunities of knowing the facts, considers it to be approximately correct; and it is affirmed by the editors of the "Year Book of Spiritualism," for

---

* Mr. Wm. Tebb has called my attention to his objections to the estimate of 8 to 11 millions of Spiritualists in the United States, published in *Human Nature*, Nov., 1871. After a careful and extensive inquiry in America, he thinks about one tenth of the amount nearer the truth. Judge Edmonds' letter on the subject (*Spiritual Magazine*, 1867, p. 327) enables us to some extent to understand how such divergent estimates could be made; and although he may be too high, it seems probable that Mr. Tebb is very much too low. "Spiritualists" is such a vague term that no approach to accuracy can be expected. The confirmed and acknowledged Spiritualists may be only about *one million*, while Judge Edmonds' estimate may include all who acknowledge that the phenomena are realities. Taken in this sense, several authorities I have consulted, including Mr. Epes Sargent, do not think Judge Edmonds' estimate to be much exaggerated.

1871. These numbers have been held to be absurdly exaggerated by persons having less information, especially by
strangers who have made superficial inquiries in America;
but it must be remembered that the Spiritualists are, to a
very limited extent, an organised body; and that the mass of
them make no public profession of their belief, but still
remain members of some denominational church—circumstances that would greatly deceive an outsider.   Nevertheless the organisation is of considerable extent.   There were
in America, in 1870, 20 State associations and 105 societies
of Spiritualists, 207 lecturers, and about the same number
of public mediums.

In other parts of the world the movement has progressed
more or less rapidly.   Several of the more celebrated
American mediums have visited this country, and not
only made converts in all classes of society, but led to the
formation of private circles and the discovery of mediumistic power in hundreds of families.   There is scarcely a
city or a considerable town in continental Europe at the
present moment where Spiritualists are not reckoned by
hundreds, if not by thousands.   There are said, on good
authority, to be fifty thousand avowed spiritualists in Paris
and ten thousand in Lyons; and the numbers in this country may be roughly estimated by the fact that there are
four exclusively spiritual periodicals, one of which has a
circulation of five thousand weekly.

DEDUCTIONS FROM THE PRECEDING SKETCH.

Before proceeding to a statement of the evidence which
has convinced the more educated and more sceptical converts, let us consider briefly the bearing of the undoubted
fact, that (to keep within bounds) many thousands of well-
informed men, belonging to all classes of society and all

professions, have, in each of the great civilised nations of the world, acknowledged the objective reality of these phenomena; although, almost without exception, they at first viewed them with dislike or contempt, as impostures or delusions. There is nothing parallel to it in the history of human thought; because there never before existed so strong, and apparently so well-founded a conviction that phenomena of this kind never have happened and never can happen. It is often said, that the number of adherents to a belief is no proof of its truth. This remark justly applies to most religions, whose arguments appeal to the emotions and the intellect but not the evidence of the senses. It is equally just as applied to a great part of modern science. The almost universal belief in gravitation, and the undulatory theory of light, does not render them in any degree more probable; because very few indeed of the believers have tested the facts which most convincingly demonstrate those theories, or are able to follow out the reasoning by which they are demonstrated. It is for the most part a blind belief accepted upon authority. But with these spiritual phenomena the case is very different. They are to most men, so new, so strange, so incredible, so opposed to their whole habit of thought, so apparently opposed to the pervading scientific spirit of the age, that they cannot and do not accept them on second-hand evidence, as they do almost every other kind of knowledge. The thousands or millions of spiritualists, therefore, represent to a very large extent men who have witnessed, examined, and tested the evidence for themselves, over and over, and over again, till that which they had at first been unable to admit *could* be true, they have at last been compelled to acknowledge *is* true. This accounts for the utter failure of all the attempted "exposures" and "explanations," to convince one solitary believer

of his error. The exposers and explainers have never got
beyond those first difficulties which constitute the *pons
asinorum* of Spiritualism which every believer has to get
over, but at which early stage of investigation no converts
are ever made. By explaining table-turning, or table-tilt-
ing, or raps, you do not influence a man who was never
convinced by these, but who, in broad daylight, sees objects
move without contact, and behave as if guided by intelligent
beings; and who sees this in a variety of forms, in a variety
of places, and under such varied and stringent conditions,
as to make the fact to him just as real as the movement
of iron to the magnet. By explaining automatic writing
(which itself convinces no one but the writer, and not
always even him), you do not affect the belief of the man
who has obtained writing when neither pencil nor
paper were touched by any one, as in the case of
Mr. Andrew Leighton of Liverpool, in whose presence the following pertinent sentence was written under
strictly test conditions—"And is this world of strife to
end in dust at last?"—or has seen a hand not attached to
a human body take up a pen and write,—as many persons
in London have seen in the presence of Mr. Home. Thus
it is that there are so few recantations or perverts in Spiritualism; so few, that it may be truly said there are none. After
much inquiry and reading I can find no example of a man
who, having acquired a good personal knowledge of all the
chief phases of the phenomena, has subsequently come to
disbelieve in their reality. If the " explanations" and " exposures" were good for anything, or if it were an imposture
to expose, or a delusion to explain, this could not be the case,
because there are numbers of men who have become convinced of the facts, but who have not accepted the spiritual
theory. These are, for the most part, in an uncomfortable and
  ttled frame of mind, and would gladly welcome an ex-

planation which really explained anything—but they find
it not. As an eminent example of this class, I may mention Dr. J. Lockhart Robertson, long one of the editors of
the *Journal of Mental Science,*—a physician who, having
made mental disease his special study would not be easily
taken in by any psychological delusions. The phenomena
he witnessed fourteen years ago were of a violent character;
a very strong table being, at his own request and in his own
house, broken to pieces while he held the medium's hands.
He afterwards himself tried to break a remaining leg of the
table, but failed to do so after exerting all his strength.
Another table was tilted over while all the party sat on it.
He subsequently had a sitting with Mr. Home, and witnessed the usual phenomena occurring with that extraordinary medium,—such as the accordion playing "most
wonderful music without any human agency," "a shadow
hand, not that of any one present which lifts a pencil and
writes with it," &c., &c.; and he says that he can "no more
doubt the physical manifestations of (so-called) Spiritualism
than he would any other fact—as, for example, the fall of
an apple to the ground of which his senses informed him."
His record of these phenomena, with the confirmation by a
friend who was present, is published in the "Dialectical
Society's Report on Spiritualism," p. 247; and, at a meeting of Spiritualists in 1870, he reasserted the facts, but
denied their spiritual origin. To such a man the
Quarterly Reviewer's explanations are worthless; yet it
may be safely said, that every advanced Spiritualist has
seen more remarkable, more varied, and even more
inexplicable phenomena than those recorded by Dr.
Robertson, and are therefore still further out of reach
of the arguments referred to, which are indeed only
calculated to convince those who know little or nothing
of the matter.

EVIDENCE OF THE FACTS.

The subject of the evidences of the objective phenomena of Spiritualism is such a large one that it will be only possible here to give a few typical examples, calculated to show how wide is their range, and how conclusively they reach every objection that the most sceptical have brought against them. This may perhaps be best done by giving, in the first place, an outline of the career of two or three well-known mediums; and, in the second, a sketch of the experiences and investigations of a few of the more remarkable converts to Spiritualism.

Career of Remarkable Mediums.—Miss Kate Fox, the little girl of nine years old, who, as already stated, was the first " medium" in the modern sense of the term, has continued to possess the same power for twenty-six years. At the very earliest stages of the movement, sceptic after sceptic, committee after committee, endeavoured to discover " the trick;" but if it was a trick this little girl baffled them all, and the proverbial acuteness of the Yankee was of no avail. In 1860, when Dr. Robert Chambers visited America he suggested to his friend, Robert Dale Owen, the use of a balance to test the lifting power. They accordingly, without pre-arrangement with the medium, took with them a powerful steelyard, and suspended from it a dining-table weighing 121 pounds. Then, under a bright gas-light the feet of the two mediums (Miss Fox and her sister) being both touched by the feet of the gentlemen, and the hands of all present being held over, but not touching the table, it was made lighter or heavier at request, so as to weigh at one time only 60, at another 134 pounds. This experiment, be it remembered, was identical with one proposed by Faraday himself as being conclusive. Mr. Owen had many sittings with Miss Fox for the purpose of test; and the precautions he took were extraordinary. He sat with her alone ; he frequently changed the room without notice ; he examined every article of furniture; he locked the doors and fastened them with strips of paper privately sealed; he held both the hands of the medium. Under these conditions various phenomena occurred, the most remarkable being the illumination of a piece of paper (which he had brought himself, cut of a peculiar size, and privately marked), showing a dark hand writing on the floor. The paper afterwards rose up on to the table with legible writing upon it, containing a promise which was subsequently verified. (" Debateable Land," p. 293.)

But Miss Fox's powers were most remarkably shown in the *séances* with Mr. Livermore, a well-known New York banker, and an entire sceptic before commencing these experiments. These sittings were more than three hundred in number, extending over five years. They took place in four different houses (Mr. Livermore's and the medium's being both changed during this period), under tests of the most rigid description. The chief phenonenon was the appearance of a tangible, visible, and audible figure of Mr. Livermore's deceased wife, sometimes accompanied by a male figure, purporting to be Dr. Franklin. The former figure was often most distinct and absolutely life-like. It moved various objects in the room. It wrote messages on cards. It was sometimes formed out of a luminous cloud, and again vanished before the eyes of the witnesses. It allowed a portion of its dress to be cut off, which though at first of strong and apparently material gauzy texture, yet in a short time melted away and became invisible. Flowers which melted away were also given. These phenomena occurred best when Mr. L. and the medium were alone; but two witnesses were occasionally admitted, who tested everything and confirmed Mr. L.'s testimony. One of these was

Mr. Livermore's physician, the other his brother-in-law; the latter previously a sceptic. The details of these wonderful *séances* were published in the *Spiritual Magazine* in 1862 and 1863; and the more remarkable are given in Owen's "Debateable Land," from which work a good idea may be formed of the great variety of the phenomena that occurred and the stringent character of the tests employed.

Miss Fox recently came to England, and here also her powers have been tested by a competent man of science, and found to be all that has been stated. She is now married to an English barrister, and some of the strange phenomena which have so long accompanied her attach themselves to her infant child, even when its mother is away, to the great alarm of the nurse. We have here, therefore, a career of twenty-six years of mediumship of the most varied and remarkable character; mediumship which has been scrutinized and tested from the first hour of its manifestation down to this day, and with one invariable result—that no imposture or attempt at imposture has ever been discovered, and no cause ever been suggested that will account for the phenomena except that advanced by Spiritualists.

Mr. Daniel D. Home is perhaps the best known medium in the world; and his powers have been open to examination for at least twenty years. Nineteen years ago Sir David Brewster and Lord Brougham had a sitting with him—sufficiently acute and eminent observers, and both, of course, thorough sceptics. In the "Home Life of Sir David Brewster," we have, fortunately, his own record of this sitting, made *at the time*. He says —"The table actually rose from the ground when no hand was upon it;" and "a small hand-bell was laid down with its mouth upon the carpet, and it actually rang when nothing could have touched it. The bell was then placed on the other side, still upon the carpet, and it came over to me and placed itself in my hand. It did the same to Lord Brougham." And he adds, speaking for both, "We could give no explanation of them, and could not conjecture how they could be produced by any kind of mechanism." Coming from the author of "Letters on Natural Magic," this is pretty good testimony, although six months later, in a letter to the *Morning Advertiser*, he made the contradictory statement—"I saw enough to satisfy myself they could all be produced by human hands and feet."

These and far more marvellous phenomena have been repeated from that day to this, many thousands of times, and almost always in private houses at which Mr. Home visits. Everybody testifies to the fact that he offers the most ample facilities for investigation; and to this I can myself bear witness, having been invited by him to examine, as closely as I pleased, an accordion, held by his one hand, keys downward, and in that position playing very sweetly. But perhaps the best attested and most extraordinary phenomenon connected with Mr. Home's mediumship is what is called the fire test. In a state of trance he takes a glowing coal from the hottest part of a bright fire, and carries it round the room, so that every one may see and feel that it is a real one. This is testified by Mr. H. D. Jencken, Lord Lindsay, Lord Adare, Miss Douglas, Mr. S. C. Hall, and many others. But, more strange still, when in this state he can detect the same power in other persons, or convey it to them. A lump of red-hot coal was once placed on Mr. S. C. Hall's head in the presence of Lord Lindsay and four other persons. Mrs. Hall, in a communication to the Earl of Dunraven (given in the *Spiritual Magazine*, 1870, p. 178), says:—

"Mr. Hall was seated nearly opposite to where I sat; and I saw Mr. Home, after standing about half a minute at the back of Mr. Hall's chair, deliberately place the lump of burning coal on his head! I have often wondered that I was not frightened, but I was not; I had perfect faith that he would not be injured. Some one said, 'Is it not hot?' Mr. Hall answered, 'Warm, but not hot.' Mr. Home had moved a little way, but returned, still in a trance; he smiled, and seemed quite pleased, and then proceeded to draw up Mr. Hall's white hair over the red coal. The white hair had the appearance of silver thread over the red coal. Mr. Home drew the hair into a sort of pyramid, the coal, still red, showing beneath the hair."

When taken off the head, without in the slightest degree injuring it or singing the hair, others attempted to touch the coal and were burnt. Lord Lindsay and Miss Douglas have also had hot coals placed in their hands, and describe them as feeling rather cold than hot; though, at the same time, they burn any one else, and even scorch the face of the holder if approached too closely. The same witnesses also testify that Mr. Home has placed red-hot coals inside his waistcoat without scorching his clothes, and has put his face into the middle of the fire, his hair falling into the flames, yet not being the least singed. The same power of resisting fire can be temporarily given to inanimate objects. Mr. H. Nisbet, of Glasgow, states (*Human Nature*, Feb., 1870) that in his own house, in Jan., 1870, Mr. Home placed a red-hot coal in the hands of a lady and gentleman, which they only felt warm; and then placed the same piece on a folded newspaper, burning a hole through eight layers of paper. He then took a fresh and blazing coal and laid it on the same newspaper, carrying it about the room for three minutes, when the paper was found, this time, not to have been the least burnt. Lord Lindsay further declares—and as one of the few noblemen who do real scientific work, his evidence must be of some value—that on eight occasions he has had red-hot coals placed on his own hand by Home without injury. Mr. W. H. Harrison (*Spiritualist*, March 15th, 1870) saw him take a large coal, which covered the palm of his hand, and stood six or seven inches high. As he walked about the room it threw a ruddy glow on the walls, and when he came to the table with it, the heat was felt in the faces of all present. The coal was thus held for five minutes. These phenomena have now happened scores of times in the presence of scores of witnesses. They are facts of the reality of which there can be no doubt; and they are altogether inexplicable by the known laws of physiology and heat.

The powers of Mr. Home have lately been independently tested by Serjeant Cox and Mr. Crookes, and both these gentlemen emphatically proclaim that he invites tests and courts examination. Serjeant Cox, in his own house, has had a new accordion (purchased by himself that very day) play by itself, in his own hand, while Mr. Home was playing the piano. Mr. Home then took the accordion in his left hand, holding it with the keys downwards while playing the piano with his right hand, " and it played beautifully in accompaniment to the piano, for at least a quarter of an hour." ("What Am I?" vol ii. p. 388.)

As to the possibility of these things being produced by trick, if further evidence than their mere statement be required, we have the following by Mr. T. Adolphus Trollope, who says,—" I may also mention that Bosco, one of the greatest professors of legerdemain ever known, in a conversation with me upon the subject, utterly scouted the idea of the possibility of such phenomena as I saw produced by Mr. Home being performed by any of the resources of his art."

Mr. Home's life has been to a great extent a public one. He has spent much of his time as a guest in the houses of people of rank and talent. He numbers among his friends many who are eminent in science, art, and literature,— men certainly not inferior in perceptive or reasoning power to those who, not having witnessed the phenomena, disbelieve in their occurrence. For twenty years he has been exposed to the keen scrutiny and never-ceasing suspicion of innumerable enquirers; yet no proof has ever been given of trickery, no particle of machinery or apparatus ever been detected. But the phenomena are so stupendous that, if impostures, they could only be performed by machinery of the most elaborate, varied, and cumbrous nature, requiring the aid of several assistants and confederates. The theory that they are delusions is equally untenable, unless it is admitted that there is no possible means of distinguishing delusion from reality.

The last medium to whose career I shall call attention is Mrs. Guppy (formerly Miss Nichol), and in this case I can give some personal testimony. I knew Miss Nichol before she had ever heard of spiritualism, table-rapping, or anything of the kind, and we first discovered her powers on asking her to sit for experiment in my house. This was in November, 1866, and for some months we had constant sittings, and I was able to watch and test the progress of her development. I first satisfied myself of the rising of a small table completely off the floor, when three or four persons (including Miss N.) placed their hands on it. I tested this by secretly attaching threads or thin strips of paper beneath the claws, so that they must be broken if any one attempted to raise the table with their feet—the only available means of doing so. The table still rose a full foot off the floor in broad daylight. In order to show this to friends with less trouble, I made a cylinder of hoops and brown paper, in which I placed the table so as to keep feet and dresses away from it while it rose, which it did as freely as before. Perhaps more marvellous was the placing of Miss N. herself on the table; for although this always happened in the dark, yet, under the conditions to be named, deception was impossible. I will relate one sitting of which I have notes. We sat in a friend's house, round a centre table, under a glass chandelier. A friend of mine, but a perfect stranger to all the rest, sat next to Miss Nichol and held both her hands. Another person had matches ready to strike a light when required. What occurred was as follows:—First, Miss Nichol's chair was drawn away from under her, and she was obliged to stand up, my friend still holding both her hands. In a minute or two more I heard a slight sound, such as might be produced by a person placing a wine-glass on the table, and at the same time a very slight rustling of clothes and tinkling of the glass pendants of the chandelier. Immediately my friend said, "She is gone from me." A light was at once struck, and we found Miss N. quietly seated in her chair on the centre of the table, her head just touching the chandelier. My friend declared that Miss N. seemed to glide noiselessly out of his hands. She was very stout and heavy, and, to get her chair on the table, to get upon it herself, in the dark, and noiselessly, and almost instantaneously, with five or six persons close around her, appeared, and still appears to me, knowing her intimately, to be physically impossible.

Another very curious and beautiful phenomenon was the production of delicate musical sounds, without any object calculated to produce them being in the room. On one occasion a German lady, who was a perfect stranger to Miss Nichol, and had never been at a séance before, was present. She sang several German songs, and most delicate music, like a fairy music-box, accompanied her throughout.

She sang four or five different songs of her own choice, and
all were so accompanied. This was in the dark, but hands
were joined all the time.

The most remarkable feature of this lady's mediumship
is the production of flowers and fruits in closed rooms.
The first time this occurred was at my own house, at a very
early stage of her development. All present were my own
friends.   Miss N. had come early to tea, it being mid-
winter, and she had been with us in a very warm gas-lighted
room four hours before the flowers appeared. The essential fact is, that upon a bare table in a small room closed
and dark (the adjoining room and passage being well
lighted), a quantity of flowers appeared, which were not
there when we put out the gas a few minutes before. They
consisted of anemones, tulips, chrysanthemums, Chinese
primroses, and several ferns. All were absolutely fresh, as
if just gathered from a conservatory. They were covered
with a fine cold dew. Not a petal was crumpled or broken,
not the most delicate point or pinnule of the ferns was out
of place. I dried and preserved the whole, and have, attached to them, the attestation of all present that they had
no share, as far as they knew, in bringing the flowers into
the room. I believed at the time, and still believe, that it
was absolutely impossible for Miss N. to have concealed
them so long, to have kept them so perfect, and, above all,
to produce them covered throughout with a most beautiful
coating of dew, just like that which collects on the outside
of a tumbler when filled with very cold water on a hot day.

Similar phenomena have occurred hundreds of times
since, in many houses and under various conditions. Sometimes the flowers have been in vast quantities, heaped upon
the table. Often flowers or fruits asked for are brought.
A friend of mine asked for a sun-flower, and one six feet
high fell upon the table, having a large mass of earth about

its roots. One of the most striking tests was at Florence, with Mr. T. Adolphus Trollope, Mrs. Trollope, Miss Blagden, and Colonel Harvey. The room was searched by the gentlemen; Mrs Guppy was undressed and redressed by Mrs. Trollope, every article of her clothing being examined. Mr. and Mrs. Guppy were both firmly held while at the table. In about ten minutes all the party exclaimed that they smelt flowers, and, on lighting a candle, both Mrs. Guppy's and Mr. Trollope's arms were found covered with jonquils, which filled the room with their odour. Mr. Guppy and Mr. Trollope both relate this in substantially the same terms. ("Dialectical Society's Report on Spiritualism," pp. 277 and 372.)

Surely these are phenomena about which there can be no mistake. What theories have ever been proposed by our scientific teachers which even attempt to account for them? Delusion it cannot be, for the flowers are real, and can be preserved, and imposture under the conditions described is even less credible. If the gentlemen who come forward to enlighten the public on the subject of "so-called spiritual manifestations" do not know of the various classes of phenomena that have now been indicated, and the weight of the testimony in support of them, they are palpably unqualified for the task they have undertaken. That they do know of them, but keep back their knowledge, while putting forward trivalities easy to laugh at or expose, is a supposition I cannot for a moment entertain. Before leaving this part of the subject, it is well to note the fact of the marked individuality of each medium. They are not copies of each other, but each one developes a characteristic set of phenomena—a fact highly suggestive of some unconscious occult power in the individual, and wholly opposed to the idea of either imposture or delusion, both of which almost invariably copy pre-existing models.

Investigations by some Notable Sceptics.—In giving some
account of how a few of the more important converts
to Spiritualism became convinced, we are of course limited
to those who have given their experience to the public.　I
will first take the case of the eminent American lawyer,
the Honourable J. W. Edmonds, commonly called Judge
Edmonds; and it may be as well to let English sceptics
know what he is thought of by his countrymen.　When
he first became a Spiritualist he was greatly abused; and
it was even declared that he consulted the spirits as to
his judicial decisions.　To defend himself, he published an
"Appeal to the Public," giving a full account of the inquiries which resulted in his conversion.　In noticing this,
the New York *Evening Mirror* said, "John W. Edmonds,
the Chief Justice of the Supreme Court of this District, is
an able lawyer, an industrious judge, and a good citizen.
For the last eight years occupying without interruption the
highest judicial stations, whatever may be his faults, no
one can justly accuse him of a lack of ability, industry,
honesty, or fearlessness.　No one can doubt his general
saneness, or can believe for a moment that the ordinary
operations of his mind are not as rapid, accurate, and reliable as ever.　Both by the practitioners and suitors at his
bar, he is recognised as the head, in fact and in merit, of
the Supreme Court for this District."　A few years later
he published a series of letters on Spiritualism in the *New
York Tribune;* and in the first of these he gives a compact
summary of his mode of investigation, from which the
following passages are extracted.　It must be remembered
that at the time he commenced the inquiry he was in the
prime and vigour of intellectual life, being fifty-two years
of age.

"It was in January, 1851, that I first began my investigations,
and it was not until April, 1853, that I became a firm believer in the

reality of spiritual intercourse. During twenty-three months of those twenty-seven, I witnessed several hundred manifestations in various forms. I kept very minute and careful records of many of them. My practice was, whenever I attended a circle, to keep in pencil a memorandum of all that took place, so far as I could, and, as soon as I returned home, to write out a full account of what I had witnessed. I did all this with as much minuteness and particularity as I had ever kept any record of a trial before me in court. In this way, during that period, I preserved the record of nearly two hundred interviews, running through some one thousand six hundred pages of manuscript. I had these interviews with many different mediums, and under an infinite variety of circumstances. No two interviews were alike. There was always something new, or something different from what had previously occurred; and it very seldom happened that only the same persons were present. The manifestations were of almost every known form, physical or mental; sometimes only one, and sometimes both combined.

" I resorted to every expedient I could devise, to detect imposture and to guard against delusion. I felt in myself, and saw in others, how exciting was the idea that we were actually communing with the dead; and I laboured to prevent any undue bias of my judgment. I was at times critical and captious to an unreasonable extreme; and when my belief was challenged, as it was over and over again, I refused to yield, except to evidence that would leave no possible room for cavil.

" I was severely exacting in my demands, and this would frequently happen. I would go to a circle with some doubt on my mind as to the manifestations at the previous circle, and something would happen aimed directly at that doubt, and completely overthrowing it as it then seemed, so that I had no longer any reason to doubt. But I would go home and write out carefully my minutes of the evening, cogitate over them for several days, compare them with previous records, and finally find some loop-hole—some possibility that it might have been something else than spiritual influence, and I could go to the next circle with a new doubt, and a new set of queries."

"I look back sometimes now, with a smile, at the ingenuity I wasted in devising ways and means to avoid the possibility of deception."

" It was a remarkable feature of my investigations, that every conceivable objection I could raise, was, first or last, met and answered."

The following extracts are from the "Appeal":—

"I have seen a mahogany table, having a centre leg, and with a lamp burning upon it, lifted from the floor at least a foot, in spite of the efforts of those present, and shaken backward and forward as one would shake a goblet in his hand, and the lamp retain its place, though its glass pendants rang again."

"I have known a mahogany chair thrown on its side and moved swiftly back and forth on the floor, no one touching it, through a room where there were at least a dozen people sitting, yet no one touched; and it was repeatedly stopped within a few inches of me, when it was coming with a violence which, if not arrested, must have broken my legs."

Having satisfied himself of the reality of the physical phenomena, he came to the question of whence comes the intelligence that was so remarkably connected with them. He says:—

"Preparatory to meeting a circle, I have sat down alone in my room, and carefully prepared a series of questions to be propounded, and I have been surprised to find my questions answered, and in the precise order in which I wrote them, without my even taking my memorandum out of my pocket, and when not a person present knew that I had prepared questions, much less what they were. My most sacred thoughts, those which I have never uttered to mortal man or woman, have been freely spoken to, as if I had uttered them; and I have been admonished that my every thought was known to, and could be disclosed by the intelligence which was thus manifesting itself."

"Still the question occurred, 'May not all this have been, by some mysterious operation, the mere reflex of the mind of some one present?' The answer was, that facts were communicated which were unknown then, but afterwards found to be true; like this, for instance: when I was absent last winter in Central America, my friends in town heard of my whereabouts and the state of my health several times; and on my return, by comparing their information with the entries in my journal, it was found to be invariably correct. So thoughts have been uttered on subjects not then in my mind and utterly at variance with my own notions. This has often happened to me and to others, so as fully to establish the fact that it was not our minds that gave forth or affected the communication."

These few extracts sufficiently show that the writer was aware of the possible sources of error in such an inquiry; and the details given in the letters prove that he was constantly on his guard against them. He himself and his daughter became mediums; so that he afterwards obtained personal confirmation of many of the phenomena by himself alone. But all the phenomena referred to in the letters and "Appeal" occurred to him in the presence of others, who testified to them as well, and thus removed the possibility that the phenomena were subjective.

We have yet to add a notice of what will be perhaps, to many persons, the most startling and convincing of all the Judge's experiences. His own daughter became a medium for speaking foreign languages of which she was totally ignorant. He says, "She knows no language but her own, and a little smattering of boarding-school French; yet she has spoken in nine or ten different tongues, often for an hour at a time, with the ease and fluency of a native. It is not unfrequent that foreigners converse with their spirit-friends through her, in their own language." One of these cases must be given.

" One evening, when some twelve or fifteen persons were in my parlour, Mr. E. D. Green, an artist of this city, was shown in accompanied by a gentleman whom he introduced as Mr. Evangelides, of Greece. Ere long a spirit spoke to him through Laura, in English, and said so many things to him that he identified him as a friend who had died at his house a few years before, but of whom none of us had ever heard. Occasionally, through Laura, the spirit would speak a word or a sentence in Greek, until Mr. E. inquired if he could be understood if he spoke Greek? The residue of the conversation for more than an hour, was, on his part, entirely in Greek, and on hers sometimes in Greek and sometimes in English. At times Laura would not understand what was the idea conveyed either by her or him. At other times she would understand him, though he spoke in Greek, and herself while uttering Greek words."

Several other cases are mentioned, and it is stated that this lady has spoken Spanish, French, Greek, Italian, Portuguese, Latin. Hungarian and Indian; and other languages which were unknown to any person present.

This is by no means an isolated case, but it is given as being on most unexceptionable authority. A man must know whether his own daughter has learnt, so as to speak fluently, eight languages besides her own, or not. Those who carry on the conversation must know whether the language is spoken, or not; and in several cases—as the Latin, Spanish, and Indian—the judge himself understood the language. And the phenomenon is connected with Spiritualism by the speaking being in the name of, and purporting to come from, some deceased person, and the subject matter being characteristic of that person. Such a case as this, which has been published sixteen years, ought to have been noticed and explained by those who profess to enlighten the public on the subject of Spiritualism.

Our next example is one of the most recent, but at the same time, one of the most useful converts to the truths of Spiritualism. Dr. George Sexton, M.D., M.A., LL.D., was for many years the coadjutor of Mr. Bradlaugh, and one of the most earnest and energetic of the secularist teachers. The celebrated Robert Owen first called his attention to the subject of Spiritualism about twenty years ago. He read books; he saw a good deal of the ordinary physical manifestations, but he always " suspected that the mediums played tricks, and that the whole affair was nothing but clever conjuring by means of concealed machinery." He gave several lectures against Spiritualism in the usual style of non-believers, dwelling much on the absurdity and triviality of the phenomena, and ridiculing the idea that they were the work of spirits. Then came another old friend and fellow-secularist, Mr. Turley, who, after investigating the subject for the purpose of exposing it, became a firm believer. Dr. Sexton laughed at this conversion, yet it made a deep impression on his mind. Ten years passed away, and his next important investigation was with the Davenport brothers; and it will be well for those who sneer at these much-abused young men to take note of the following account of Dr. Sexton's proceedings with them, and especially of the fact that they cheerfully submitted to every test the doctor suggested. He tells us (in his lecture, "How I became a Spiritualist,") that he visited them again and again, trying in vain to find out the trick. Then, he says,—

"My partner—Dr. Barker—and I invited the Brothers to our houses, and, in order to guard against anything like trickery, we requested them not to bring any ropes, instruments, or other apparatus; all these we ourselves had determined to supply. Moreover, as there were four of them, viz., the two Brothers Davenport, Mr. Fay, and Dr. Ferguson, we suspected that the two who were not tied might really do all that was done. We therefore requested only two to come. They unhesitatingly complied with all these requests. We formed a circle, consisting entirely of members of our own families and a few private friends, with the one bare exception of Mrs. Fay. In the circle we all joined hands, and as Mrs. Fay sat at one end she had one of her hands free, while I had hold of the other. Thinking that she might be able to assist with the hand that was thus free, I asked as a favour that I might be allowed to hold both her hands—a proposition which she at once agreed to. Now, without entering here at all into what took place, suffice it to say that we bound the mediums with our own ropes, placed their feet upon sheets of writing paper and drew lines around their boots, so that if they moved their feet it should be impossible for them to place them again in the same position; we laid pence on their toes, sealed the ropes, and in every way took precautions against their moving. On the occasion to which I now refer, Mr. Bradlaugh and

Mr. Charles Watts were present; and when Mr. Fay's coat had
been taken off, the ropes still remaining on his hands, Mr. Bradlaugh requested that his coat might be placed on Mr. Fay, which
was immediately done, the ropes still remaining fastened. We got
on this occasion all the phenomena that usually occurred in the presence of these extraordinary men, particulars of which I shall
probably give on another occasion.   Dr. Barker became a believer
in Spiritualism from the time that the Brothers visited at his house.
I did not see that any proof had been given that disembodied spirits
had any hand in producing the phenomena; but I was convinced
that no tricks had been played, and that therefore these extraordinary physical manifestations were the result of some occult force in
nature which I had no means of explaining in the present state of
my knowledge.   All the physical phenomena that I had seen now
became clear to me; they were not accomplished by trickery, as I
had formerly supposed, but were the result of some undiscovered
law of nature which it was the business of the man of science to
use his utmost endeavours to discover."

While he was maintaining this ground, Spiritualists
often asked him how he explained the intelligence that was
manifested; and he invariably replied that he had not yet
seen proofs of any intelligence other than what might be
that of the medium or of some other persons present in
the circle, adding, that as soon as he did see proofs of such
intelligence he should become a Spiritualist.   In this position he stood for many years, till he naturally believed he
should never see cause to change his opinion.   He continued the inquiry, however, and in 1865 began to hold
séances at home; but it was years before any mental
phenomena occurred which were absolutely conclusive,
although they were often of so startling a nature as would
have satisfied any one less sceptical.   At length, after
fifteen years of enlightened scepticism—a scepticism not
founded upon ignorance, but which refused to go one step
beyond what the facts so diligently pursued, absolutely
demonstrated—the needful evidence came:

"The proofs that I did ultimately receive are, many of them, of a character that I cannot describe minutely to a public audience, nor, indeed, have I time to do so. Suffice it to say, that I got in my own house, in the absence of all mediums other than members of my own family and intimate private friends in whom mediumistic powers became developed, evidence of an irresistible character that the communications came from deceased friends and relatives. Intelligence was again and again displayed which could not possibly have had any other origin than that which it professed to have. Facts were named known to no one in the circle, and left to be verified afterwards. The identity of the spirits communicating was proved in a hundred different ways. Our dear departed ones made themselves palpable both to feeling and to sight; and the doctrine of spirit-communion was proved beyond the shadow of a doubt. I soon found myself in the position of Dr. Fenwick in Lord Lytton's 'Strange Story.' 'Do you believe,' asked the female attendant of Margrave, 'in that which you seek?' 'I have no belief,' was the answer. 'True science has none; true science questions all things, and takes nothing on credit. It knows but three states of mind— denial, conviction, and the vast interval between the two, which is not belief, but the suspension of judgment.' This describes exactly the phases through which my mind has passed."

Since Dr. Sexton has become a Spiritualist he has been as energetic an advocate for its truths as he had been before for the negations of secularism. His experience and ability as a lecturer, with his long schooling in every form of manifestation render him one of the most valuable promulgators of its teachings. He has also done excellent service in exposing the pretensions of those conjurers who profess to expose Spiritualism. This he does in the most practical way, not only by explaining how the professed imitations of spiritual manifestations are performed, but by actually performing them before his audience; and at the same time pointing out the important differences between what these people do and what occurs at good séances. Any one who wishes to comprehend how Dr. Lynn, Messrs. Maskelyne and Cook, and Herr Dobler perform some of their most curious feats have only to read his

lecture, entitled, " Spirit Mediums and Conjurers," before
going to witness their entertainments.   We can hardly
believe that the man who does this, and who during fifteen
years of observation and experiment held out against the
spiritual theory, is one of those who, as Lord Amberley
tells us, " fall a victim to the most patent frauds, and are
imposed upon by jugglery of the most vulger order:" or
who, as viewed by Professor Tyndall's high scientific stand-
point, are in a frame of mind before which science is
utterly powerless—"dupes beyond the reach of proof, who
like to believe and do not like to be undeceived." These
be brave words; but we leave our readers to judge whether
they come with a very good grace from men who have the
most slender and inadequate knowledge of the subject they
are criticising, and no knowledge at all of the long-con-
tinued and conscientious investigations of many who are
included in their wholesale animadversions.

Yet one more witness to these marvellous phenomena
we must bring before our readers ;—a trained and experienced physicist, who has experimented in his own labora-
tory, and has applied tests and measurements of the most
rigid and conclusive character.   When Mr. Crookes—the
discoverer of the metal thallium, and a Fellow of the Royal
Society—first announced that he was going to investigate
so-called spiritual phenomena, many public writers were
all approval; for the complaint had long been that men
of science were not permitted by mediums to inquire too
scrupulously into the facts.   One expressed " profound
satisfaction that the subject was about to be investigated
by a man so well qualified;"—another was "gratified to
learn that the matter is now receiving the attention of cool
and clear-headed men of recognised position in science;"—
while a third declared that "no one could doubt Mr.

Crookes' ability to conduct the investigation with rigid philosophical impartiality." But these expressions were evidently insincere—were only meant to apply, in case the result was in accordance with the writers' notions of what it ought to be. Of course, a "scientific investigation" would explode the whole thing. Had not Faraday exploded table turning? They hailed Mr. Crookes as the Daniel come to judgment,—as the prophet who would curse their enemy, Spiritualism, by detecting imposture and illusion. But when the judge, after a patient trial lasting several years, decided against them, and their accepted prophet blessed the hated thing as an undoubted truth, their tone changed; and they began to suspect the judge's ability, and to pick holes in the evidence on which he founded his judgment.

In Mr. Crookes' latest paper, published in the *Quarterly Journal of Science* for January last, we are informed that he has pursued the inquiry for four years; and besides attending séances elsewhere, has had the opportunity of making numerous experiments in his own house with the two remarkable mediums already referred to, Mr. D. D. Home and Miss Kate Fox. These experiments were almost exclusively made in the light, under conditions of his own arranging, and with his own friends as witnesses. Such phenomena as percussive sounds; alterations of the weight of bodies; the rising of heavy bodies in the air without contact by any one; the levitation of human beings; luminous appearances of various kinds; the appearance of hands which lift small objects, yet are not the hands of any one present; direct writing by a luminous detached hand or by the pencil alone; phantom forms and faces; and various mental phenomena, —have all been tested so variously and so repeatedly that Mr. Crookes is thoroughly satisfied of their objective reality.

These phenomena are given in outline in the paper above
referred to, and they will be detailed in full in a volume
now preparing. I will not, therefore, weary my readers by
repeating them here, but will remark, that these experiments have a weight as evidence vastly greater than would
be due to them as resting on the testimony of any man of
science, however distinguished, because they are, in almost
every case, confirmations of what previous witnesses in
immense numbers have testified to, in various places and
under various conditions, during the last twenty years.
In every other experimental inquiry without exception,
confirmation of the facts of an earlier observer is held to
add so greatly to their value, that no one treats them with
the same incredulity with which he might have received
them the first time they were announced. And when the
confirmation has been repeated by three or four independent observers under favourable conditions, and there is
nothing but theory or negative evidence against them, the
facts are admitted—at least provisionally—and until disproved by a greater weight of evidence or by discovering
the exact source of the fallacy of preceding observers.

But here, a totally different—a most unreasonable and a
most unphilosophical course is pursued. Each fresh observation, confirming previous evidence, is treated as though it
were now put forth for the *first* time ; and fresh confirmation
is asked of it. And when the fresh and independent confirmation comes, yet more confirmation is asked for, and so
on without end. This is a very clever way to ignore and
stifle a new truth ; but the facts of Spiritualism are ubi-
quitous in their occurrence and of so indisputable a nature
as to compel conviction in every earnest inquirer. It thus
happens that although every fresh convert requires a large
proportion of the series of demonstrative facts to be reproduced before he will give his assent to them, the number

of such converts has gone on steadily increasing for a quarter of a century. Clergymen of all sects, literary men and lawyers, physicians in large numbers, men of science not a few, secularists, philosophical sceptics, pure materialists, all have become converts through the overwhelming logic of the phenomena which Spiritualism has brought before them. And what have we *per contra?* Neither science nor philosophy, neither scepticism nor religion, has ever yet in this quarter of a century made one single convert from the ranks of Spiritualism! This being the case, and fully appreciating the amount of candour and fairness, and knowledge of the subject, that has been exhibited by their opponents, is it to be wondered at that a large proportion of spiritualists are now profoundly indifferent to the opinion of men of science, and would not go one step out of their way to convince them? They say, that the movement is going on quite fast enough. That it is spreading by its own inherent force of truth, and slowly permeating all classes of society. It has thriven in spite of abuse and persecution, ridicule and argument, and will continue to thrive whether endorsed by great names or not. Men of science, like all others, are welcome to enter its ranks; but they must satisfy themselves by their own persevering researches, not expect to have its proofs laid before them. Their rejection of its truths is their own loss, but cannot in the slightest degree affect the progress of Spiritualism. The attacks and criticisms of the press are borne good-humouredly, and seldom excite other feelings than pity for the wilful ignorance and contempt for the overwhelming presumption of their writers. Such are the sentiments that are continually expressed by spiritualists; and it is as well, perhaps, that the outer world, to whom the literature of the movement is as much unknown as the Vedas, should be made acquainted with them.

M

Investigation by the Dialectical Committee.—There are
many other investigators who ought to be noticed in any
complete sketch of the subject, but we have now only
space to allude briefly to the " Report of the Committee of
the Dialectical Society." Of this committee, consisting of
thirty-three acting members, only eight were, at the com-
mencement, believers in the reality of the phenomena,
while not more than four accepted the spiritual theory.
During the course of the inquiry at least twelve of the
complete sceptics became convinced of the reality of many
of the physical phenomena through attending the experimental sub-committees, and almost wholly by means of
the mediumship of members of the committee. At least
three members who were previously sceptics pursued their
investigations outside the committee meetings, and in
consequence have become thorough Spiritualists. My own
observation, as a member of the committee and of the
largest and most active sub-committee, enables me to state
that the degree of conviction produced in the minds of the
various members was, allowing for marked differences of
character, approximately proportionate to the amount of
time and care bestowed on the investigation. This fact,
which is what occurs in all investigation into these phenomena, is a characteristic result of the examination into
any natural phenomena. The examination into an imposture or delusion has, invariably, exactly opposite results;
those who have slender experience being deceived, while
those who perseveringly continue the inquiry inevitably
find out the source of the deception or the delusion. If
this were not so, the discovery of truth and the detection
of error would be alike impossible. The result of this
inquiry on the members of the committee themselves is,
therefore, of more importance than the actual phenomena
they witnessed, since these were far less striking than

many of the facts already mentioned. But they are also of importance as confirming, by a body of intelligent and unprejudiced men, the results obtained by previous individual inquirers.

Before leaving this report, I must call attention to the evidence it furnishes of the state of opinion among men of education in France. M. Camille Flammarion, the well-known astronomer, sent a communication to the committee which is well worth consideration. Besides declaring his own acceptance of the objective reality of the phenomena after ten years of investigation, he makes the following statement:—

" My learned teacher and friend, M. Babinet, of the Institute, who has endeavoured, with M. E. Liais (now Director of the Observatory of Brazil,) and several others of my colleagues of the Observatory of Paris, to ascertain their nature and cause, is not fully convinced of the intervention of spirits in their production ; though this hypothesis, by which alone certain categories of these phenomena would seem to be explicable, has been adopted by many of our most esteemed *savants*, among others by Dr. Hœffle, the learned author of the ' History of Chemistry' and the ' General Encyclopædia ;' and by the diligent labourer in the field of astronomic discovery whose death we have recently had to deplore, M. Hermann Goldschmidt, the discoverer of fourteen planets."

It thus appears that in France, as well as in America and in this country, men of science of no mean rank have investigated these phenomena and have found them to be realities ; while some of the most eminent hold the spiritual theory to be the only one that will explain them.*

---

* That the names we are able to quote of men who have publicly acknowledged their conviction of the reality of the phenomena of modern Spiritualism, form only a small portion of those who are really convinced, but who for social, religious, or other reasons do not make public their belief, every Spiritualist knows. As an example of the latter class we may refer to the late Dr. Robert Chambers, a man as remarkable for his powers of observation, scientific knowledge, and literary ability as for his

This seems the proper place to notice the astounding assertion of some writers, that there is not " a particle of evidence" to support the spiritual theory,—that those who accept it betray " hopeless inability to discriminate between adequate and inadequate proof of facts,"—that the theory is " formed apart from facts,"—and, that those who accept it are so unable to reason, as to "jump to the conclusion" that it must be spirits that move tables, merely because they do not know how else they can be moved. The preceding account of how converts to Spiritualism have been made, is a sufficient answer to all this ignorant assertion. The spiritual theory, as a rule, has only been adopted as a last resource, when all other theories have hopelessly broken down; and when fact after fact, phenomenon after phenomenon, has presented itself, giving direct proof that the so-called dead are still alive. The spiritual theory is the logical outcome of the whole of the facts. Those who deny it, in every instance with which I am acquainted, either from ignorance or disbelief, leave half the facts out of view. Take the one case (out of many almost equally conclusive) of Mr. Livermore, who during five years, on hundreds of occasions, saw, felt, and heard the movements of, the figure of his dead wife in absolute, unmistakable, living form. A form which could move objects, and which repeatedly wrote to him in her own handwriting and her own language, on cards which remained after the figure had disappeared. A form which was equally visible and tangible to two friends, which

caution in forming and expressing his opinions. I am glad to be now able to give the following extract from a letter received from him in February, 1867 :—" I have for many years *known* that these phenomena are real, as distinguished from impostures; and it is not of yesterday that I concluded they were calculated to explain much that has been doubtful in the past; and, when fully accepted, revolutionise the whole frame of human opinion on many important matters."

appeared in his own house, in a room absolutely secured, with the presence of only a young girl, the medium. Had these three men " not a particle of evidence" for the spiritual theory? Is it, in fact, possible to conceive or suggest any more complete proof? The facts must be got rid of before you can abolish the theory; and simple denial or disbelief does not get rid of facts testified during a space of five years by three witnesses, all men in responsible positions, and carrying on their affairs during the whole period in a manner to win the respect and confidence of their fellow-citizens.*

---

* The objection will here inevitably be made : " These wonderful ∨.⌐↝p. things always happen in America. When they occur in England it will be time enough to inquire into them." Fortunately for these objectors, after this article was in the press, the final test was obtained, which demonstrated the occurrence of similar phenomena in London. A short statement may, therefore, be interesting for those who cannot digest American evidence. For some years a young lady, Miss Florence Cook, has exhibited remarkable mediumship, which latterly culminated in the production of an entire female form purporting to be of spiritual origin, and which appeared barefooted and in white flowing robes while she lay entranced, in dark clothing and securely bound in a cabinet or adjoining room. Notwithstanding that tests of an apparently conclusive character were employed, many visitors, Spiritualists as well as sceptics, got the impression that all was not as it should be ; owing in part to the resemblance of the supposed spirit to Miss Cook, and also to the fact that the two could not be seen at the same time. Some supposed that Miss C. was an impostor, who managed to conceal a white robe about her (although she was often searched), and who, although she was securely tied with tapes and sealed, was able to get out of her bonds, dress and undress herself, and get into them again, all in the dark, and in so complete and skilful a manner as to defy detection. Others thought that the spirit released her, provided her with a white dress, and sent her forth to personate a ghost. The belief that there was something wrong led one gentleman—an ardent Spiritualist be it remembered—to seize the supposed spirit and endeavour to hold it, in the hope that some other person would open the cabinet door and see if Miss Cook was really there. This was, unfortunately, not done ; but the great resemblance of the being he seized to Miss Cook, its perfect solidity, and the vigorous struggles it made to

Spirit-Photographs.

We now approach a subject which cannot be omitted in any impartial sketch of the evidences of Spiritualism, since it is that which furnishes perhaps the most unassailable demonstration it is possible to obtain, of the objective reality of spiritual forms, and also of the truthful nature

---

escape from him convinced that gentleman that it was Miss Cook herself, although the rest of the company a few minutes afterwards found her bound and sealed just as she had been left an hour before. To determine the question conclusively, experiments were made by two scientific men. Mr. C. F. Varley, F.R.S., the eminent electrician, made use of a galvanic battery and cable-testing apparatus, and passed a current through Miss Cook's body (by fastening sovereigns soldered to wires to her arms). The apparatus was so delicate that any movement whatever was instantly indicated, while it was impossible for the young lady to dress and act the ghost without breaking the circuit. Yet, under these conditions, the spirit-form did appear, exhibited its arms, spoke, wrote, and touched several persons; and this happened, not in the medium's own house, but in that of a private gentleman in the West End of London. For nearly an hour the circuit was never broken, and at the conclusion of the experiment Miss Cook was found in a deep trance. Subsequently Mr. Crookes, F.R.S., obtained more satisfactory evidence. He contrived a phosphorus lamp, and armed with this, was allowed to go into the dark room accompanied by the spirit, and there both saw and felt Miss Cook, dressed in black velvet, lying in a trance on the floor, while the spirit-form, in white robes, stood close beside her. During the evening this spirit-form had been for nearly an hour walking and talking with the company; and Mr. Crookes, by permission, did what the sceptical gentleman had done without —clasped the figure in his arms, and found it to be apparently that of a real living woman. Yet this figure is not that of Miss Cook nor of any other living human being, since it appeared and disappeared in closed and carefully guarded rooms in Mr. Crookes' own house, as readily and completely as in that of the medium herself. The full statements of Messrs. Crookes and Varley, with a mass of interesting details on the subject, appeared in the *Spiritualist* newspaper in March and April last; and they serve to show that whatever marvels occur in America can be reproduced here, and that men of science are *not* (as it is continually asserted they are) precluded from investigating these phenomena with scientific instruments and by scientific methods.

The preceding remarks formed a note to the article as it appeared in

of the evidence furnished by seers when they describe figures visible to themselves alone. It has been already indicated—and it is a fact, of which the records of Spiritualism furnish ample proof—that different individuals possess the power of seeing such forms and figures in very variable degrees. Thus, it often happens at a séance, that some will see distinct lights of which they will describe the form, appearance, and position, while others will see nothing at all. If only one or two persons see the lights, the rest will naturally impute it to their imagination; but there are cases in which only one or two of those present are unable to see them. There are also cases in which all see them, but in very different degrees of distinctness; yet that they see the same objects is proved by their all agreeing as to the position and the movement of the lights. Again,

---

the *Fortnightly Review;* but since that article appeared, the demonstration has been carried still further. Miss Cook came to Mr. Crookes' house alone, with a very small bag as her only luggage, and stayed there about a week. She slept with one of the ladies of the house, and was constantly under the observation of one or other of the family. Yet the spirit-form appeared constantly : Mr. Crookes both saw and felt it and Miss Cook at the same time; and he obtained a series of photographs of the spirit-form, and a comparative series of Miss Cook, showing it to be that of a woman at least half a head taller, just as it appeared to be to all observers. The photographs (which I have had the opportunity of examining) are to all appearance those of a human being, whose features are like those of Miss Cook, as a sister might be like, but by no means identical ; dressed in flowing white robes, while Miss Cook was always dressed in ordinary dark clothes ; and by measurement, as well as by comparison with Mr. Crookes, who is photographed by the side of both, very much taller. This figure, after being seen, felt, conversed with, and photographed, absolutely disappeared from a small room, out of which there was no means of exit but through the adjoining room filled with spectators. We must also remember that the photographs are so clear and distinct, and the form and features of the spirit are so well known to a considerable number of people, that if it were a human being who, in different houses in various parts of London always manages to accompany Miss Cook, and act the spirit, that person could hardly maintain a perpetual incognito,

what some see as merely luminous clouds, others will see
as distinct human forms, either partial or entire.   In other
cases all present see the form—whether hand, face, or entire
figure—with equal distinctness.   Again, the objective
reality of these appearances is sometimes proved by their
being touched, or by their being seen to move objects,—in
some cases heard to speak, in others seen to write, by
several persons at one and the same time; the figure seen
or the writing produced being sometimes unmistakeably
recognisable as that of some deceased friend.   A volume
could easily be filled with records of this class of appearances, authenticated by place, date, and names of witnesses;
and a considerable selection is to be found in the works of
Mr. Robert Dale Owen.

Now, at this point, an inquirer, who had not pre-judged

---

and for years avoid detection. But any such supposition is even more
incredible than the fact of a "spiritual manifestation," when we consider
that this unknown person would have had to obtain entrance, and to live
for a week in a private house without once being seen, except in a room
where concealment is impossible and which is carefully secured before
each séance. During this week she must either live without food, or get
in and out of the house continually without ever being perceived, and this
in a house fully occupied by a rather large family ! Since these manifestations have ceased with Miss Cook, they have occurred with other mediums
in Manchester, in Newcastle, in Melbourne, and especially in America,
under conditions, if possible, still more stringent. Mr. Robert Dale Owen
testifies to having seen the spirit-form come out of an empty cabinet, *when
the mediums were visible, and sitting among the spectators.* And on several
occasions he and others have seen this apparently living, solid, moving,
speaking form actually vanish before their eyes, and after a time be reproduced. The figure *faded out from the head downwards.* On another
occasion, on a bare floor of polished boards, the form appeared rising out
of the floor ; first, the head and shoulders, then the entire body, which
afterwards walked out among the spectators. Yet another time, three
distinct figures appeared from the cabinet, spoke to the witnesses, and
were touched by them. Those who know nothing of the subject, of
course, *cannot* believe this ; but to all who know that many spiritual
phenomena are facts, the evidence must be conclusive.

the question, and who did not believe his own knowledge
of the universe to be so complete as to justify him in re-
jecting all evidence for facts which he had hitherto considered to be in the highest degree improbable, might fairly
say, "Your evidence for the appearance of visible, tangible,
spiritual forms, is very strong; but I should like to have
them submitted to a crucial test, which would quite settle
the question of the possibility of their being due to a coincident delusion of several senses of several persons at the
same time ; and, if satisfactory, would demonstrate their
objective reality in a way nothing else can do.   If they
really reflect or emit light which makes them visible to
human eyes, *they can be photographed.*   Photograph them,
and you will have an unanswerable proof that your human
witnesses are trustworthy."   Two years ago we could only
have replied to this very proper suggestion, that we believed
it had been done and could be again done, but that we had
no satisfactory evidence to offer.   Now, however, we are
in a position to state, not only that it has been frequently
done, but that the evidence is of such a nature as to satisfy
any one who will take the trouble carefully to examine it.
This evidence we will now lay before our readers, and we
venture to think they will acknowledge it to be most remarkable.

Before doing so it may be as well to clear away a popular
misconception.   Mr. G. H. Lewes advised the Dialectical
Committee to distinguish carefully between "facts and
inferences from facts."   This is especially necessary in the
case of what are called spirit-photographs.   The figures
which occur in these, when not produced by any human
agency, may be of "spiritual" origin, without being figures
"of spirits."   There is much evidence to show that they
are, in some cases, forms produced by invisible intelligences,
but distinct from them.   In other cases the intelligence ap-

pears to clothe itself with matter capable of being perceived by us; but even then it does not follow that the form produced is the actual image of the spiritual form. It may be but a reproduction of the former mortal form with its terrestrial accompaniments, *for purposes of recognition.*

Most persons have heard of these " ghost-pictures," and how easily they can be made to order by any photographer, and are therefore disposed to think they can be of no use as evidence. But a little consideration will show that the means by which sham ghosts can be manufactured being so well known to all photographers, it becomes easy to apply tests or arrange conditions so as to prevent imposition. The following are some of the more obvious:—

1. If a person with a knowledge of photography takes his own glass plates, examines the camera used and all the accessories, and watches the whole process of taking a picture, then, if any definite form appears on the negative besides the sitter, it is a proof that some object was present capable of reflecting or emitting the actinic rays, although invisible to those present. 2. If an unmistakeable likeness appears of a deceased person totally unknown to the photographer. 3. If figures appear on the negative having a definite relation to the figure of the sitter, who chooses his own position, attitude, and accompaniments, it is a proof that invisible figures were really there. 4. If a figure appears draped in white, and partly behind the dark body of the sitter without in the least showing through, it is a proof that the white figure was there at the same time, because the dark parts of the negative are transparent, and any white picture in any way superposed would show through. 5. Even should none of these tests be applied, yet if a medium, quite independent of the photographer, sees and describes a figure during the sitting, and an exactly

corresponding figure appears on the plate, it is a proof that such a figure was there.

Every one of these tests have now been successfully applied in our own country, as the following outline of the facts will show.

The accounts of spirit-photography in several parts of the United States caused many spiritualists in this country to make experiments, but for a long time without success. Mr. and Mrs. Guppy, who are both amateur photographers, tried at their own house, and failed. In March, 1872, they went one day to Mr. Hudson's, a photographer living near them (not a spiritualist) to get some *cartes de visite* of Mrs. Guppy. After the sitting the idea suddenly struck Mr. Guppy that he would try for a spirit-photograph. He sat down, told Mrs. G. to go behind the background, and had a picture taken. There came out behind him a large, indefinite, oval, white patch, somewhat resembling the outline of a draped figure. Mrs. Guppy, behind the background, was dressed in black. This is the first spirit-photograph taken in England, and it is perhaps more satisfactory on account of the suddenness of the impulse under which it was taken, and the great white patch which no impostor would have attempted to produce, and which taken by itself, utterly spoils the picture. A few days afterwards, Mr. and Mrs. Guppy and their little boy went without any notice. Mrs. G. sat on the ground holding the boy on a stool. Mr. Guppy stood behind looking on. The picture thus produced is most remarkable. A tall female figure, finely draped in white, gauzy robes, stands directly behind and above the sitters, looking down on them and holding its open hands over their heads, as if giving a benediction. The face is somewhat Eastern, and, with the hands, is beautifully defined. The white robes pass behind the sitters' dark figures without in the least showing through.

A second picture was then taken as soon as a plate could be prepared, and it was fortunate it was so, for it resulted in a most remarkable test. Mrs. G. again knelt with the boy ; but this time she did not stoop so much, and her head was higher. The same white figure comes out equally well defined, but *it has changed its position in a manner exactly corresponding to the slight change of Mrs. G.'s position.* The hands were before on a level ; now one is raised considerably higher than the other, so as to keep it about the same distance from Mrs. G.'s head as it was before. The folds of the drapery all correspondingly differ, and the head is slightly turned. Here, then, one of two things are absolutely certain. Either there was a living, intelligent, but invisible being present, or Mr. and Mrs. Guppy, the photographer, and some fourth person, planned a wicked imposture, and have maintained it ever since. Knowing Mr. and Mrs. Guppy so well as I do, I feel an absolute conviction that they are as incapable of an imposture of this kind as any earnest inquirer after truth in the department of natural science. *

The report of these pictures soon spread. Spiritualists in great numbers came to try for similar results, with varying degrees of success ; till after a time rumour of imposture arose, and it is now firmly believed by many, from suspicious appearances on the pictures and from other circumstances, that a large number of shams have been produced. It is certainly not to be wondered at if it were so. The photographer, remember, was not a spiritualist,

* It is an important circumstance that the face of the spirit form is well defined, and as recognisable as the portrait of any living person. Had an imposture been attempted this would have been carefully avoided, since it would almost certainly lead to the discovery of the person who was dressed up for the occasion. Yet no such person has been found, although, during the discussions that subsequently arose, many were eager to find proofs of imposture.

and was utterly puzzled at the pictures above described. Scores of persons came to him, and he saw that they were satisfied if they got a second figure with themselves, and dissatisfied if they did not. He *may* have made arrangements by which to satisfy everybody. One thing is clear; that if there has been imposture, it was at once detected by spiritualists themselves; if not, then spiritualists have been quick in noticing what appeared to indicate it. Those, however, who most strongly assert imposture allow that a large number of genuine pictures have been taken. But, true or not, the cry of imposture did good, since it showed the necessity for tests and for independent confirmation of the facts.

The test of clearly recognisable likenesses of deceased friends has often been obtained. Mr. William Howitt, who went without previous notice, obtained likenesses of two sons, many years dead, and of the very existence of one of which even the friend who accompanied Mr. Howitt was ignorant. The likenesses were instantly recognised by Mrs. Howitt; and Mr. H. declares them to be "perfect and unmistakeable." (*Spiritual Magazine*, Oct., 1872.) Dr. Thomson of Clifton obtained a photograph of himself, accompanied by that of a lady he did not know. He sent it to his uncle in Scotland, simply asking if he recognised a resemblance to any of the family deceased. The reply was that it was the likeness of Dr. Thomson's own mother, who died at his birth; and there being no picture of her in existence, he had no idea what she was like. The uncle very naturally remarked, that he "could not understand how it was done." (*Spiritual Magazine*, Oct., 1873.) Many other instances of recognition have since occurred, but I will only add my personal testimony. A few weeks back I myself went to the same photographer's for the first time, and obtained a most unmistakeable likeness of a deceased relative. * We will now pass to a better class of evidence, the private experiments of amateurs.

Mr. Thomas Slater, an old established optician in the Euston Road, and an amateur photographer, took with him to Mr. Hudson's a new camera of his own manufacture and his own glasses, saw everything done and obtained a portrait with a second figure on it. He then began experi-

---

* The particulars of this case are as follows. On March 14th, 1874, I went to Hudson's, by appointment, for the first and only time, accompanied by Mrs. Guppy, as medium. I expected that if I got any spirit picture it would be that of my eldest brother, in whose name messages had frequently been received through Mrs. Guppy. Before going to Hudson's I sat with Mrs. G., and had a communication by raps to the effect that my mother would appear on the plate if she could. I sat three times, always choosing my own position. Each time a second figure appeared in the negative with me. The first was a male figure with a short sword; the second a full length figure, standing apparently a few feet on one side and rather behind me, looking down at me and holding a bunch of flowers. At the third sitting, after placing myself, and after the prepared plate was in the camera, I asked that the figure would come close to me. The third plate exhibited a female figure standing *close* in front of me, so that the drapery covers the lower part of my body. I saw all the plates developed, and in each case the additional figure started out the moment the developing fluid was poured on, while my portrait did not become visible till, perhaps, twenty seconds later. I recognised none of these figures in the negatives; but the moment I got the proofs, the first glance showed me that the third plate contained an unmistakeable portrait of my mother, —like her both in features and expression; not such a likeness as a portrait taken during life, but a somewhat pensive, idealised likeness— *yet still, to me, an unmistakeable likeness.* The second figure is much less distinct; the face is looking down; it has a different expression to the other, so that I at first concluded it was a different person. The male figure I know nothing of. On sending the two female portraits to my sister, she thought that the second was much more like my mother than the third,—was, in fact, a good likeness though indistinct, while the third seemed to her to be like in expression, but with something wrong about the mouth and chin. This was found to be due, in part, to the filling up of spots by the photographer; for when the picture was washed it became thickly covered with whitish spots, but a *better likeness of my mother.* Still I did not see the likeness in the second

menting in his own private house, and during last summer obtained some remarkable results. The first of his successes contains two heads by the side of a portrait of his sister. One of these heads is unmistakeably the late Lord Brougham's; the other, much less distinct, is recognised by Mr.

picture till a few weeks back I looked at it with a magnifying glass, when I at once saw a remarkable special feature of my mother's natural face, an unusually projecting lower lip and jaw. This was most conspicuous some years ago, as latterly the mouth was somewhat contracted. A photograph taken 22 years ago shows this peculiarity very strongly, and corresponds well with the second picture, in which the mouth is partly open and the lower lip projects greatly. This figure had always given me the impression of a younger person than that in the third picture, and it is remarkable that they correspond respectively with the character of the face as seen in photographs taken at intervals of about twelve years; yet without the least resemblance to these photographs either in attitude or expression. Both figures carry a bunch of flowers exactly in the same way; and it is worthy of notice that, while I was sitting for the second picture, the medium said—"I see some one, and it has flowers"—intimating that she saw the flowers distinctly, the figure only very faintly. Here, then, are two different faces representing the aspect of a deceased person's countenance at two periods of her life; yet both the figures are utterly unlike any photograph ever taken of her during her life. How these two figures, with these special peculiarities of a person totally unknown to Mr. Hudson could appear on his plates, I should be glad to have explained. Even if he had by some means obtained possession of all the photographs ever taken of my mother, they would not have been of the slightest use to him in the manufacture of these pictures. I see no escape from the conclusion that some spiritual being, acquainted with my mother's various aspects during life, produced these recognisable impressions on the plate. That she herself still lives and produced these figures may not be proved; but it is a more simple and natural explanation to think that she did so, than to suppose that we are surrounded by beings who carry out an elaborate series of impostures for no other apparent purpose than to dupe us into a belief in a continued existence after death. While these sheets were passing through the press, I received a letter from my brother in California, to whom I had sent a proof of the third picture. He says—"As soon as I opened the letter, I looked at the photograph attentively, and recognised your face, and remarked that the other one was something like Fanny (my sister). I then handed it across the table to Mrs. W., and she exclaimed at once, 'Why,

Slater as that of Robert Owen, whom he knew intimately up to the time of his death. He has since obtained several excellent pictures of the same class.   One in particular, shows a female in black and white flowing robes, standing by the side of Mr. Slater.   In another the head and bust appear, leaning over his shoulder. The faces of these two are much alike, and other members of the family recognise them as likenesses of Mr. Slater's mother, who died when he was an infant.   In another a pretty child figure, also draped, stands beside Mr. Slater's little boy. Now, whether these figures are correctly identified or not, is not the essential point. The fact that *any* figures, so clear and unmistakeably human in appearance as these, should appear on plates taken in his own private studio by an experienced optician and amateur photographer, who makes all his apparatus himself, and with no one present but the mem- bers of his own family,—is the real marvel.   In one case a second figure appeared on a plate with himself, taken by Mr. Slater when he was absolutely alone—by the simple process of occupying thé sitter's chair after uncapping the camera. He and his family being themselves mediums, they require no extraneous assistance; and this may, perhaps, be the reason why he has succeeded so well. One of the most extraordinary pictures obtained by Mr. Slater is a full- length portrait of his sister, in which there is no second figure, but the sitter appears covered all over with a kind of transparent lace drapery, which on examination is seen to be wholly made up of shaded circles of different sizes, quite unlike any material fabric I have seen or heard of.

it's your mother!' We then compared it with a photograph of her we had here, and there could be no doubt of the general resemblance, but it has an appearance of sickness or weariness." Neither my brother nor his wife know anything of Spiritualism, and both are prejudiced against it. We may therefore accept their testimony as to the resemblance to my mother, in confirmation of myself and my sister, as conclusive.

Mr. Slater has himself shown me all these pictures and explained the conditions under which they were produced. That they are not impostures is certain; and as the first independent confirmations of what had been previously obtained only through professional photographers, their value is inestimable.

A less successful, but not perhaps on that account less satisfactory confirmation has been obtained by another amateur, who, after eighteen months of experiment, obtained a partial success. Mr. R. Williams, M.A., Ph. D., of Hayward's Heath, succeeded last summer in obtaining three photographs, each with part of a human form besides the sitter, one having the features distinctly marked. Subsequently another was obtained, with a well-formed figure of a man standing at the side of the sitter, but while being developed, this figure faded away entirely. Mr. Williams assures me (in a letter) that in these experiments there was "no room for trick or for the production of these figures by any known means."

The editor of the *British Journal of Photography* has made experiments at Mr. Hudson's studio, taking his own collodion and new plates, and doing everything himself, yet there were "abnormal appearances" on the pictures although no distinct figures.

We now come to the valuable and conclusive experiments of Mr. John Beattie of Clifton, a retired photographer of twenty years' experience, and of whom the above-mentioned editor says :—" Everyone who knows Mr. Beattie will give him credit for being a thoughtful, skilful, and intelligent photographer, one of the last men in the world to be deceived, at least in matters relating to photography, and one quite incapable of deceiving others."

Mr. Beattie has been assisted in his researches by Dr. Thomson, an Edinburgh M.D., who has practised photography, as an amateur, for twenty-five years. They experimented at the studio of a friend, who was not a spiritualist (but who became a medium during the experiments), and had the services of a tradesman with whom they were well acquainted, as a medium. The whole of the photographic work was done by Messrs. Beattie and Thomson, the other two sitting at a small table. The pictures were taken in series of three, within a few seconds of each other, and several of these series were taken at each sitting. The figures produced are for the most part not human, but white shaded patches, variously formed, and which in successive pictures are seen to change, and develop as it were into a more perfect or complete type. Thus, one set of five begins with two white somewhat angular patches over the middle sitter, and ends with a rude but unmistakeable white female figure, covering the larger part of the plate. The other three show intermediate states, indicating a continuous change of form from the first figure to the last. Another set (of four pictures) begins with a white vertical cylinder over the body of the medium, and a shorter one on his head. These change their form in the second and third, and in the last become laterally spread out into luminous masses resembling nebulæ. Another set of three is very curious. The first has an oblique flowing luminous patch from the table to the ground; in the second this has changed to a white serpentine column, ending in a point above the medium's head; in the third the column has become broader and somewhat double, with the curve in an opposite direction, and with a head-like termination. The change of the curvature may have some connection with a change in the position of the sitters, which is seen to have taken place between the second and the third of this set. There are two others, taken, like all the preceding, in 1872, but which the medium described during the exposure. The first, he said, was a thick white fog; and the picture came out all shaded white, with not a trace of any of the sitters. The other was described as a fog with a figure standing in it; and here a white human figure is alone seen in the almost uniform foggy surface. During the experiments made in 1873, the medium, *in every case*, minutely and correctly described the appearances which afterwards came out on the plate. In one there is a luminous rayed star of large size, with a human face faintly visible in the centre. This is the last of three in which the star developed, and the whole were accurately described by the medium. In another set of three, the medium first described,—"a light behind him, coming from the floor." The next,—"a light rising over another person's arms, coming from his own boot." The third,—"there is the same light, but now a column comes up through the table, and it is hot to my hands." Then he suddenly exclaimed,—"What a bright light up there! Can you not see it?" pointing to it with his hand. All this most accurately describes the three pictures, and in the last, the medium's hand is seen pointing to a white patch which appears overhead. There are other curious developments, the nature of which is already sufficiently indicated; but one very startling single picture must be mentioned. During the exposure one medium said he saw on the background a black figure, the other medium saw a light figure by the side of the black one. In the picture both these figures appear, the light one very faintly, the black one much more distinctly, of a gigantic size, with a massive coarse-featured face and long hair.

Mr Beattie has been so good as to send me for examination a complete set of these most extraordinary photographs, thirty-two in number, and has furnished me with any particulars I desired. I have described them as correctly as

I am able; and Dr. Thomson has authorised me to use his name as confirming Mr. Beattie's account of the conditions under which they appeared. These experiments were not made without labour and perseverance. Sometimes twenty consecutive pictures produced absolutely nothing unusual. Hundreds have been taken, and more than half have been complete failures. But the successes have been well worth the labour. They demonstrate the fact that what a medium or sensitive sees (even where no one else sees anything) may often have an objective existence. They teach us that perhaps the bookseller, Nicolai of Berlin—whose case has been quoted *ad nauseam* as the type of a "spectral illusion"—saw real beings after all; and that, had photography been then discovered and properly applied, we might now have the portraits of the invisible men and women who crowded his room.*   They give us hints of a process

---

* The efforts men of science have to make in order to avoid recognising the possibility of such forms being actual beings, visible only during the peculiar state induced by disease or insanity, is well shown by the following curious passage from the recent work of Mr. G. H. Lewes' "Problems of Life and Mind" (Vol. I. p. 255):—"In the course of my observations in English and German asylums I have been forcibly impressed with the fact, abundantly illustrated in the records of insanity, that patients belonging to very different classes of society, and to different nations, have precisely similar hallucinations, which they express in terms so closely alike, that the one might have been a free translation of the other. The pauper lunatic in England will often have the same illusion as the insane German merchant ; and the insane soldier in Bohemia will seem to be repeating the absurdities of the insane farmer in Sussex. Not only does the fact of cerebral congestion determine hallucination in the Englishman as in the German, but determines the precise form which that hallucination will take. Twenty different patients, of both sexes, and of different age, country, and states, will be found having similar morbid sensations ; and will all form a similar hypothesis to explain what they feel. Not only will they agree in attributing their distressing sensations to the malevolent action of invisible enemies ; but will also agree in describing *how* these enemies molest them ; even when such imaginary explanations take peculiar shapes—for example, that the enemy blows poisonous vapours through the keyhole, or chinks in the wall, strikes them with galvanic

by which the figures seen at séances may have to be gradually formed or developed, and enable us better to understand the statements repeatedly made by the communicating intelligences—that it is very difficult to produce definite, visible, and tangible forms, and that it can only be done under a rare combination of favourable conditions.

We find, then, that three amateur photographers, working independently in different parts of England, separately confirm the fact of spirit-photography—already demonstrated to the satisfaction of many who had tested it through professional photographers. The experiments of Mr. Beattie and Dr. Thomson are alone absolutely conclusive; and, taken in connection with those of Mr. Slater and Dr.

batteries hidden under the table, roars and threatens them from underground cellars, &c.   To hear in Germany a narrative which one has already heard in England, gravely particularising the same preposterous details, almost as if the thoughts of the one were the echo of the thoughts of the other, has a startling effect.   I do not refer simply to the well-known general types of hallucination, in which patients fancy themselves emperors, Christs, great actors, or great statesmen, or fancy themselves doomed to perdition, made of glass and liable to break in pieces if they move,—I refer to the singular resemblance noticeable in the expression of these forms, so that one patient has the same irrational conceptions as another.   This identity of conception rests on *identity* of *congestion*. Remove the congestion and the hallucination vanishes." Now this explanation is so untenable and so contrary to the laws of physiological pyschology, that we venture to say Mr. Lewes' friend, Herbert Spencer, will not endorse it.   For it asserts that the product of two factors can be constantly identical with the product of two other factors, one of which is widely different from the corresponding one.   It asserts that race, nation, education, life-long habits and associations and ideas, being *all* different in two individuals, a similar or identical cerebral disease will produce an identical mental result, and that the radical differences in the most important of the two factors go absolutely for nothing!   There could hardly be a more striking proof of the theory that so-called spectral illusions are often actual objective forms than the facts adduced by Mr. Lewes ; and if his explanation is satisfactory to himself, we can hardly have a stronger case of the blinding influence of preconceived ideas, even on the most powerful intellects.

Williams, and the test photographs, like those of Mrs. Guppy, establish as a scientific fact the objective existence of invisible human forms, and definite invisible actinic images.   Before leaving the photographic phenomena we have to notice two curious points in connection with them. The actinic action of the spirit-forms is peculiar, and much more rapid than that of the light reflected from ordinary material forms; for the figures start out the moment the developing fluid touches them, while the figure of the sitter appears much later.   Mr. Beattie noticed this throughout his experiments, and I was myself much struck with it when watching the development of three pictures recently taken at Mr. Hudson's.   The second figure, though by no means bright, always came out long before any other part of the picture.   The other singular thing is, the copious drapery in which these forms are almost always enveloped, so as to show only just what is necessary for recognition of the face and figure.   The explanation given of this is, that the human form is more difficult to materialise than drapery. The conventional "white-sheeted ghost" was not then all fancy, but had a foundation in fact—a fact, too, of deep significance, dependent on the laws of a yet unknown chemistry.

SUMMARY OF THE MORE IMPORTANT MANIFESTATIONS, PHYSICAL AND MENTAL.

As we have not been able to give an accountof many curious facts which occur with the various classes of mediums, the following catalogue of the more important and well-characterized phenomena may be useful.   They may be grouped provisionally, as, Physical, or those in which material objects are acted on, or apparently material bodies produced; and, Mental, or those which consist in the exhibition by the medium of powers or faculties not possessed in the normal state.

The principal physical phenomena are the following:—

1. *Simple Physical Phenomena.*—Producing sounds of all kinds, from a delicate tick to blows like those of a heavy sledge-hammer. Altering the weight of bodies. Moving bodies without human agency. Raising bodies into the air. Conveying bodies to a distance out of and into closed rooms. Releasing mediums from every description of bonds, even from welded iron rings, as has happened in America.

2. *Chemical.*—Preserving from the effects of fire, as already detailed.

3. *Direct Writing and Drawing.*—Producing writing or drawing on marked papers, placed in such positions that no human hand (or foot) can touch them. Sometimes, visibly to the spectators, a pencil rising up and writing or drawing apparently by itself. Some of the drawings in many colours have been produced on marked paper in from ten to twenty seconds, and the colours found wet. (See Mr. Coleman's evidence, in "Dialectical Report." p. 143, confirmed by Lord Borthwick, p. 150.) Mr. Thomas Slater, of 136 Euston Road, is now obtaining communications in the following manner:—A bit of slate pencil an eighth of an inch long is laid on a table; a clean slate is laid over this, in a well-lighted room; the sound of writing is then heard, and in a few minutes a communication of considerable length is found distinctly written. At other times the slate is held between himself and another person, their other hands being joined. Some of these communications are philosophical discussions on the nature of spirit and matter, supporting the usual spiritual theory on this subject.

4. *Musical Phenomena.*—Musical instruments, of various kinds, played without human agency, from a hand-bell to a closed piano. With some mediums, and where the conditions are favourable, original musical compositions of a very high character are produced. This occurs with Mr. Home.

5. *Spiritual Forms.*—These are either luminous appear-

ances, sparks, stars, globes of light, luminous clouds, &c.; or, hands, faces, or entire human figures, generally covered with flowing drapery, except a portion of the face and hands. The human forms are often capable of moving solid objects, and are both visible and tangible to all present. In other cases they are only visible to seers, but when this is the case it sometimes happens that the seer describes the figure as lifting a flower or a pen, and others present see the flower or the pen apparently move by itself. In some cases they speak distinctly; in others the voice is heard by all, the form only seen by the medium. The flowing robes of these forms have in some cases been examined, and pieces cut off, which have in a short time melted away. Flowers are also brought, some of which fade away and vanish; others are real, and can be kept indefinitely. It must not be concluded that any of these forms are actual spirits; they are probably only temporary forms produced by spirits for purposes of test, or of recognition by their friends. This is the account invariably given of them by communications obtained in various ways; so that the objection once thought to be so crushing—that there can be no "ghosts" of clothes, armour, or walking-sticks—ceases to have any weight.

6. *Spiritual Photographs.*—These, as just detailed, demonstrate by a purely physical experiment the trustworthiness of the preceding class of observations.

We now come to the mental phenomena, of which the following are the chief:—

1. *Automatic Writing.*—The medium writes involuntarily, sometimes in a state of trance, and often matter which he is not thinking about, does not expect, and does not like. Occasionally definite and correct information is given of facts of which the medium has not, nor ever had, any knowledge. Sometimes future events are accurately

predicted. The writing takes place either by the hand or through a planchette. Often the handwriting changes. Sometimes it is written backwards; sometimes in languages the medium does not understand.

2. *Seeing, or Clairvoyance and Clairaudience.*—This is of various kinds. Some mediums see the forms of deceased persons unknown to them, and describe their peculiarities so minutely that their friends at once recognise them. They often hear voices, through which they obtain names, date, and place, connected with the individuals so described. Others read sealed letters in any language, and write appropriate answers.

3. *Trance-speaking.*—The medium goes into a more or less unconscious state, and then speaks, often on matters and in a style far beyond his own capacities. Thus, Serjeant Cox—no mean judge on a matter of literary style—says, " I have heard an uneducated barman, when in a state of trance, maintain a dialogue with a party of philosophers on ' Reason and Foreknowledge, Will and Fate,' and hold his own against them. I have put to him the most difficult questions in psychology, and received answers, always thoughtful, often full of wisdom, and invariably conveyed in choice and elegant language. Nevertheless a quarter of an hour afterwards, when released from the trance, he was unable to answer the simplest query on a philosophical subject, and was even at a loss for sufficient language to express a commonplace idea." (" What am I ?" vol. ii., p. 242.) That this is not overstated I can myself testify, from repeated observation of the same medium. And from other trance-speakers—such as Mrs. Hardinge, Mrs. Tappan, and Mr. Peebles—I have heard discourses which, for high and sustained eloquence, noble thoughts, and high moral purpose, surpassed the best efforts of any preacher or lecturer within my experience.

4. *Impersonation.*—This occurs during trance. The medium seems taken possession of by another being; speaks, looks, and acts the character in a most marvellous manner; in some cases speaks foreign languages never even heard in the normal state; as in the case of Miss Edmonds, already given. When the influence is violent or painful, the effects are such as have been in all ages imputed to possession by evil spirits.

5. *Healing.*—There are various forms of this. Sometimes by mere laying on of hands, an exalted form of simple mesmeric healing. Sometimes, in the trance state, the medium at once discovers the hidden malady, and prescribes for it, often describing very exactly the morbid appearance of internal organs.

The purely mental phenomena are generally of no use as evidence to non-spiritualists, except in those few cases where rigid tests can be applied; but they are so intimately connected with the physical series, and often so interwoven with them, that no one who has sufficient experience to satisfy him of the reality of the former, fails to see that the latter form part of the general system, and are dependent on the same agencies.

With the physical series the case is very different. They form a connected body of evidence, from the simplest to the most complex and astounding, every single component fact of which can be, and has been, repeatedly demonstrated by itself; while each gives weight and confirmation to all the rest. They have all, or nearly all, been before the world for twenty years; the theories and explanations of reviewers and critics do not touch them, or in any way satisfy any sane man who has repeatedly witnessed them; they have been tested and examined by sceptics of every grade of incredulity, men in every way qualified to detect imposture or to discover natural causes—trained physicists, medical men, lawyers, and men of business—but in every case the investigators have either retired baffled, or become converts.

There have, it is true, been some impostors who have attempted to imitate the phenomena; but such cases are few in number, and have been discovered by tests far less severe than those to which the genuine phenomena have been submitted over and over again; and a large proportion of these phenomena have never been imitated, because they are beyond successful imitation.

Now what do our leaders of public opinion say, when a scientific man of proved ability again observes a large portion of the more extraordinary phenomena, in his own house, under test conditions, and affirms their objective reality; and this not after a hasty examination, but after four years of research?   Men "with heavy scientific appendages to their names" refuse to examine them when invited; the eminent society of which he is a fellow refuses to record them; and the press cries out that it wants better witnesses than Mr. Crookes, and that such facts want "confirmation" before they can be believed.   But why more confirmation?   And when again "confirmed," who is to confirm the confirmer?   After the whole range of the phenomena had been before the world ten years, and had convinced sceptics by tens of thousands—sceptics, be it remembered, of common sense and more than common acuteness, Americans of all classes—they were *confirmed* by the first chemist in America, Professor Robert Hare. Two years later they were again confirmed by the elaborate and persevering inquiries of one of the first American lawyers, Judge Edmonds.   Then by another good chemist, Professor Mapes.   In France the truth of the simpler physical phenomena was *confirmed* by Count A. de Gasparin in 1854; and since then French astronomers, mathematicians, and chemists of high rank have *confirmed* them. Professor Thury, of Geneva, again confirmed them in 1855.   In our own country. such men as Professor de Morgan, Dr. Lockhart Robertson, T. Adolphus Trollope, Dr. Robert Chambers, Serjeant Cox, Mr. C. F. Varley, as well as the sceptical Dialectical Committee, have independently *confirmed* large portions of them; and lastly comes Mr. William Crookes, F.R.S., with four years of research and unrestricted experiment with the two oldest and most remarkable mediums in the world, and again *confirms* almost the whole series! But even this is not all. Through an independent set of most competent observers we have the crucial test of photography; a witness which cannot be deceived, which has no preconceived opinions, which cannot register "subjective" impressions; a thoroughly scientific witness, who is admitted into our law courts, and whose testimony is good as against any number of recollections of what did happen or opinions as to what ought to and must have happened. And what have the other side brought against this overwhelming array of consistent and unimpeachable evidence ? They have merely made absurd and inadequate suppositions, but have not disproved or explained away one weighty fact !

My position, therefore, is that the phenomena of Spiritualism in their entirety do *not* require further confirmation. They are proved, quite as well as any facts are proved in other sciences; and it is not denial or quibbling that can disprove any of them, but only fresh facts and accurate deductions from those facts.   When the opponents of Spiritualism can give a record of their researches approaching in duration and completeness to those of its advocates; and when they can discover and show in detail, either how the phenomena are produced or how the many sane and able men here referred to have been deluded into a coincident belief that they have witnessed them; and when they can prove the correctness of their theory by producing a like belief in a body of equally sane and able unbelievers, —then, and not till then, will it be necessary for spiritualists to produce fresh confirmation of facts which are, and always have been, sufficiently real and indisputable to satisfy any honest and persevering inquirer.

This being the state of the case as regards evidence and proof, we are fully justified in taking the *facts* of modern Spiritualism (and with them the spiritual theory as the only tenable one) as being fully established. It only remains to give a brief account of the more important uses and teachings of Spiritualism.

Historical Teachings of Spiritualism.

The lessons which modern Spiritualism teaches may be classed under two heads. In the first place, we find that it gives a rational account of various phenomena in human history which physical science has been unable to explain, and has therefore rejected or ignored; and, in the second, we derive from it some definite information as to man's nature and destiny, and, founded on this, an ethical system of great practical efficacy. The following are some of the more important phenomena of history and of human nature which science cannot deal with, but which Spiritualism explains.

1. It is no small thing that the spiritualist finds himself able to rehabilitate Socrates as a sane man, and his "demon" as an intelligent spiritual being who accompanied him through life,—in other words, a guardian spirit. The non-spiritualist is obliged to look upon one of the greatest men, in human history, not only as subject all his life to a mental illusion, but as being so weak, foolish, or superstitious as never to discover that it was an illusion. He

is obliged to disbelieve the fact asserted by contemporaries
and by Socrates himself, that it forewarned him truly of
dangers; and to hold that this noble man, this subtle
reasoner, this religious sceptic, who was looked up to with
veneration and love by the great men who were his pupils,
was imposed upon by his own fancies, and never during a
long life found out that they were fancies, and that their
supposed monitions were as often wrong as right. It is a
positive mental relief not to have to think thus of Socrates.

2. Spiritualism allows us to believe that the oracles of
antiquity were not all impostures; that a whole people,
perhaps the most intellectually acute who ever existed,
were not all dupes.   In discussing the question, "Why
the Prophetess Pythia giveth no Answers now from the
Oracle in Verse," Plutarch tells us that when kings and
states consulted the oracle on weighty matters that might
do harm if made public, the replies were couched in
enigmatical language; but when private persons asked
about their own affairs they got direct answers in the plainest terms, so that some people even complained of their
simplicity and directness as being unworthy of a divine
origin.   And he adds this positive testimony: "Her
answers, though submitted to the severest scrutiny, have
never proved false or incorrect.   On the contrary, the veri-
fication of them has filled the temple with gifts from all
parts of Greece and foreign countries."   And again, "The
answer of Pythoness proceeds to the very truth, without any
diversion, circuit, fraud, or ambiguity.   It has never yet,
in a single instance, been convicted of falsehood."   Would
such statements be made by such a writer, if these oracles
were all the mere guesses of impostors?   The fact that
they declined and ultimately failed, is wholly in their
favour; for why should imposture cease as the world became less enlightened and more superstitious?   Neither

does the fact that the priests could sometimes be bribed
to give out false oracles prove anything, against such statements as that of Plutarch and the belief during many
generations, supported by ever-recurring experiences, of
the greatest men of antiquity. That belief could only have
been formed by demonstrative facts; and modern Spiritualism enables us to understand the nature of those facts.

3. Both the Old and the New Testaments are full of
Spiritualism, and spiritualists alone can read the record
with an enlightened belief. The hand that wrote upon the
wall at Belshazzar's feast, and the three men unhurt in
Nebuchadnezzar's fiery furnace, are for them actual facts
which they need not explain away. St. Paul's language
about "spiritual gifts," and "trying the spirits," is to them
intelligible language, and the "gift of tongues" a simple
fact. When Christ cast out "devils" or "evil spirits," he
really did so—not merely startle a madman into momen-
tary quiescence; and the water changed into wine, as well
as the bread and fishes continually renewed till five thousand men were fed, are credible, as extreme manifestations
of a power which is still daily at work among us.

4. The miracles of the saints, when well attested, come
into the same category. Those of St. Bernard, for instance,
were often performed in broad day before thousands of
spectators, and were recorded by eye-witnesses. He was
himself greatly troubled by them, wondering why this
power was bestowed upon him, and fearing lest it should
make him less humble. This was not the frame of mind,
nor was St. Bernard's the character of a deluded enthusiast.
The spiritualists need not believe that all this never happened; or that St. Francis d'Assisi and Sta. Theresa were
not raised into the air, as eye-witnesses declared they were.

5. Witchcraft, and witchcraft trials, have a new interest
for the spiritualist. He is able to detect hundreds of

ourious and minute coincidences with phenomena he has himself witnessed; * he is able to separate the *facts* from the absurd *inferences*, which people imbued with the frightful superstition of diabolism drew from them, and from which false inferences all the horrors of the witch-craft mania arose. Spiritualism, and Spiritualism alone, gives a rational explanation of witchcraft, and determines how much of it was objective fact, how much subjective illusion.

6. Modern Roman Catholic Miracles become intelligible

---

* At a trial for Witchcraft, at Cork, in 1661, a young girl was believed to be bewitched. She had violent fits, and, during these, several witnesses declared that, while they were present, she was "removed strangely, in the twinkling of an eye, out of the bed, sometimes into the bottom of a chest with linen, under all the linen, and the linen not at all disordered, sometimes betwixt the two beds she lay on, sometimes under a parcel of wool; and once she was laid on a small deal board, which lay on the top of the house between two sollar beams, where it was necessary to rear up ladders to have her fetched down." At the same trial, it was declared, that little stones were thrown at her wherever she went, and the witnesses saw great quantities of these come and hit her, and fall to the ground, and then vanish, so that none of them could be found. But once the girl caught one, and the witness another, and she tied them in her purse, but they vanished in a little time, although the knot remained unopened.

These facts are very analogous to some of the more powerful manifestations of modern Spiritualism. Such occurrences as these are to be met with in the record of witchcraft trials by thousands, generally witnessed by numbers of persons educated and uneducated; and if any one will take the trouble to read the reports of these trials, they will see that the testimony of single witnesses, to extraordinary phenomena, was not accepted, unless corroborated by similar facts witnessed by several persons. It is generally the fashion to pass over these testimonies, as not worthy of a moment's notice; but this is surely not satisfactory ; and, when we find that phenomena of an exactly similar nature are witnessed in our own day, by men of talent and education, whose prepossessions are all against them, this concurrence of ancient and modern testimony, must be held to prove that, some, at least, of the facts witnessed, were realities.

facts. Spirits whose affections and passions are strongly excited in favour of Catholicism, produce those appearances of the Virgin, and of saints, which they know will tend to increased religious fervour. The appearance itself may be an objective reality; while it is only an inference that it is the Virgin Mary,—an inference which every intelligent spiritualist would repudiate as in the highest degree improbable.

7. Second-sight, and many of the so-called superstitions of savages may be realities. It is well known that mediumistic power is more frequent and more energetic in mountainous countries; and as these are generally inhabited by the less civilised races, the beliefs that are more prevalent there may be due to facts which are more prevalent, and be wrongly imputed to the coincident ignorance. It is known to spiritualists that the pure dry air of California led to more powerful and more startling manifestations than in any other part of the United States.

8. The recently discussed question of the efficacy of prayer receives a perfect solution by Spiritualism. Prayer may be often answered, though not directly by the Deity. Nor does the answer depend wholly on the morality or the religion of the petitioner; but as men who are both moral and religious, and are firm believers in a Divine response to prayer, will pray more frequently, more earnestly, and more disinterestedly, they will attract towards them a number of spiritual beings who sympathise with them, and who, when the necessary mediumistic power is present, will be able, as they are often willing, to answer the prayer. A striking case is that of George Müller, of Bristol, who has now for forty-four years depended wholly for his own support, and that of his wonderful charities, on answer to prayer. His " Narrative of Some of the Lord's Dealings with George Müller" (6th Edit., 1860), should have been

o

referred to in the late discussion, since it furnishes a better
demonstration that prayer is sometimes really answered
than the hospital experiment proposed by Sir Henry Thomson
could possibly have done.   In this work we have a precise
yearly statement of his receipts and expenditure for many
years.   He never asked any one, or allowed any one to be
asked, directly or indirectly, for a penny.   No subscriptions
or collections were ever made; yet from 1830 (when he
married without any income whatever) he has lived,
brought up a family, and established institutions which
have steadily increased, till now four thousand orphan children are educated and in part supported.   It has happened
hundreds of times that there has been no food in his house,
and no money to buy any, or no bread or milk or sugar for
the children.   Yet he never took a loaf or any other article
on credit even for a day; and during the thirty years over
which his narrative extends, neither he nor the hundreds
of children dependent upon him for their daily food have
ever been without a regular meal !   They have lived literally
from hand to mouth; and his one and only resource has
been secret prayer.   Here is a case which has been going
on in the midst of us for forty years, and is still going on;
it has been published to the world for many years, yet a
warm discussion is carried on by eminent men as to the fact
of whether prayer is or is not answered, and not one of them
exhibits the least knowledge of this most pertinent and
illustrative phenomenon !   The spiritualist explains all this
as a personal influence.   The perfect simplicity, faith,
boundless charity, and goodness of George Müller have
enlisted in his cause beings of a like nature; and his
mediumistic powers have enabled them to work for him by
influencing others to send him money, food, clothes, &c., all
arriving, as we should say, just in the nick of time.   The
numerous letters he received with these gifts, describing

the sudden and uncontrollable impulse the donors felt to send him a certain definite sum at a certain fixed time, such being the exact sum he was in want of, and had prayed for, strikingly illustrates the nature of the power at work. All this might be explained away if it were partial and discontinuous; but when it continued to supply the daily wants of a life of unexampled charity, *for which no provision in advance was ever made* (for that Müller considered would show want of trust in God), no such explanation can cover the facts.

9. Spiritualism enables us to comprehend and find a place for that long series of disturbances and occult phenomena of various kinds which occurred previous to what are termed the modern Spiritual manifestations. Robert Dale Owen's Works give a rather full account of this class of phenomena, which are most accurately recorded and philosophically treated by him. This is not the place to refer to them in detail; but one of them may be mentioned as showing how large an amount of unexplained mystery there was, even in our own country, before the world heard anything of modern Spiritualism. In 1841, Major Edward Moor, F.R.S., published a little book called " Bealings Bells," giving an account of mysterious bell-ringing in his house at Great Bealings, Suffolk, and which continued for fifty-three days. Every attempt to discover the cause, by himself, friends, and bell-hangers, was fruitless; and by no efforts, however violent, could the same clamorous and rapid ringing be produced. He wrote an account to the newspapers, requesting information bearing on the subject, when, in addition to certain wise suggestions—of rats or a monkey as efficient causes—he received fourteen communications, all relating cases of mysterious bell-ringing in different parts of England, many of them lasting much longer than Major Moor's, and all remaining equally un-

explained.   One lasted eighteen months; another was in
Greenwich Hospital, where neither clerk-of-the-works, bell-
hanger, nor men of science could discover the cause.   One
clergyman wrote of disturbances of a most serious kind
continued in his parsonage for *nine years*, and he was able
to trace back their existence in the same house for *sixty
years*.   Another case had lasted *twenty years*, and could be
traced back for a *century*.   Some of the details of these cases
are most instructive.   Trick is absolutely the most incredible
of all explanations.   Spiritualism furnishes the explanation
by means of analogous facts occurring every day, and forming part of the great system of phenomena which demonstrates the spiritual theory.   Major Moor's book is very
rare; but a good abstract of it is given in " Owen's Debateable Land," pp. 239-258.

*10. Spiritualism, if true, furnishes such proofs of the
existence of ethereal beings, and of their power to act upon
matter, as must revolutionise philosophy.   It demonstrates
the actuality of forms of matter, and modes of being, before
inconceivable; it demonstrates mind without brain, and
intelligence disconnected from what are termed a material
body; and, it thus cuts away all presumption against our
continued existence after the physical body is disorganised
and dissolved.   Yet more, it demonstrates, as completely
as the fact can be demonstrated, that the so-called dead
are still alive; that our friends are still with us, though
unseen, and guide and strengthen us when, owing to
absence of proper conditions, they cannot make their
presence known.   It thus furnishes that *proof* of a future
life which so many crave, and for want of which so many
live and die in anxious doubt, so many in positive disbelief.

---

* This paragraph did not appear in the article, as published in the
Fortnightly Review, but its omission was a great oversight, as it is
essential to a complete sketch of the " teachings" of Spiritualism.

How valuable the *certainty* gained by spiritual communications is, may be gathered from what was said to a friend of mine, by a clergyman who had witnessed the modern phenomena :—"Death is a different thing to me *now*, from what it ever has been; from the greatest depression because of the death of my sons I am full of confidence and cheerfulness; I am a changed man." This is the effect of modern Spiritualism, on a man who had all that a belief in Christianity could give him before ; and this is the answer to those who ask, "What use is it ?" It substitutes a definite, real, and practical conviction, for a vague, theoretical, and unsatisfying faith. It furnishes actual knowledge on a matter of vital importance to all men, and as to which the wisest men, and most advanced thinkers, have held that no knowledge was attainable.

MORAL TEACHINGS OF SPIRITUALISM.

We have now to explain the Theory of Human Nature, which is the outcome of the phenomena taken in their entirety, and is also more or less explicitly taught by the communications which purport to come from spirits. It may be briefly outlined as follows :

1. Man is a duality, consisting of an organised spiritual form, evolved coincidently with and permeating the physical body, and having corresponding organs and development.

2. Death is the separation of this duality, and effects no change in the spirit, morally or intellectually.

3. Progressive evolution of the intellectual and moral nature is the destiny of individuals; the knowledge, attainments, and experience of earth-life forming the basis of spirit-life.

4. Spirits can communicate through properly-endowed

mediums. They are attracted to those they love or sympathise with, and strive to warn, protect, and influence them
for good, by mental impression when they cannot effect
any more direct communication; but, as follows from
clause 2, their communications will be fallible, and must
be judged and tested just as we do those of our fellow-
men.

The foregoing outline propositions, will suggest a number
of questions and difficulties, for the answers to which
readers are referred to the works of R. D. Owen, Hudson
Tuttle, Professor Hare, and the records of Spiritualism
passim. Here I must pass on to explain with some amount
of detail, how the theory leads to a pure system of morality
with sanctions far more powerful and effective than any
which either religious systems or philosophy have put
forth.

This part of the subject cannot, perhaps, be better
introduced, than by referring to some remarks of Professor
Huxley, in a letter to the Committee of the Dialectical
Society. He says,—"But supposing the phemonena to be
genuine—they do not interest me. If anybody would
endow me with the faculty of listening to the chatter of
old women and curates at the nearest cathedral town, I
should decline the privilege, having better things to do.
And if the folk in the spiritual world do not talk more
wisely and sensibly than their friends report them to do, I
put them in the same category." This passage, written with
the caustic satire in which the kind-hearted Professor occasionally indulges, can hardly mean, that if it were proved
that men live after the death of the body, that fact would not
interest him, merely because some of them talked twaddle?
Many scientific men deny the spiritual source of the manifestations, on the ground that real, genuine spirits might
reasonably be expected not to indulge in the common-

place trivialities which do undoubtedly form the staple of ordinary spiritual communications. But surely Professor Huxley, as a naturalist and philosopher, would not admit this to be a reasonable expectation. Does he not hold the doctrine that there can be no effect, mental or physical, without an adequate cause; and that mental states, faculties, and idiosyncrasies, that are the result of gradual development and life-long—or even ancestral—habit, cannot be suddenly changed by any known or imaginable cause? And if (as the professor would probably admit) a very large majority of those who daily depart this life are persons addicted to twaddle, persons whose pleasures are sensual rather than intellectual,—whence is to come the transforming power which is suddenly, at the mere throwing off the physical body, to change these into beings able to appreciate and delight in high and intellectual pursuits? The thing would be a miracle, the greatest of miracles, and surely Professor Huxley is the last man to contemplate innumerable miracles as part of the order of nature; and all for what? Merely *to save these people from the necessary consequences of their misspent lives.* For the essential teaching of Spiritualism is, that we are, all of us, in every act and thought, helping to build up a "mental fabric," which will be, and constitute ourselves, more completely after the death of the body, than it does now. Just as this fabric is well or ill built, so will our progress and happiness be aided or retarded. Just in proportion as we have developed our higher intellectual and moral nature, or starved it by disuse and by giving undue prominence to those faculties which secure us mere' physical or selfish enjoyment, shall we be well or ill-fitted for the new life we enter on. The noble teaching of Herbert Spencer, that men are best educated by being left to suffer the natural consequences of their actions, is the teaching of Spiritualism as regards the transition to another phase of life. There will be no imposed rewards or punishments; but every one will suffer the natural and inevitable consequences of a well or ill-spent life. The well-spent life is that in which those faculties which regard our personal physical well-being, are subordinated to those which regard our social and intellectual well-being, and the well-being of others; and that inherent feeling—which is so universal and so difficult to account for—that these latter constitute our higher nature, seems also to point to the conclusion that we are intended for a condition in which the former will be almost wholly unnecessary, and will gradually become rudimentary through disuse, while the latter will receive a corresponding development.

Although, therefore, the twaddle and triviality of so many of the communications is not one whit more interesting to sensible spiritualists than it is to Professor Huxley, and is never voluntarily listened to, yet the fact that such poor stuff is talked (supposing it to come from spirits) is both a fact that might have been anticipated and a lesson of deep import. We must remember, too, the character of the séances at which these common-place communications are received. A miscellaneous assemblage of believers of various grades and tastes, but mostly in search of an evening's amusement, and of sceptics who look upon all the others as either fools or knaves, is not likely to attract to itself the more elevated and refined denizens of the higher spheres, who may well be supposed to feel too much interest in their own new and grand intellectual existence to waste their energies on either class. If the fact is proved, that people continue to talk after they are dead with just as little sense as when alive, but that, being in a state in which sense, both common and uncommon, is of far greater importance to happiness than it is here (where fools pass very comfortable lives,) they suffer the penalty of having neglected to cultivate their minds; and being so much out of their element in a world where all pleasures are mental, they endeavour to recall old times by gossiping with their former associates whenever they can —Professor Huxley will not fail to see its vast importance as an incentive to that higher education which he is never weary of advocating. He would assuredly be interested in anything having a really practical bearing on the present as well as on the future condition of men; and it is evident that even these low and despised phenomena of Spiritualism, "if true," have this bearing, and, combined with its higher teachings, constitute a great moral agency which may yet regenerate the world.

For the spiritualist who, by daily experience gets absolute knowledge of these facts regarding the future state—who knows that, just in proportion as he indulges in passion, or selfishness, or the exclusive pursuit of wealth, and neglects to cultivate the affections and the varied powers of his mind, so does he inevitably prepare for himself misery in a world in which there are no physical wants to be provided for, no sensual enjoyments except those directly associated with the affections and sympathies, no occupations but those having for their object social and intellectual progress—is impelled towards a pure, a sympathetic, and an intellectual life by motives far stronger than any which either religion or philosophy can supply. He dreads to give way to passion or to falsehood, to selfishness or to a life of luxurious physical enjoyment, because he knows that the natural and inevitable consequences of such habits are future misery, necessitating a long and arduous struggle in order to develop anew the faculties, whose exercise long disuse has rendered painful to him. He will be deterred from crime by the knowledge that its unforeseen consequences may cause him ages of remorse; while the bad passions which it encourages will be a perpetual torment, to himself in a state of being in which mental emotions cannot be laid aside or forgotten amid the fierce struggles and sensual pleasures of a physical existence. It must be remembered that these beliefs (unlike those of theology) will have a living efficacy, because they depend on *facts* occurring again and again in the family circle, constantly reiterating the same truths as the result of personal knowledge, and thus bringing home to the mind even of the most obtuse, the absolute reality of that future existence in which our degree of happiness or misery will be directly dependent on the "mental fabric" we construct by our daily thoughts and words and actions here.

Contrast this system of natural and inevitable reward and retribution, dependent wholly on the proportionate development of our higher mental and moral nature, with the arbitrary system of rewards and punishments dependent on stated acts and beliefs only, as set forth by all dogmatic religions; and who can fail to see that the former is in harmony with the whole order of nature—the latter opposed to it. Yet it is actually said that Spiritualism is altogether either imposture or delusion, and all its teachings but the product of "expectant attention" and "unconscious cerebration!" If none of the long series of demonstrative facts which have been here sketched out existed, and its only product were this theory of a future state, that alone would negative such a supposition. And when it is considered that mediums of all grades, whether intelligent or ignorant, and having communications given through them in various direct and indirect ways, are absolutely in accord as to the main features of this theory, what becomes of the gross misstatement that nothing is given through mediums but what they know and believe themselves? The mediums have, almost all, been brought up in some of the usual orthodox beliefs. How is it, then, that the usual orthodox notions of heaven are *never* confirmed through them? In the scores of volumes and pamphlets of spiritual literature I have read I have found no statement of a spirit describing "winged angels," or "golden harps," or the "throne of God"—to which the humblest orthodox Christian thinks he will be introduced if he goes to heaven at all. There is no more startling and radical opposition to be found between the most diverse religious creeds, than that between the beliefs in which the majority of mediums have been brought up and the doctrines as to a future life that are delivered through them; there is nothing more marvellous in the history of the human mind than the fact that, whether in the backwoods of America or in country towns in England, ignorant men and women, having almost all been brought up in the usual sectarian notions of heaven and hell, should, the moment they become seized by the strange power of mediumship, give forth teachings on this subject which are philosophical rather than religious, and which differ wholly from what had been so deeply ingrained into their minds. And this statement is not affected by the fact that communications purport to come from Catholic or Protestant, Mahomedan or Hindoo spirits. Because, while such communications maintain special *dogmas* and *doctrines* yet they confirm the *very facts* which really constitute the spiritual theory, and which in themselves contradict the theory of the sectarian spirits. The Roman Catholic spirit, for instance, does not describe himself as being in either the orthodox purgatory, heaven, or hell; the Evangelical Dissenter who died in the firm conviction that he should certainly "go to Jesus," never describes himself as being with Christ, or as ever having seen Him, and so on throughout. Nothing is more common than for religious people at séances to ask questions about God and Christ. In reply they never get more than opinions, or more frequently the statement that they, the spirits, have no more direct knowledge of those subjects than they had while on earth.   So that the facts are all harmonious; and the very circumstance of there being sectarian spirits bears witness in two ways to the truth of the spiritual theory—it shows that the mind, with its ingrained beliefs, is not suddenly changed at death; and it shows that the communications are not the reflection of the mind of the medium, who is often of the same religion as the communicating spirit, and, because he does not get his own ideas confirmed, is obliged to call in the aid of "Satanic influence" to account for the anomaly.

The doctrine of a future state and of the proper preparation for it as here developed, is to be found in the works of all spiritualists, in the utterances of all trance-speakers, in the communications through all mediums; and this could be proved, did space permit, by copious quotations. But it varies in form and detail in each; and just as the historian arrives at the opinions or beliefs of any age or nation, by collating the individual opinions of its best and most popular writers, so do spiritualists collate the communications on this subject. They know well that absolute dependence is to be placed on no individual communications.   They know that these are received by a complex physical and mental process, both communicator and recipient influencing the result; and they accept the teachings as to the future state of man only so far as they are repeatedly confirmed in substance (though they may differ in detail) by communications obtained under the most varied circumstances, through mediums of the most different characters and acquirements, at different times, and in distant places. Fresh converts are apt to think that, once satisfied the communications come from their deceased friends, they may implicitly trust to them, and apply them universally; as if the vast spiritual world was all moulded to one pattern, instead of being, as it almost certainly is, a thousand times more varied than human society on the earth is, or ever has been. The fact that the communications do not agree as to the condition, occupations, pleasures, and capacities, of individual spirits, so far from being a difficulty, as has been absurdly supposed, is what ought to have been expected; while the agreement on the essential features of what we have stated to be the spiritual theory of a future state of existence, is all the more striking, and tends to establish that theory as a fundamental truth.

The assertion so often made, that Spiritualism is the survival or revival of old superstitions, is so utterly unfounded as to be hardly worth notice. A science of human nature which is founded on observed facts; which appeals only to facts and experiment; which takes no beliefs on trust; which inculcates investigation and self-reliance as the first duties of intelligent beings; which teaches that happiness in a future life can be secured by cultivating and developing to the utmost the higher faculties of our intellectual and moral nature *and by no other method,*—is and must be the natural enemy of all superstition. Spiritualism is an experimental science, and affords the only sure foundation for a true philosophy and a pure religion. It abolishes the terms "supernatural" and "miracle" by an extension of the sphere of law and the realm of nature; and in doing so it takes up and explains whatever is true in the superstitions and so-called miracles of all ages. It and it alone, is able to harmonise conflicting creeds; and it must ultimately lead to concord among mankind in the matter of religion, which has for so many ages been the

source of unceasing discord and incalculable evil;—and it
will be able to do this because it appeals to evidence instead of faith, and substitutes facts for opinions; and is
thus able to demonstrate the source of much of the teaching that men have so often held to be divine.

It will thus be seen, that those who can form no higher
conception of the uses of Spiritualism, "even if true," than
to detect crime or to name in advance the winner of the
Derby, not only prove their own ignorance of the whole
subject, but exhibit in a marked degree that partial mental
paralysis, the result of a century of materialistic thought,
which renders so many men unable seriously to conceive
the possibility of a natural continuation of human life after
the death of the body. It will be seen also that Spiritualism is no mere "psychological" curiosity, no mere indication
of some hitherto unknown "law of nature;" but that it is
a science of vast extent, having the widest, the most important, and the most practical issues, and as such should
enlist the sympathies alike of moralists, philosophers, and
politicians, and of all who have at heart the improvement
of society and the permanent elevation of human nature.

In concluding this necessarily imperfect though somewhat lengthy account of a subject about which so little is
probably known to most of my readers, I would earnestly
beg them not to satisfy themselves with a minute criticism of single facts, the evidence for which in my brief
survey, may be imperfect; but to weigh carefully the mass
of evidence I have adduced, considering its wide range and
various bearings. I would ask them to look rather at the
great results produced by the evidence than at the evidence itself as imperfectly stated by me; to consider the
long roll of men of ability who, commencing the inquiry as
sceptics left it as believers, and to give these men credit

for not having overlooked, during years of patient inquiry,
difficulties which at once occur to themselves. I would
ask them to ponder well on the fact, that no earnest and
patient inquirer has ever come to a conclusion adverse
to the reality of the phenomena; and that no spiritualist
has ever yet given them up as false. I would ask them,
finally, to dwell upon the long series of facts in human
history that Spiritualism explains, and on the noble and
satisfying theory of a future life that it unfolds. If they
will do this, I feel confident that the result I have alone
aimed at will be attained; which is, to remove the prejudices and misconceptions with which the whole subject
has been surrounded, and to incite to unbiassed and persevering examination of the facts. For the cardinal maxim
of Spiritualism is, that every one must find out the truth
for himself. It makes no claim to be received on hearsay
evidence; but on the other hand, it demands that it be not
rejected without patient, honest, and fearless inquiry.

APPENDIX.

I.

SINCE my article appeared in the *Fortnightly Review*, I have seen Dr. Carpenter's latest work, "The Principles of Mental Physiology." One or two of the learned doctor's statements have been noticed in foot-notes to this book, but there are a few others calling for remark, which I will now refer to.

At p. 296 Dr. Carpenter says, that the only answer spiritualists give to Faraday's experiments is, that—"Faraday's performers moved the tables with their hands, whereas we know that we do not;"—and he then continues—"Those who make this assertion are (of course) scientifically bound to demonstrate it, by showing that in *their* case the table *does* go round without any deflection of the index by lateral pressure, but they have uniformly refused to apply this test to their own performance although repeatedly challenged to do so." But Dr. C. omits to tell us who are the spiritualists whose "only answer" is above given, and who are they who have been "repeatedly challenged" and have "uniformly refused" to accept the challenge. On inquiry it may be found that it is the men of science who have "uniformly refused" to witness the proof of what they say spiritualists are scientifically bound to demonstrate.

In the spring of 1867, when I had obtained the proofs of force in lifting (not turning) a table (as detailed at p. 132) I invited Dr. Carpenter to attend some sittings with every probability of being able to show the phenomena. He came once. The sitting was not very successful, raps and taps of varying character being alone produced. Although strongly pressed to do so, he *never came again.* With Professor Tyndall exactly the same thing occurred. He came once, and declined to come again; although informed of phenomena which had repeatedly occurred in my own house, which he could not explain, and which I had every reason to believe would occur in his presence if he would only give three or four short sittings to these investigations. More recently Dr.

Sharpey and Professor Stokes, Secretaries of the Royal Society, refused the invitation of one of their own Fellows, Mr. Crookes, to witness experiments which formed the subject of a paper offered to the Society. Where we are vaguely and generally accused of "uniformly refusing" to produce certain proofs, it is only right that the public should know how our scientific opponents receive our offers to exhibit even more conclusive proofs. We must also remember that Dr. Carpenter is acquainted with the evidence of the Dialectical Committee, of Serjeant Cox, of Mr. Crookes, of Mr. Varley, and of myself, as to the movement of heavy objects entirely without contact of the medium or any other person; yet in 1874 he can adduce nothing but the utterly exploded and almost forgotten "table turning" of the time of Faraday, as worthy of notice!

The theory of "unconscious cerebration" is Dr. Carpenter's special hobby, yet in his application of it to explaining the phenomena of dreams we find a remarkable amount of contradiction and false reasoning.

At p. 586, for example, he notices the "suspension of our power to form common sense judgments,".the "suspension of our moral sense," and the "entire want of coherence between the ideas that successively present themselves," as characteristics of dreams, and to be explained as the normal result of "unconscious cerebration." But he imputes to the very same cause an exaltation of the imaginative and reasoning powers and their action in strict logical succession, so as to produce results which the whole working powers of the mind were unable to achieve; and in many cases the committal of these results to paper without a single error. And all this is still to be accepted as explained by the magical words, "unconscious cerebration."

As an illustration of Dr. Carpenter's mode of reasoning we give the narrative of a student at an Amsterdam University, adduced by him as supporting his views. The Professor having to perform a laborious and difficult mathematical calculation found that he could not get the correct result, owing to errors occurring in some of numerous figures employed. He therefore gave the problem to ten of his pupils. The narrator worked at it unsuccessfully for three evenings, but always without effect; and after sitting up till one in the morning on the third trial, went to bed much disappointed at not having been able to do the work correotly, as it was particularly required the next day. On getting up in the morning he found to his astonishment on his writing table the problem correctly solved in his own handwriting, not a single figure being wrong. But the important fact is, that the work was done by a shorter and better method than the student had attempted during his three evenings' work. The work he had already done and with which his mind must have been imbued was not done over again without error, but an altogether new and better class of work was performed; and the Professor himself was astonished at it, and declared that he "had never once thought of a solution so simple and concise."

Now here is evidently a case in which the ordinary rules of unconscious cerebration do not apply. For something is done in a way the doer had never thought of when awake. The student had been trying over and over again to find out the numerical error in his calculation, not to perform the calculation itself by any other method. When asleep he does not find out this error —which, if done, *might* have been imputed to the repetition of the former cerebral action, uninfluenced by the disturbing causes which had led to error—but he begins, *de novo*, in a way he had never attempted when awake, and solves the problem by a process which even his mathematical tutor had not thought of! This is exactly analogous to those cases of trance mediums who do in trance what they *cannot* do when awake—speak languages they have never learnt, for example; and to impute such actions to "unconscious cerebration" is not to explain them, but merely to give a name, and, like a child or a savage, accept the name as a sufficient explanation. It is exactly an analogous case to that of Mr. Lewes (given at page 196), in which preconceived ideas completely shut out the plainest logical consequences of the facts adduced.

II.

I have been informed by some of my correspondents that, because I have not referred to any cases of new information of practical utility having been derived from spiritual communications, I am supposed to admit that such do not exist. This is an error. I believe there are many such instances, but as bearing on the question whether Spiritualism is a reality or a delusion, I did not think them of much importance, and they could not have been introduced, with the necessary evidence, without altering the plan and much increasing the length of my article. If Spiritualism is a delusion—that is, if it is a product of known or unknown natural forces *plus* the minds of the assistants—then no new information of the kind referred to can possibly be derived from it. If, on the other hand, it is a reality —that is, if it proves that intelligent beings of another order of existence than our own can and do communicate with us (whether those beings are the spirits of deceased men or no)—this fact alone is of such vast and overwhelming importance, and involves such tremendous issues, scientific, philosophical, and religious, that the question whether these beings can and will improve our telegraphs or our steam-engines, is an altogether subordinate one. Since the question of what is called *practical results*, implies the truth and reality of the spiritual theory, it appears to me to be out of place to bring up that question while the primary question remains unsettled; for I can no more imagine a rational man being influenced in his acceptance of Spiritualism by the probability of his getting out of it such *practical* results, than I can imagine an earnest enquirer after religious truth being influenced in his acceptance of Christianity by the probability of its ministers being able to affect the weather by their prayers. When once a man is satisfied of the reality of spiritual communications, he will meet with abundant practical results. So long as he is not satisfied, such results, like all the other evidence, will be ignored or explained away.

III.

The *Spectator*, the *Academy*, and *Pall Mall Gazette* thought my paper in the *Fortnightly Review* worthy of more or less lengthy notice, but they have all declined to discuss the nature and bearing of the evidence I have adduced and referred to for the reality of the phenomena, while they take various objections to the moral and historical teachings deduced therefrom. Here I must decline to join issue with them. I hold that spiritualists alone are as yet competent to decide what theory best explains the facts, and what are the teachings which arise out of them, for the sufficient reason that they alone know these facts in their wide range and countless details. I could only sketch generally the *nature* of the phenomena, and was obliged to omit all the infinitude of characteristic mental details which constitute their chief value. My critics also express their views as to the contemptible and unsatisfactory nature of the phenomena and of the communications, even if true ; but here again they are evidently too ignorant of what they criticise to be enabled to form an opinion. I felt it my duty to give some idea of the teachings which are satisfying to most spiritualists, whatever may have been their previous opinions. Whether those teachings are agreeable to sceptics or no, is of little importance ; the facts of Spiritualism remain, and must be dealt with before the critics are in a position to give any opinion worth listening to as to the truth of the theory.

IV.

I here give a few extracts strikingly illustrative of our subject. In the following passage from Jamblichus on Divination, quoted in Maurice's "Moral and Metaphysical Philosophy," we find mention in a short space of a number of the most startling phenomena of modern Spiritualism :—

" Often at the moment of inspiration, or when the afflatus has subsided, a *fiery appearance* is seen—the entering or departing power. Those who are skilled in this wisdom can tell by the character of this glory the rank of the divinity who has seized for the time the reins of the mystic's soul, and guides it as he will. Sometimes the body of the man is *violently agitated*, sometimes it is *rigid and motionless*. In some instances *sweet music is heard*, in others discordant and fearful sounds. The person of the subject has been known to dilate and *tower to a superhuman height*, in other cases it has been *lifted into the air*. Frequently not merely the ordinary exercise of reason, but sensation and animal life would appear to have been suspended; and the subject of the afflatus has *not felt the application of fire*, has been pierced with spits, cut with knives, and not been sensible to pain."

The next passage throws much light on what is so often a stumbling-block to sceptics—the action of suspicion, or too rigid inquiry in checking the manifestations. Dr. Frederick L. H. Willis, professor of *Materia Medica* in the New York Medical College, thus describes his experience with a musical medium (*Spiritual Magazine*, 1867, p. 209):—

" One evening the medium went into the dark room alone, and took her seat at the piano. I was in the sitting-room adjoining (the door between was open), the light from which made every object in the circle-room distinctly visible. Scarcely had the medium struck the first note upon the piano, when the tambourine and the bells seemed to leap from the floor and join in unison. Carefully and noiselessly I stole into the room, and for several seconds it was my privilege to witness a rare and wonderful sight. I saw the bells and tambourine in motion. I saw the bells lifted as by invisible hands and chimed, each in its turn, accurately and beautifully with the piano. I saw the tambourine dexterously and scientifically manipulated with no mortal hand near it. But suddenly, by a slight turn of the head, the medium became aware of my presence; instantly, like the severing of the connection between a galvanic battery and its poles, everything ceased. Mark this; so long as my presence in the room was known only to the invisibles, so long the manifestations continued in perfection; the moment the medium became aware of it, everything stopped. A wave of mental emotion passed over her mind, which was in itself sufficient to stop the phenomena at once. The incident proved to my mind most clearly that, in most cases, it is the condition of the medium that renders it so difficult for spirits to perform these wonders in the light rather than any lack of power or disposition on their part."

From the numerous cases referred to at pages 77 and 211, which have been investigated by the police authorities, I adduce the following taken from *La Gazette des Tribunaux* (the official organ of the French Police), of February 2, 1849, because in this case a friend of mine, a literary man, has verified the extract at the British Museum, and assures me that the translation is exact:—

"A fact most extraordinary, and which has been repeated every evening, every night, for the last three weeks, without the most active researches, the most extended and persevering surveillance, having been able to discover the cause, has thrown into commotion all the populous quarter of La Montagne-Sainte-Geneviève, the Sorbonne, and Place Saint-Michel. This is what has taken place, in accordance with the public clamorous demand, and a double inquiry, judicial and administrative, which has been going on many days, without throwing any light on the mystery.

"In the work of demolition going on to open a new street, which shall join the Sorbonne to the Pantheon and l'Ecole de Droit, in traversing the Rue de Grès up to the old church, they came to a wood and coal yard, with an inhabited house connected with it, of only one storey and an attic. This house, at some distance from the street, and separated from the houses in course of destruction by large excavations, has been assailed every evening, and through the whole night, by a hail of projectiles, which, from their bulk, and the violence with which they have been thrown, have done such destruction, that it has been laid open to the day, and the woodwork of the doors and windows, reduced to shivers, as if it had sustained a siege, aided by a catapult or grape-shot.

"Whence came these projectiles, which are paving stones, fragments of the demolished walls near, and ashlar stones entire, which from their weight, and the distance they are hurled, are clearly from no mortal hand? This is just what, up to this moment, it has been impossible to discover. In vain has a surveillance been exercised, day and night, under the personal direction of the Commissary of Police, and able assistants. In vain has the head of the Service of Safety been continually on the spot. In vain have they let loose every night watchdogs in the adjoining enclosures. Nothing has been able to explain the phenomena, which, in its credulity, the people has attributed to mysterious means. The projectiles have continued to rain down with great noise on the house, launched forth at a great height above the heads of those who have placed themselves in observation on the roofs of the small surrounding houses, and, seeming to come from a great distance, reaching their aim, with a precision, as it were, mathematical, and without deviating from the parabolic evidently designed for them.

"We shall not enter into the ample details of these facts, which will, without doubt, receive a speedy explanation; thanks to the solicitude which they have awakened. Nevertheless, we will remark that, in circumstances somewhat analogous, and which equally excited a certain sensation in Paris, where, for example, a rain of pieces of small money drew together the loungers of Paris every evening, in the Rue de Montesquieu, or when all the bells were rung in a house in the Rue de Malte, by an invisible hand, it was found impossible to make any discovery, to find any palpable cause for the phenomena. Let us hope that this time we shall arrive at a result more precise."

My friend informs me, that he found a later short notice saying that "the phenomena remain inexplicable," and then the matter seems to have been no further noticed; so we may conclude that, as in the other cases referred to, "it was found impossible to make any discovery."

The sneer of the writer at the people's "credulity," in attributing the phenomena to "mysterious means," is quite amusing, in face of the statement just made that they "are clearly from no mortal hand," and the undoubted fact that they were "mysteries," since it was found "impossible" to discover them in a month's close examination, by the police force of Paris. If we read the narrative carefully, giving due weight to all the facts that occurred and the completeness of the investigation into them, we shall be driven to the conclusion, that had any *human beings* with the *necessary machinery* been engaged *they must have been discovered.* It is a case strictly analogous to that of Bealing's Bells (see p. 211) and others there referred to, and it by no means stands alone, for Mr. Howitt has published a remarkable collection of cases of "stone-throwing," most of them strictly investigated at the time, without *any human agents being in any case discovered.*

INDEX.

AMBERLEY, LORD, on spiritual phenomena and the character of mediums, 140.

ANIMAL Magnetism, 59.

ANTIQUITY of Man, evidence of, long denied or ignored, 18.

APPARITIONS, evidence of the reality of, 69; date of a War Office certificate shown to be erroneous by, 72; at the "Old Kent Manor House," 74.

ATKINSON, H. G., clairvoyant experiment with Adolphe Didier, 66.

AYMAR, JAQUES, discovery of a murderer by, 57.

BARING GOULD, on Jaques Aymar, 57, 59.

BEALINGS Bells, 211.

BEATTIE, MR. JOHN, his experiments in spirit photography, 193.

BRAY, CHARLES, testimony to clairvoyance, 105; his theory of a "thought atmosphere" unintelligible, 106.

BREWSTER, SIR DAVID, his account of his sitting with Mr. Home, 159.

BURTON, Captain, testimony as to the Davenport Brothers, 98.

CARPENTER, Dr., misstatement by, 31; criticism on Mr. Rutter, 56; omission of facts opposed to his views in his "Mental Physiology," 68; criticism on, 224; "unconscious cerebration" misapplied, 226.

CHALLIS, Professor, on the conclusiveness of the testimony, 98.

CHAMBERS, Dr. ROBERT, experiment by, 156; extract from letter of, 180 (note).

CLAIRVOYANCE, tests of, 60, 61.

CLARK, Dr. T. EDWARDS, on a medical case of clairvoyance, 67.

CONVERTS from the ranks of Spiritualism never made, 177.

COOK, Miss FLORENCE, tested by Mr. Varley and Mr. Crookes (in note), 181.

COX, Sergeant, on trance speaking, 201.

CRITICISM on the "Fortnightly" article replied to, 228.

CROOKES, Mr., his investigation of the phenomena, 175; on materialisations through Miss Cook, 182 (note); his treatment by the press, 203; by the Secretaries of the Royal Society, 226.

DECLINE of belief in the supernatural due to a natural law, 22 (note).

DE MORGAN, Professor, on spiritual phenomena, 81.

DEITY, the popular and spiritualistic notions of compared, 116.

DIALECTICAL Committee, investigation by, 178.

DISTURBANCES, unexplained, before rise of modern spiritualism, 211.

DIVINING rod, 56.

DUNPHY, Mr., versus Lord Amberley, 141.